A Rose Worth Saving

Alicia Rivoli

This novel is a work of fiction. Names, places, and characters are figments of the author's imagination. Any resemblance to those persons, living or dead, events or locales is purely coincidental. The author holds all rights to this work. It is illegal to reproduce this novel without written expressed consent from the author herself.

Alicia Rivoli Books

http://www.aliciarivoli.com

https://www.facebook.com/AliciaRivoli

Cover illustration by:

https:/www.bookcoverscre8tive.com

Copyediting by Amanda Zelaya

ISBN: 9798752609886

Copyright © 2019 Alicia Rivoli

First Paperback Edition: December 2021

In Dedication

To everyone who encouraged me to pursue my passions.

Contents

Prologue	1
One	11
Two	31
Three	47
Four	57
Five	83
Six	97
Seven	107
Eight	121
Nine	139
Ten	153
Eleven	179
Twelve	197
Thirteen	211
Fourteen	223
Fifteen	239
Sixteen	249
Seventeen	255
Eighteen	263
Nineteen	271
Twenty	285
Epilogue	291
Acknowledgments	297
About the Author	299

Prologue

London England
1807

Olivia was homesick. London would never compare to her family's country home. Being forced to come to the city for Charles' first Season wasn't where she wished to be. She was almost sixteen. She wanted to be home enjoying time with her rose garden and riding her horse across her father's estate. What if being gone for so long unraveled all the training she had worked on with Buttercup over the years? Complaining to her mother had done nothing when she also begged not to leave her roses, but Mr. Smith and Henry, the gardener and stablemaster, promised they would take care of things while she was away. Olivia felt she had no choice but to trust them.

"Come away from the window, darling. Victoria and her family will be here any minute," her mother reprimanded.

Olivia rolled her eyes and looked down at the dress her mother had picked out for her to wear. "We were just with Lord and Lady Pembrooke for over a month." she grumbled, running a hand down the front and sighing in frustration. "Why do I have to wear this day dress? We are only having afternoon tea with your dearest friend."

"I already told you, Victoria is bringing her son," her mother explained. "You remember him, don't you?"

Holding back a sigh, Olivia said, "Yes, Mama. I saw him a few summers ago at the Pembrooke's estate. He and Charles were always good friends."

Her mother raised an eyebrow at her words. "If I remember correctly, they included you in most of their escapades. I still can't forget you always coming home covered in mud, your dresses ruined."

Memories began pulling at the threads of her mind making Olivia want to laugh at her antics as a young girl. Following her brother and his friend around the estate had been something she'd looked forward to each time they were all together. It was a period in her life which she remembered fondly. Charles was kind to her and made sure to include her in any mischief the two boys got into. Sometimes she missed her carefree days as a young girl where the only thing she needed to worry about was how she would escape her governess. It would be strange to see her brother's friend again and for a reason she couldn't explain, she felt nervous. "That was a long time ago, Mama. I'm certain Lord Hanley won't wish to traipse through the river and catch frogs or play in the mud."

Laughing at her mother, Olivia gave an exasperated sigh. "Don't worry, Mama, I'll be on my best behavior. I'll only tease him a little."

Olivia held back a grin as she teased her mother, which had become one of her favorite hobbies.

Her mother's eyes grew large at the threat. "Olivia Barton, you will behave like a lady! I don't want you embarrassing your father and me with your appalling jokes."

Olivia held up her hands in surrender. "I promise, I will not embarrass you or father."

"Or Charles," her mother added.

"Yes, mother," Olivia said, exasperated. "Charles will also be safe from my unladylike jokes." Olivia rolled her eyes.

Lady Elmwood eyed her daughter suspiciously then returned to her embroidery. She and Lady Pembrooke had grown up near each other as girls and had quickly become like sisters. Olivia was quite fond of Lady Pembrooke. She took Olivia shopping during every visit, and Lady Pembrooke insisted on buying Olivia a ribbon, bonnet, dress, or frippery because she didn't have a daughter of her own.

Olivia tossed her head back and sighed dramatically.

Could boredom kill a person? She wondered.

She was tired of standing around waiting in this posh room. The ornate furniture, walls lined with paintings of scenery surrounding her family estate in Nottinghamshire, and the feel of being confined would drive her to bedlam. Olivia knew if she didn't do something to keep her mind busy, she'd go crazy. Eyeing the embroidery she'd put in a basket the day before, she cringed. In her opinion, embroidery was the worst of the approved activities for young ladies, and was the last thing she desired to do to keep herself from fidgeting. Instead, she turned and saw the grand piano forte in the corner. Olivia had become a proficient musician, but wasn't as talented as other girls her age could claim.

"Can I at least play the piano forte until they arrive?" Olivia whined.

Her mother nodded and Olivia hurried to the instrument. She had been working hard at a particular piece by Mozart, and it was nearly perfect. Before she could begin the song, Marcus, their ever-proper butler, entered the room.

"Lord and Lady Pembrooke and Lord Hanley, my lady," he said in a regal tone, addressing Olivia's mother.

"Olivia," her mother whispered loudly, holding out her hand.

She groaned, sliding her legs slowly over the bench to go stand next to her mother.

"Best behavior!" her mother whispered through tight lips.

Olivia gave her a bright smile. "Always, Mama."

Her mother turned her attention back toward the door, waiting for their anticipated guests to enter the room.

"Victoria!" her mother squealed in delight, embracing her dearest friend. "It's been far too long since you have joined us for tea."

"Catherine," Lady Pembrooke grinned, returning the hug. "It's so good to see you."

Holding her head high, Olivia prepared herself as Lady Pembrooke turned to her. It didn't matter how much she enjoyed the countess's company, she was always nervous to greet the kindly woman for the first time, even after only a short time between visits. Olivia didn't know why she reacted in such a way, she wasn't afraid of Lady Pembrooke, but she had never been able to stifle the anxiety.

"Oh, but Lady Olivia, don't you look lovely," Lady Pembrooke praised. "Is this the gown we bought over the summer?"

Olivia took a nervous breath and nodded. She wasn't surprised by the elegance the countess exuded as she stood regally in her lavender colored gown. "Yes, my lady."

She smiled brightly at Olivia. "You remember my husband of course, but allow me to reintroduce our son, Lord William Hanley," she said proudly.

Olivia curtsied to Lord Pembrooke before turning for the first time to address their son.

"Lord Hanley, it's a pleasure to see you again." She curtsied before raising her eyes to his face. When their gazes locked, Olivia's breath caught in her throat. She hadn't looked at the gentleman when he'd walked in, and she was surprised to find that he had most certainly changed over the years. No longer was he a gangly boy who pulled on her braids and kicked mud at her. Now, he stood tall, his brown hair falling softly over his forehead, highlighting his deep brown eyes. He was dressed impeccably in white trousers, shining black Hessians, and a mathematical knot in his cravat. His waistcoat and jacket were a dark blue, and when he smiled at her, she felt her knees go weak.

"Lady Olivia," he said, reaching for her outstretched hand and bowing over it. "It's a pleasure to see you again."

Olivia gulped as his touch sent tingles across her fingertips and up her arm.

"Olivia," her mother called across the room. "Are you going to join us?"

She looked over her shoulder, noticing her mother had already set up tea for their guests. "Of course, Mama," she said, stepping to the side to allow Lord Hanley to join his parents on the settee.

Olivia sat near her mother and folded her hands primly in her lap, keeping her eyes on the floor. She hated blushing and knew if Lord Hanley kept watching her as he was currently doing, she wouldn't be able to hide it.

"How do you like your tea, Lord Hanley?" her mother asked, silently elbowing Olivia in the side to remind her of her duty to their guests.

She took a breath and looked up at their guests, her eyes instantly moving toward the man sitting directly across from her. He stared at her through his lashes, their gazes locking onto one another. Lord Hanley's lips rose in a rather coy smile, and she immediately blushed. Raising a hand to her overly warm cheek, Olivia quickly looked away. Lord Hanley chuckled and turned toward Olivia's mother.

"With milk. If it won't be any trouble, my lady," he said, answering the question.

Olivia felt another jab into her side. Startling at her mother's prodding, she reached for the porcelain pot, her fingers trembling, and poured the tea. Olivia attempted to ignore the handsome gentleman as she handed him his cup.

"And how is Lord Elmwood?" Lord Hanley asked her.

Olivia forced herself to gain control of the emotions Lord Hanley's attentions had induced in her and looked up. "He is well. Thank you."

"My husband should be joining us shortly," her mother answered, saving Olivia from further comments.

"Will Lord Barton be joining us as well?" Lady Pembrooke asked before lifting her teacup daintily to her mouth.

"My son has stepped out to check on his new litter of dogs," her mother said in exasperation. "He's obsessed with those animals."

"A new litter, you say?" Lord Pembrooke asked in a deep voice. "What are his plans for the pups?"

"Knowing Charles, it's going to be something ridiculous," Olivia muttered. She immediately threw her hand over her mouth. *Why did she say it aloud?* She wondered. Her mother had made it clear Olivia was to keep her true thoughts to herself.

"Ridiculous?" Charles said from the doorway. "Livvie, you wound me."

She looked up and smiled as her brother strode into the room. "They will be my hunting hounds if I train them correctly. I will use them to track birds and small rodents."

"I didn't know you were interested in hounds," Lord Pembrooke said.

"Indeed," Charles explained as he stepped into the room. "During a hunting trip over the summer, I discovered I had a way with the hounds. I asked to help a friend with his, but he convinced me to purchase a dame who was ready to welp pups. Now, I have six glorious yapping puppies, and a mother who would rather not let me near them."

Lord Pembrooke laughed, "I can only imagine. I have never been good with animals, but it doesn't stop me from liking them."

"And what of you, my lady?" Lord Hanley asked Olivia while the others in the room were listening to Charles. "What are your plans for your first Season?"

"I'm not quite sixteen, so I really haven't given it much thought," Olivia answered truthfully. "In all honesty, I am not looking forward to it."

Lord Hanley raised an eyebrow. "And why is that?"

She shrugged, "The thought of dancing for hours doesn't sound enjoyable."

He smiled, mischief playing in his gaze. "Ah, but it depends entirely on your partner."

She felt the blood rush up her neck and back into her cheeks causing her blush to deepen, making Lord Hanley grin. How is it she had gone most of her life without ever blushing, and now she couldn't stop? She was going to need to learn how to control it before her first Season. She had no desire to be the debutante who blushed at every gentleman who smiled at her.

Olivia lifted her hand to fidget with the ends of her braid before she remembered it was piled atop her head in an elegant style her mother insisted on. She sighed and tried to put her discomfort aside.

Lord Hanley continued peppering her with questions about what she wanted to do during her first Season, which Olivia answered as calmly as she could. When she turned to answer someone else's question, she felt his eyes on her. Olivia was enjoying conversing with Lord Hanley. Her fondness for him grew the longer they talked. Thinking about her future, she realized she would eventually need to become the lady her mother and governess had been trying to teach her to be since she was four years old. She knew that even though she hated everything about the *ton* she may want to become the type of woman Lord Hanley would notice.

"Olivia, darling," Lady Pembrooke said, pulling Olivia's gaze away from Lord Hanley. "What are your plans for the next couple of months? Will you be attending any of the nightly entertainments with your brother?"

She shook her head. "No, my lady," she answered. "I have every intention of avoiding society as long as possible. I don't care for the gossips and ruthless behaviors the *ton* puts on display." She silently chided herself as soon as the words left her mouth. It seemed she was incapable of keeping her thoughts to herself. She had already forgotten that she wanted to change her ways.

Her mother gasped quietly and glared at her but didn't say anything. Olivia cringed. She knew from her mother's reaction she would be in her black books. It wasn't that she was trying to be impertinent or unladylike. Olivia was only being honest. Apparently, her mother didn't agree.

Lord Pembrooke laughed loudly. "Here, here, my dear," he said. "I couldn't have said it better myself."

Olivia smiled sweetly at him, knowing she needed to correct her mistake if she wanted to avoid a tongue lashing after their guests had left. "Of course, I shall enjoy making new acquaintances during my Season."

Lord Hanley's smile brightened and Olivia knew she was in serious trouble if one man could have such an effect on her. How was she going to withstand the attention of more than one gentleman at a time? She heard his subtle laugh, and her cheeks flamed under his scrutiny. She was going to need to learn to keep her blush in check, or she was going to have a very long first Season.

Alicia Rivoli

One

Nottinghamshire England
Three years later

Spending two full days traipsing across England in the rain, was more than should be required of a lady. Her father had been horrified when Olivia had suggested she return to the estate by horseback rather than a carriage. But once she'd explained why she thought it would be the best way to leave London and avoid suspicion, he had to comply.

Rain wasn't Olivia's favorite type of weather, which seemed rather ironic considering it rained all the time in England. But the wet, cold, muddy earth was worse while she was on horseback. The sloshing of her mare's hooves in the thick mud coupled with Olivia's cold, soaking wet clothing, and drooping bonnet was enough to drive her crazy. Her brother and a few of the hired guards, had wished to stop at an inn and push their journey back a day, but Olivia wanted to be in her own home and out of this horrid weather, so they had pushed onward.

They had spent the previous night before in Northampton at an inn called the Misty Dragon. It was clean with good food and overall, quite pleasant. But the noises of the bustling town in the early hours of the morning had been agonizing. She had attempted to drown out the sounds by smothering her face in her pillow or blankets, but the silence was worse. It brought back memories of her last few weeks in London which she was still trying to recover from.

Olivia had been thrilled at the thought of her first Season in London, much to her surprise. She had spent the last few years perfecting the art of being a debutante and felt she had become rather good at being the perfect lady. At home, she usually spent her free time with her horses or tending to her rose garden, which she was content with; however, an afternoon tea three years earlier changed her view of what a Season in London could be like, and she'd given a real go at learning how to be the lady she was expected to be.

Lord William Hanley, the son of the Earl of Pembrooke, had taken her by surprise all those years ago. At the age of fifteen, she had already convinced herself she wanted to become a spinster. She didn't want to be constantly entertaining guests with her husband and doing whatever he told her to do. She didn't want to give up her freedom and become nothing more than her husband's property to do with as he pleased.

Olivia loved two things in her life, training horses and growing beautiful flowers. She had always dreaded trips to London, hated the crowds of people, the smell of too many animals and unclean streets, and the lack of open spaces to ride her horse. She had convinced her mother, more than once, to stay at Elmwood Manor in Nottinghamshire under the ruse of continuing Olivia's education. It had, of course, been an excuse she'd concocted so she could stay close to her hobbies.

When Lord Hanley had accompanied his parents to her family's London townhome three years prior, Olivia's priorities shifted. While she still had a deep love for flowers and horses, she no longer desired to be a spinster. She had known the Pembrooke's for as long as she could remember, and Lord Hanley had always been her brother's annoying friend who teased her relentlessly. Three years ago, he'd become more, and that made her nervous.

She hadn't missed Lord Hanley when she didn't see him very often after he and Charles left for Cambridge when she was eight. It had given her time to work with her horses and develop her talent with growing beautiful roses. She had had her father's complete attention, and he'd taught her all she knew about horses. It also helped her develop a very close relationship with him. She and her father were inseparable. He continually provided her with plenty of laughs, but it was the love he offered to her freely that truly made a difference in her life. Olivia's father taught her to be strong and to not give up, even if the road becomes difficult. It was because of him that she'd become the woman she currently was. If her brother had still been around, taking her father's attention away, she didn't think she would have learned nearly as much.

When Lady Pembrooke came to visit Elmwood Manor, Lord Hanley had always remained with his father in London or at their country home, learning the ins and outs of being an earl. Seeing him three years ago, Olivia realized he was no longer the boy who teased her. He had grown up and become a very handsome gentleman.

She looked forward to her first Season after his visit and hadn't been disappointed when her time finally came three years later. She had first run into Lord Hanley at the Everly's musicale during the last Season. She was asked to perform and had been extremely nervous. She'd scanned the room, not entirely sure what, or who she was looking for when she found him watching her. Lord Hanley sought her out, and they had each made a point to find one another throughout the rest of the Season. They danced at every ball, he sat nearby at all the musicales, and visited their family's box at the theatre. His particular attention to her had only increased her own attention in him. What had been a young woman's crush bloomed into something else.

Her mother claimed Olivia had been the Season's *diamond* among the debutantes. Olivia had always been surrounded by gentlemen, and the sheer number of flowers showing up at her door after every event stunned her. Her dance card was almost always full, even before the night's activities had begun. This seemed to confirm her mother's words. Olivia had, much to her dismay, blushed at the compliment.

During one particular night of games, she was approached by a different gentleman, a viscount named, Lord Franklin Greenly. She'd seen him previously, but wasn't impressed by his actions toward the other ladies of the *ton*. He was a shorter man, with long black hair tied back with a piece of string, and dark eyes which seemed to take more advantages of a lady's figure than they ought. He wore fashionable clothing, but she noticed he looked somewhat disheveled most nights, appearing more like a rake than a true gentleman. She didn't know the man would eventually cause her so much trouble.

When he had asked her to be his whist partner, Olivia reluctantly agreed. After a few hands, Lord Greenly had become quite drunk and moved on to a game with larger stakes. She'd watched as he lost quite a few pounds, before excusing herself. After that, Lord Greenly began to seek her out at every event, and she had agreed to dance with him at a couple of balls. When he tried more than once to get her to meet him in the gardens or had become a little too forward, she'd begun refusing his advances. Her brother and father had stepped in to help her escape more than once. Her father even went so far as to threaten Lord Greenly with bodily harm if he didn't leave Olivia alone, which had only made her love for her father even more powerful than before. She had also seen Lord Hanley watching her carefully from around the room. He'd even stood close by her brother during a very particular encounter at the theatre

A week after she had refused to dance with him at a well-attended ball, he'd found Olivia walking around a garden near Hyde Park. She was grateful her father insisted she take a footman and maid with her when he approached her. She didn't know how the viscount knew where she would be walking, and she'd found it quite disconcerting. Niceties were exchanged, and he had the audacity to offer for her hand. She had stifled a laugh and gently refused him. Three years earlier, she may have slapped him, but her training had taught her easier ways to refuse unwanted attention.

Later the same night, she had overheard a conversation between Lord Greenly and a few gentlemen she wasn't acquainted with. When her name was mentioned during their conversation, she inched closer to hear them better. She had been appalled at his words. Lord Greenly had referred to her as a *bird of paradise* he would very much like to get alone. The very next day, her father explained Lord Greenly had the audacity to ask for Olivia's hand in marriage, but he had refused him, knowing Olivia had no desire to marry the man and had already rejected him. She was disgusted; the man was a tyrant.

Olivia's thoughts returned to the present when her mare stumbled slightly on the muddy path. She was grateful for her wool riding habit. It kept her from being extremely cold even though the material was wet. She did feel like someone had doused her in the river, but the clothing did its job of keeping her mostly warm. She watched her horse's breath come out in a misty puff every time she exhaled. Sweet Pea was a superb mare, and when her father had given her the animal at the beginning of the London Season, she had been impressed by the mare's disposition and was thrilled to be able to have a horse to ride while in the city.

The red sorrel tossed her head, prancing slightly as they came to a small stream. She knew Sweet Pea wasn't fond of the water, but since she and Charles had been forced to stay off main roads and avoid larger towns, they had needed to cross a lot of rivers and creeks.

After a few gentle praises, Olivia was able to convince her horse to join Charles on the other side of the stream and continue toward Elmwood Manor. Recognizing the rolling hills of the countryside, she knew they were getting close to home. Wiping the rain from her face, she groaned from her sore muscles. She wished, not for the first time, she could have gone with her parents in their carriage. But she knew the importance of making a quick escape from London.

Olivia let herself fall into a rhythm with the horse's movements, as nightmarish memories of the masquerade ball began to wash over her. Each recollection made her shiver in fear and disgust. As the horse's gait lulled her into a trance, it became impossible for her to put aside her feelings as she felt her mind drift.

Olivia stared at herself in the mirror, turning first one direction, then twisting to look at her other side. The gown, made of the finest silk, had been made special for the last ball she would attend this Season. The light-purple, two-toned fabric, split down the center of her bust line and grew wider before gently falling to the floor. The shape highlighted her curves, and the inner darker purple velvet layer made her feel like a princess. Olivia ran her hands down the beautiful stitching and special embroidered butterflies along the waist, admiring the same pattern on the bottom of the hem, and along either side of the split.

Sally, her lady's maid, had twisted her long hair into an elaborate knot atop her head and left a few soft curls to frame her face and neck. Purple and gold ribbons were weaved throughout her hair, along with several white flowers. A beautiful golden butterfly comb, gave her coiffure the perfect touch.

"Will there be anything else, my lady?" Sally asked, her eyes lowered.

Olivia turned to look at her maid. "Sally, it's absolutely amazing. I especially love how you were able to include the ribbons. It completes the look."

Sally smiled. "Thank you, my lady." The maid gave a quick curtsy and left the room with a blush on her cheeks from Olivia's praise.

Olivia left her bedchamber, then descended the grand staircase, careful not to trip on her gown and stepped into the entrance hall. Charles turned and flashed her a large grin.

"You look stunning," he said after a moment. "I almost didn't recognize you." His tone was teasing as he spoke to her.

She smiled and ran her hands down the length of her purple gown and smoothed the thin fabric which seemed to shimmer and dance in the soft candlelight.

Olivia pointed to the jeweled mask with its soft purples and yellow glittering sequins which covered the top half of her face. One side of the mask presented the large shape of a butterfly in flight and blended beautifully with the rest of the ensemble. Mama said she found the mask at a shop on Bond Street and knew it would be the perfect match with my gown," Olivia remarked.

"Mother was correct," Charles exclaimed. "Butterflies are all the rage this Season. Your butterfly mask will stun your many suitors into pure shock."

Olivia rolled her eyes. "I don't have many suitors."

Charles turned with a slight lift of his eyebrows and glanced into the open door of the small sitting room. "Then why does the entire house smell like a hot house?"

"Don't be ridiculous, Charles," she sighed. "You know every dance partner sends flowers to the ladies he had the honor of dancing with. I happen to be an excellent dancer; therefore, my partners were obligated to send them."

Charles laughed. "Are you blushing, my dear sister?"

Olivia swatted playfully at his arm and rolled her eyes.

"You look lovely, Olivia. The entire costume is perfect on you, as I said it would be." Her mother preened. Olivia barely suppressed her laughter when Charles dramatically rolled his eyes.

"Here, here," her father cheered as he pulled his daughter into a hug. "Charles, we best be on our guard tonight. Your sister is going to have a very difficult time keeping all her suitors at bay," he teased.

Charles laughed and winked at her. "Told you so," he whispered.

"Father," Olivia sighed, glaring at her brother before turning away from him. "Don't be ridiculous."

He pulled her gloved hands up to his mouth and gently kissed the backs of each one, smiling as he did. "You are beautiful, my dear girl."

Olivia smiled and hugged her father, surprised to see tears glistening in his eyes. She held on to him tightly, wanting to make sure he knew how much she loved him. Her father had been her strength over the years as she grew from a young girl to a woman. His support of her and everything she wanted or tried meant the world to her.

"Shall we go?" Her mother said, taking her husband's offered arm. "We're going to be late."

Olivia gave a nervous sigh as a cape was draped over her shoulders and she walked to their awaiting carriage. The weather was unseasonably cold for a summer night in London. Charles and her father stood at either side of the door and helped each lady inside before taking their seats. The rocking and swaying as they traveled the cobblestone-lined path churned Olivia's stomach, making her feel slightly nauseous. She took a deep breath in an attempt to calm herself. Tonight was not the night to fall ill. When the carriage pulled to a stop in front of the Pembrooke's London townhouse, she began to fidget, the nerves she felt by being the bell of the ball finally getting the better of her.

Charles leaned over to her. "Breathe Olivia. The ton won't bite."

She smiled weakly at him before accepting the hand of the footman as he assisted her from the carriage. Charles tucked her arm into his and led her into the house.

The front entry was lined with people waiting to greet the host and hostess. The glittery crystal vases scattered around the entrance were full of white roses, the aroma making Olivia's already tender stomach, flip even more. She felt her hand trembling on Charles's arm, and he patted her fingers reassuringly.

"I have never seen you so anxious, Olivia," he remarked. "Are you alright?"

She gave him a weak smile and nodded. "I'm always nervous before a ball."

Although the statement was mostly true, the real reason for her jitters, besides all the eyes of the ton continually watching her, was the gentleman who had captured her complete attention. She'd been thinking about Lord Hanley a lot over the last couple of days, and up until now, she'd been excited to show off her costume. Now she wasn't so sure. Her family was biased, and she couldn't help but wonder if she looked as beautiful as they claimed. She felt pretty, but her feelings weren't important. All that mattered to her was Lord Hanley's opinion.

"There will be no introductions or formalities at tonight's activities," Lady Pembrooke said to the group, smiling. "It makes the evening more mysterious."

"Of course, my lady," her father said, bowing to kiss her offered hand.

Olivia curtsied and took her brother's arm once more, following her family into the large ballroom. Ladies and gentlemen stood on each side of the room, their faces hidden behind masks creating a very colorful array of ribbons, feathers, and jewels. She touched the pearl necklace hanging around her neck, the small stones somehow calming her nerves.

Her mother had given her the necklace for her twelfth birthday, and she wore it to nearly every festivity of the Season, save a few of the more elegant events. She rubbed the pearls between her fingers as she looked around the room. How was she supposed to know who she was dancing with? She never dreamed a mask could hide a person's identity so fully.

Charles, looking rather mysterious in his black domino, led her to a chair near their mother and father. "If it's alright, mother, I think I shall go locate some of my friends." He bowed to his parents, winked at Olivia, and darted into the sea of people.

Olivia eyed the gentleman in the room, several were already headed in her direction, but she was looking for a very particular man. A man who had swept her off her feet over the course of the Season. Her stomach flipped as she thought about the time she had spent with him. The thoughts made her smile.

Someone cleared their throat, and Olivia glanced up. A masked man stood in front of her then bowed. She didn't recognize him, but curtsied and gave him a small smile.

"I can't deny, my lady, I simply couldn't go through the night without requesting a dance from the very stunning butterfly," he said. "May I?" He held out his hand for her and her mother nodded.

Olivia took the stranger's hand and was swept onto the dance floor. She listened to the sound of his voice as they discussed the different masks and weather, but even though there was a little familiarity to his tone, she couldn't place him. It felt as if the man was intentionally using a different voice to throw her off, and she found it a rather intriguing mystery. She asked multiple questions, all in an attempt to unmask her dance partner, but he had avoided most of the personal questions by changing the subject. After returning her to her seat, he bowed low and smiled. She watched him walk away, her frustration rising when she couldn't determine who she had danced with.

Olivia sighed, turning her attention to her next partner who had immediately taken the first gentleman's place. Her night continued in this way. She was barely able to catch her breath before another man asked her to dance. Her legs and feet ached as the dinner dance ended, and when her partner returned her to her family, she was ready to collapse into a nearby chair. Olivia's father held out a hand to his wife, who rose elegantly, taking her husband's offered arm.

"May I escort you to dinner, my lady?" her previous dance partner asked.

Olivia turned slowly, her sore body protesting and gave a quick curtsy, "Of course sir," she answered, smiling.

At the beginning of the night, Olivia had worried about being approached by unknown men, who refused to share their name. It felt as though it would be a terrible idea, especially for a young unmarried woman. But as the night went on, she came to find the mystery quite enjoyable. She did recognize several of her dance partners, as their masks only covered their eyes, and she could recognize their voices. But for the most part, the dim candlelight prevented her from knowing whom she danced with.

"Miss?" the man whom she still didn't recognize even after their dance and who was leading her into dinner asked, looking at her with concern in his eyes.

She shook her head, embarrassed to be caught wool-gathering. "I apologize, sir," she said. "I seemed to be elsewhere."

"No matter," the jovial man said. "I asked if you were enjoying the ball?"

Olivia looked at the man, trying to determine who he was. His mask covered his entire face, and he wore all black, including a hooded cloak. "Yes sir, I find it very agreeable."

He smiled. "It seems to be quite the crush. Lady Pembrooke is beaming."

Olivia glanced down the table at her hostess who was smiling brightly as she conversed with the small group surrounding her.

The man stopped and Olivia waited as he held out her chair, then took his own at her side.

"What have you thought about the Season?" the deep-voiced stranger asked.

She smiled at him. "I have enjoyed it very much. I have barely had a full night's sleep these past months."

He chuckled. "It does seem that way sometimes."

She shifted to allow the footman to set her plate in front of her. She looked at the small offering of thick slices of lamb, boiled potatoes, and a mixture of hot steaming vegetables. She wasn't a fan of this particular meal, but she gingerly began slicing her meat and took small bites, trying to avoid spilling any of the accompanying red sauce onto her gown.

"What of your family?" her partner asked after he too had taken a few bites.

She turned to respond but a rather large man who was sitting on her other side, stood abruptly sending his chair flying across the room as he choked on his dinner. The woman beside him shrieked and pleaded for someone to help her husband. In a flash, a gentleman a few seats away raced behind him and began pounding the gentleman forcefully on the back. The plump man continued to choke, but with a final slap on his back, a small piece of meat flew from his mouth and landed in the middle of the table. The women around the grey mass screamed, hurrying from the room with their hands covering their mouths. Olivia grabbed a glass of water and handed it to the now panting man. He quickly downed the liquid and motioned for another. Olivia complied and filled his glass once more before handing it back to him.

"Many thanks," he wheezed, nodding toward the other gentleman who had assisted him. He smiled warmly at her, bowing his head in acknowledgment of her assistance, making Olivia blush.

People quickly returned to their meals and conversations, but Olivia's attention returned to the choking man, afraid he may collapse after experiencing something so frightening. Her masked partner stood and excused himself, so he could assist the man and his wife out of the dining room. Olivia followed her dinner partner and the couple out into the hallway, wanting to help. When she turned the corner, she froze. The man who had escorted her to dinner had left the couple alone and had walked to a small corner and pulled his mask from his face. His hair had fallen from where it was being held out of sight and he wiped the sweat from his brow, revealing the very man she had been trying to avoid for the last couple of weeks.

How could she be so foolish as to not even recognize his voice? Did he realize it was her under her mask, or was it only a coincidence? She cringed as she remembered when Lord Greenly had made it all too clear Olivia, and her large dowry, were his for the taking.

She hurried in the opposite direction and out onto the back veranda. Inhaling the cool night air, she put a hand to her heart as she took slow deliberate breaths. She shivered as her mind reeled. Had Lord Greenly known her? She wondered as she stared out at the dark garden, inhaling the air around her. She needed to calm herself and return to the ballroom. Dropping her face into one of her hands, she gripped her middle with the other. A slight pain began pulsing in her head. She closed her eyes against the oncoming headache.

"There you are," a deep voice cut into her thoughts. "I was wondering where you had disappeared too."

Olivia froze, the hair on the back of her neck prickled as she now recognized the voice of the horrid man standing behind her.

"Are you feeling alright?" He asked when she didn't turn toward him.

Olivia nodded but didn't answer.

"Are you certain? I can fetch you some refreshment, or maybe, guide you to a chair," he said kindly.

"No, thank you," she replied, trying to steady her shaking words. "I only needed some air."

He stood silent for a moment. "May I join you?"

Now that she had recognized him, his overly polite tone made her cringe.

"I think I'd rather be alone for a while, sir," she answered without turning, her voice sharp. At the sound of Lord Greenly's steps coming closer, she whipped around and glared at him.

"You know," he said stepping up to her, a sly smile lighting his face. "I do believe you are the most beautiful woman I have ever seen," he reached out to touch one of her curls, but she stepped out of his reach.

He shook his head. "I tried everything I could think of to get you to agree to marry me, I even went so far as to seek permission from your father. But he also turned me away. It seems, my dear, we have a problem." His voice dripped with barely held anger.

She glared at him. "I don't believe we do. You've received your answer, not only from myself, but also from my father."

He tsked. "Oh, but your father can't save you if he can't find you," he took a quick step toward her and before she could react, grabbed her arm.

"Release me this instant!" she yelled before realizing she was alone with this man, and no one could hear her call for help.

He ignored her and pulled her down the steps onto the grassy path. He moved quickly toward the darkened side of the house. She looked around frantically, hoping someone would come help her even if she would be ruined in the process. Olivia would rather take her chances with the ton than with this wicked viscount. She yanked her arm, hoping to free herself. His grip tightened at the failed attempt, his fingers digging into her skin. The feelings of panic grew inside her, and not caring if she ruined her reputation, Olivia released an ear-piecing scream. He stopped immediately at the sound, and turned toward her. Lord Greenly lifted his hand as if to strike her before he suddenly jerked to a stop. His gaze darkened, and his hand lowered, as a sneer formed on his lips.

"I don't know Colfelt, I think the butterfly wishes to be free. Don't you?"

Olivia watched as two men stepped out from behind Lord Greenly, their faces shadowed in the black of night. One man held a long silver sword against Lord Greenly's back.

"I believe you're right my good man," the man known as Colfelt answered, smiling.

Olivia felt Lord Greenly's hold slacken slightly. She jerked her arm free from his grasp and took several steps back toward the veranda. He snarled and made a gesture of taking a step toward her but stopped as the man holding the sword pressed the tip harder into his back.

"OLIVIA!" The shout came from Charles as he raced to her side. He pulled her safely behind him and glared at the loathsome viscount.

"Olivia," he said, not trying to muffle the seething in his voice. "Lord and Lady Elmwood are looking for you. Please tell them I'll be there in a moment." His eyes never left Lord Greenly's face as his words flowed around the area. The other two men stood silent, keeping Lord Greenly securely in one spot.

Olivia grabbed the back of Charles's jacket. "Please, Charles," she whispered.

Charles pushed her gently away from him. "Go, Olivia."

Olivia backed slowly away from the men, then turned and ran back inside and straight to her parents. Her father had been furious when she'd explained what had happened, and stormed off to make sure the man never came near her again. She let her mother hold her tightly, trying to hold back the flurry of emotions building inside of her and trying to force their way to the surface. She didn't feel safe until her father and brother joined her mother and herself in the carriage and they pulled away from the ball.

Charles explained later to herself and her parents that it had been Lord Hanley who had come to her rescue. The words had filled Olivia with such an overwhelming feeling of warmth toward her brother's friend, she could only smile. Lord Pembrooke had had the viscount immediately thrown from their home. She also discovered from her father that Lord Greenly was in an exorbitant amount of debt. He'd attempted to kidnap her to force her father's acceptance of a union between himself and Olivia.

Lord Greenly knew her family was planning to leave London the day after the ball, everyone in the *ton* did. It hadn't been kept a secret. Lord Greenly knew it would have been his last chance to get to her. Knowing there wasn't a judge in all of England who would convict a member of the peerage for something so miniscule, Olivia's parents and brother had spent several hours after leaving the ball planning how to get Olivia out of London safely. They weren't sure, but they had a suspicion Lord Greenly would try to get her again. Her father wanted her back in the safe confines of their country estate as quickly as possible.

Olivia had presented the idea of her leaving with Charles on horseback before the sun rose, taking a couple of armed footmen, and returning her to Elmwood Manor. Their parents would send their personal carriage with their luggage and follow in a hired coach. Olivia trusted her brother to keep her safe.

"Olivia?" Charles called from a few paces ahead, "we're here."

Olivia snapped out of her musings and sat up straighter to see where Charles was pointing. A short distance away, she could make out the outline of their home through the heavy rain. She sighed in relief.

"Come," Charles ordered. "Let's hurry and get warm and dry. I don't know about you, but I think this rain made our journey quite taxing."

She nodded, and they kicked their tired horses into a slow gallop to avoid them slipping and falling in the mud.

As soon as she and her brother entered the house, Olivia called for hot water to be taken to her room. She hoped a hot bath would stop her from shivering. Sally wouldn't be arriving until later. She was riding in the servant's carriage that followed with all their luggage, so a different maid assisted Olivia out of her wet clothing.

Lowering herself into the steaming basin, Olivia laid back, closing her eyes as she felt the chill slowly dissipate. Every bone in her body ached from the long ride to Nottinghamshire and for the first time in almost forty-eight hours, she was able to relax.

Alicia Rivoli

Two

William wasn't ready to get out of bed when his valet opened the thick curtains, allowing light to pour into the room. Even though the Masquerade Ball had taken place a week earlier, William had been dreaming throughout the night of a lovely young woman in a shimmering butterfly mask. He groaned, covering his head with his pillow.

"Why haven't I thrown you out, Sam?" William's muffled voice asked dryly.

"Come now, sir, it's a beautiful morning," Sam said, whistling a happy tune as he disappeared into William's dressing room. "Would you care for the grey or black jacket today?"

William threw off the covers and put his bare feet on the floor, dropping his face into his hands in an attempt to rub the sleep from his eyes. "I don't care Sam. Whatever you think will make me the talk of the town," he said sarcastically.

"In that case, maybe I should go buy those yellow trousers we saw in the shop window a couple of days ago. It would go nicely with a bright orange jacket adorned with the animal of the day."

William stared open-mouthed at his valet. "You would never let me leave the house in such a way. People would think you'd lost your mind, because you know I would blame it entirely on you."

Sam chuckled and brought a basin of clean water and a towel to the bedside table before returning to choosing William's attire for the day.

William grabbed the small towel and plunged it into the water, dropping it quickly as the freezing cold liquid enveloped his hands. "Sam, this is cold!" he exclaimed.

"That's what happens when you take too long to get out of bed," Sam's crooked grin pulled a laugh from William.

"You are pure evil," William said, returning to the bowl and the towel. Before he could convince himself otherwise, he began rubbing the cold wet towel on his face and hands washing away the sweat of the night.

He shivered as he walked over to the fireplace. Placing his hands over the flames, the warmth instantly made him sigh. He stared at the flickering flames for a few moments, his thoughts straying toward a beautiful butterfly.

"Grey," he said when he heard Sam return from the dressing room. His valet held up two jackets for him to choose from.

Once dressed and his cravat tied, he took the stairs two at a time to the breakfast room.

"Good morning, mother. You look radiant today," he said, kissing her on the cheek, and bowed toward his father who sat at the head of the table.

"You're in a good mood this morning," his mother teased.

"It's a beautiful, sunny day," he shrugged. Moving to the sideboard, he filled his plate with food and sat beside his mother.

His father lowered the paper he was reading and turned to his son. "Do you have any plans this afternoon?"

William swallowed his piece of fruit and wiped his mouth before answering. "I thought a ride in Hyde Park would be to my liking," he answered. "Was there something you would like me to do?"

"With the end of the Season only a few weeks away, Parliament wants to close out any open business. I was hoping you would join me and get a feel for how it's accomplished," his father responded before taking a sip of his tea.

"Of course," William said. "What time should I be ready to leave?"

"The part of the meeting I wish for you to attend isn't until later this afternoon, around three o'clock," he answered, lifting his paper to continue whatever article had caught his eye. "You can ride over after you take your stroll thru the park."

William didn't enjoy sitting in a room full of tobacco smoke and crazed men trying to make their voices heard over each other, but he knew someday it would be his responsibility to undertake. He needed to be prepared for when that day finally came. William moved his fork along his plate and stared at the selection of meats and cheeses along with a pile of fresh fruit. Grateful they had fresh blueberries now that the weather had warmed, he popped several in his mouth, savoring the sweet flavor.

"William?" his mother said, bringing his attention back to the present. "What are your plans for the summer?"

He eyed her suspiciously. His mother was always trying to plan some way for him to meet eligible young ladies, but he wasn't interested. He took a deep breath and prepared himself for whatever scheme his mother had cooked up. "I haven't made any real plans yet," he answered, narrowing his eyes. "Why?"

She smiled. "I have been invited to Elmwood Manor for a few weeks, and the invitation included you and your father."

William felt his heart stutter. He had always enjoyed his visits to the marquess's estate in Nottinghamshire. Lord Barton had become one of his closest friends during their summer visits. However, Charles was not the reason for his quickened heartbeat. His friend's now very grown-up sister was the reason he was looking forward to a trip to the countryside.

William had always seen Olivia as Charles's pesky little sister. She followed them around, and he and Charles were scolded constantly by their parents when her gowns were ruined by their antics. It wasn't their fault she followed them across streams and played in the mud. But Charles adored her, so she was always included in whatever he and his friend decided to do. When William went off to school, his summers changed drastically. He no longer spent any time in Nottinghamshire, or at his family estate in Shropshire. He spent his summers in London, learning the ins and outs of running his father's holdings and finances.

He had been shocked to see Lady Olivia's transformation from an awkward girl to a stunning woman during the afternoon tea three years prior. He hadn't seen her for a few years, and the emerald green dress she wore had captured his complete attention. It drew his eyes to her lovely chestnut-colored hair which no longer laid across her shoulder in a long braid, but twisted into an elegant knot at the top of her head. He had a difficult time paying attention to anything else, and had thoroughly enjoyed making her blush. The light pink hue on her cheeks brightened her blue eyes, and they captivated him.

It was the last time he had been in her company, or even seen her, before their encounter at the musicale earlier in the Season. He had told his friend, Robert, all about the beautiful woman in the green dress when he had returned to school. As soon as he saw her standing across the room, he pointed Lady Olivia out to his friend.

Robert had whistled quietly under his breath. "I don't think you gave her enough praise, she's lovely." he'd said with wide eyes.

William had watched her walk toward the piano forte to perform and was mesmerized by her talent at the instrument. He didn't remember her being able to play so well, but he had been young during their childhood visits to each other's estates. He probably didn't really care what she did. The musicale set the precedence for the rest of the Season. He found he desired her attention and company above all the other debutants.

It hadn't taken long before she had become the most sought-after lady of the *ton*. He knew it shouldn't have bothered him, but jealousy ate at him as he watched her interact or dance with other men. He'd enjoyed her company, but it shouldn't mean he should care who she talked to. He'd already determined he wasn't ready to marry, so his reaction to her was ridiculous. It wasn't until Lord Greenly, a pompous cad if he ever saw one, had focused his attention on Lady Olivia, that William began to worry.

The viscount was greedy and didn't have a sterling reputation when it came to women. He also had a well-known gambling addiction. The arrogant man had, on more than one occasion, been entirely inappropriate in his actions toward Lady Olivia, but he could only stand back and watch her brother or father step in to help as William wasn't her husband or relation in any way. But he always kept a close eye on the viscount after he had witnessed her reject him, worried about how he might react. William hadn't missed the way the man's eyes seemed to darken and he sneered at her every chance he could.

When one of the servants explained Lord Greenly had followed Lady Olivia during the masquerade, he and his friend, Robert, immediately pursued them, arriving not a moment too soon. William's blood had boiled when he witnessed Lord Greenly raise a hand to strike Olivia after she had screamed for help. If Robert hadn't stopped him, William would have run the man through with his sword.

William was entirely taken by Lady Olivia, so the thought of going to her home for several weeks this summer, although exciting, scared him. Something about her pulled him to her and took away his ability to think clearly.

"William?" his mother called, bringing him out of his wonderings.

"Sorry, mother. What did you ask me?" he asked, putting his napkin onto the table.

"I asked if you would join us at Elmwood Manor," she responded, watching him curiously.

He gave her a small lift of his lips. "I would love to join you," he said before he could change his mind.

She clasped her hands in front of her. "Fantastic! I know Catherine will be ecstatic at your acceptance."

He narrowed his eyes suspiciously. "What else are you planning, mother?"

"Nothing," she answered innocently. "I only know they have missed having you visit these last years."

Fulwell, their ever-faithful butler, gave a small tap on the door interrupting their conversation. He walked inside the room bringing William's father a letter.

"This was just delivered, my lord," he said in a leisurely tone as he held a silver platter before the earl.

"Thank you, Fulwell," his father took the paper and turned the letter over to inspect the seal. "It's from Elmwood Manor," he said.

William's mother looked up from her plate excitedly. "Well, what does it say?"

His father opened the letter and slowly flattened out the creases. William stifled a laugh, knowing his father was deliberately doing so to get his wife to react.

"George, if you don't read the letter, so help me…" she said in a raised voice.

He chuckled. "Yes, dear."

William watched as his father's smile disappeared, his face losing all color.

"Father," William asked, his stomach lurching. "Is everything alright?"

"I…it's…Lord…here," his father mumbled before shoving the letter into William's hand. His mother hurried from her chair and stood behind him so she could read it as well.

Lord Pembrooke,

Six days ago, while my parents were traveling from London to our country estate, their carriage was attacked. Even though they had armed guards, my father and mother were gravely injured. Neither remains awake for long and both have lost a lot of blood. We're unsure if either will survive, and our hearts are grieving.

I beg your assistance in trying to locate and bring the men to justice who have committed this heinous crime against my family. Unfortunately, I have very little information about their attackers. I only know what one of the surviving guards was able to recall. He said there were four men on horseback. The man who shot my parents was shorter and wearing a black mask. The others also wore masks and were all average in height. One man had a large scar on his left arm. They shot and nearly killed not only my parents, but also, the guards and coachman. A local farmer who had heard the gunfire hurried to help, and when he recognized my father, drove them in their carriage to our estate. The highwaymen didn't attempt to take anything else, which makes me think they were after my parents, and not their fortunes. I'm sorry I don't have any other information to help you discover their whereabouts, but my sister and I would be grateful for your assistance.

Sincerely,

Lord Charles Barton

"George!" his mother cried out in shock. William watched as she collapsed into a nearby chair. Overcome by the brutality of the situation. She waved her fan nervously, her eyes overflowing with moisture.

William's stomach twisted into knots as he read the missive. He had to read it a second time, then a third, before he felt like he could grasp the depth of horror the letter revealed. Why would anyone attack a marquess and marchioness unless they were after their jewels and notes? To perform such heinous acts and not take anything was suspicious.

"What do we do, father?" William asked his sire. "Is there anyone we can alert and seek help from?"

His father had risen from his chair and was standing at the window with his hands clasped behind his back. He stared blankly at the sunlit sky, but color was still absent on his face.

Turning toward William, his father nodded. "Yes, we should go immediately to the House of Lords. Francis and Catherine's standing in the aristocracy will greatly help us find their attackers," he said in a somber tone. "Let Fulwell know we plan to depart and need the carriage prepared."

William didn't hesitate. He hurried from the room and minutes later, he and his father were on their way to Westminster Palace.

The next three days were a blur. William didn't know the last time he slept for more than an hour or eaten a hearty meal. He'd gone with a few men around London to some less than reputable inns and gaming hells, trying to get information on the men who had attacked the marquess and his wife. At one extremely dirty establishment, they received information about a man who had been there a few days earlier with a large scar on his arm. But the proprietor had no other information. William and his companions hit a dead end, and he was exhausted.

He shuffled into the front entry of his family's London home and barely made it to his bedchamber before his exhaustion crippled him, and he fell into a restless sleep. He'd been startled awake on more than one occasion from nightmares of Lady Olivia being attacked, so when his valet pulled the drapes open, William felt like he hadn't slept at all.

"Sorry, my lord," Sam said in a regretful tone. "Your father has asked for you to join him in his study."

William shot up. "Has he learned something new? Did they catch the highwaymen?" he asked excitedly.

Sam shook his head. "I don't know, my lord."

William dressed quickly and hurried down the stairs to his father's study. The room was very masculine. Heavy leather chairs sat beneath large windows where the sun streamed through, bathing the entire space in a warm light. A large wooden desk sat in the center of the room, and paintings of past earls lined every wall.

"William," his father said, stifling a yawn. "We haven't received any further correspondence from Lord Barton on the well-being of his parents. Your mother will be going to Elmwood Manor, so she may help any way she's able. She's tired of waiting and not knowing."

"Do you think traveling to Nottinghamshire will be safe?" William asked. "We can't send her alone."

"We've done all we can at the moment. I have Bow Street Runners scouring the countryside for more clues, so we will be going with her," he explained, stifling another yawn. "We have sent a letter informing Lord Barton and Lady Olivia of our impending arrival. We will be there by Friday evening if our journey isn't delayed in any way."

"We haven't been invited to join them. Isn't our showing up a little presumptuous?"

"We were set to leave for Elmwood Manor in a week's time. Your mother believes we'll be welcome as we've already been invited to stay for part of the summer. The Season doesn't end for several weeks yet, but your mother has decided she has had enough."

William rubbed his eyes with his fists. "If we are to be there by Friday, we need to leave immediately," he said sleepily.

His father nodded. "Yes, your mother has already asked the servants to begin closing the house and to pack our luggage for the trip. I've also hired several well-armed men to accompany us. I won't take any chances."

William stood up to leave. "I'll go make sure all the preparations are in order. I will also ensure that the carriage is readied for our departure."

"Thank you, William," his father said, smiling at his son. "Oh, and William," his father exclaimed, stopping him. "We've been watching Lord Greenly, but he's done nothing of suspicion. I know you believe he may have had something to do with the attack, but so far we have turned up nothing to prove his involvement."

William took a deep breath. "After the viscount's behavior at mother's ball, I wouldn't put it past the man to try and regain control of the situation. I think we should continue to have him watched. However, if Lord Greenly suspects he's being watched, I believe he will avoid contacting any of the men involved. The Runners need to be well hidden."

His father nodded. "I'll have them continue to keep an eye on the man. I'll also see if they can find anyone who may have been complicit in the deed."

William gave a curt nod before leaving to find his mother. He wanted to make sure she was getting everything she needed for the trip.

He found her in her room, keeping watch over the maid who was packing her trunk. It was being filled with all the gowns and accessories she would need for a prolonged stay at Elmwood Manor.

"William, did your father talk to you?" she asked, moving from her dressing room to her writing desk and back again. She picked up several sheets of paper and a couple of quills.

He nodded. "I'm sure Lord and Lady Elmwood have paper and quills mother. I don't think you're expected to bring your own." He tried for a lightly teasing tone, but from his mother's glare, he failed in his attempt.

"Are you here to tell me what I do and do not need to bring or is there something else I can do for you?" she snapped. She pushed out a heavy breath and rubbed the sides of her head with her fingers, resting the other hand on her hip. "I'm sorry, William. I'm only worried something else has happened to Catherine or Francis while I'm not there to help."

He gave her a small smile. "Don't worry, mother. We will be there in no time."

She walked over and patted the sides of his cheeks like she did when he was a little boy. "We're so lucky you're our son." Her voice was quiet and smooth. William had no doubt she meant what she said. He smiled in return, then watched his mother dictate to her maid for a few more minutes, before walking from the room.

He shuffled his feet. His head ached from a lack of sleep and he was hungry. He needed to get everything packed and ready for the trip, but all he wanted to do, was lay down and rest. He pushed open his door and was greeted happily by Sam.

"Hello, my lord," Sam said casually. "I hope you don't mind, but I took the liberty of having a tray brought up."

William felt like kissing the man as he hurried over and began picking through the sampling of treats. Sam poured him a warm cup of tea, and William collapsed into a nearby chair, propping his feet on the windowsill.

"I've also begun packing your luggage," Sam said from behind him. "If there's something else you wish to take, let me know and I'll pack it for you."

William turned around and smiled at his valet. "Are you looking for a raise in your wages or something?" he teased. "You know you are already the best-paid valet in the country." He chuckled when Sam narrowed his eyes at him.

"You are ridiculous, my lord," he smirked. "Next time I'll make sure you have to pack your own trunk."

William laughed aloud, grateful for the man's friendship. He and Sam had grown up almost like brothers. His father's stable master brought his son, Sam, to the estate every day when he came to work. He and William would run around the countryside causing all sorts of havoc. When Sam's father passed away after an accident with one of the horses, William's father started paying the boy wages for doing labor around the stables and house. Eventually, William asked his father if Sam could be his valet, and his father had heartily agreed. Sam enjoyed the job, and because they were so familiar with each other, they teased each other mercilessly.

William held up a hand in surrender. "You and I both know I haven't a clue how to pack that thing," he said, pointing to a large trunk laying at the foot of his bed. "Besides, if I did these things myself, what would you do with yourself?"

Sam shook his head, laughing. "All you aristocrats are spoiled, you do realize that? I know for a fact you wouldn't survive without having me here to help you."

William put his plate and teacup down and slapped his legs. "Well, you've got part of it right, we aristocrats are spoiled."

Sam laughed, moving to the open trunk. "I packed a couple of pairs of riding boots, as well as riding attire. Do you think you'll need formal wear?"

William shrugged. "I honestly have no idea. I'm going to leave Barak here in London. Charles has given me an open invitation to ride any horse in their stables when I visit. I also don't suspect any large parties." His lips raised slowly into a grin. "Although, Lady Olivia will be there. I'm hoping by the time we arrive Lord and Lady Elmwood will have recovered and I can spend time getting to know Lady Olivia better."

Sam laughed. "I wondered if the girl still interested you. I can see from the glaze in your eyes and sheepish grin on your face, she's still in the running as the next Lady Hanley," he said, checking the items one last time before closing and locking the trunk.

"We've enjoyed one another's company the last few months, but the circumstances of this visit may not allow for a lot of dancing and laughing." William sighed deeply. "I hope our family is welcomed, and we aren't in the way. We have no idea what we are going to find when we arrive."

Sam nodded but said nothing.

William turned his attention back to the window and watched as a few birds flitted by and perched themselves on the branches of a tree. He'd always compared the flight of a bird to a bruising ride on his horse. The wind rushed past, whipping his hair and the flaps of his jacket wildly behind him. If he closed his eyes, he could imagine himself like those birds; flying high and free. He stood up, brushed some cake crumbs from his pants, and grabbed his coat. He needed fresh air before he spent the next two days in a stuffy carriage.

Alicia Rivoli

Three

Olivia was exhausted. She had spent nearly a week of restless nights at her parent's side. She would never get the image of both of her parents being carried inside covered in blood, with their complexions pale. She had always considered herself to be strong when it came to injuries or blood with how much she worked with horses, but she had done nothing but gape as the servants carried her parents up the stairs and out of sight.

Once she had been apprised of what had happened, she sat near her mother or father unceasingly, forcing them to drink whenever they awoke, or tried to get some food into their bodies. The doctor tried to get her to leave every time he wanted to explain a medical issue to her brother or to change bandages, but she refused. After a few attempts that earned her a glare, he stopped insisting. Charles bounced back and forth. He was caught between checking in on their parents and handling the estate business. She knew he was stretched beyond his limits at only twenty-three years of age, but he never complained.

Olivia moved to the window. She sat and watched the outside world continue to shift and move without her, and she couldn't decide if she even cared. She touched the window, her fingers tracing the pattern of a large puffy cloud. The chill of the air pressed against the glass and rushed up her arm, causing a shiver to run through her body. It was early summer, but the English weather seemed to want to keep hold of winter as long as possible.

She dropped her head into her hands and not for the first time, she sobbed. According to the doctor, her mother seemed to be doing better. But after the fourth day, then the fifth without her regaining any coherency, Olivia wasn't sure what to think. Her father had lost a significant amount of blood, and the doctor said it would take him longer to recover. So far, she had seen no sign he was getting better.

Olivia was scared. She insisted the doctor give her something to do, but he told her she needed to take care of herself and left her alone.

"My lady," Sally, her maid, said with a brief knock on the door. "Lord Barton has ordered a bath for you."

Charles had been doing a lot for her lately because she rarely did anything on her own to care for herself. She felt guilty she was adding to his stress. Olivia walked slowly out the door and followed her maid, thinking it would help give her brother one less thing to worry about if she at least looked like she was okay. She hadn't given a single thought as to how she appeared and had barely eaten anything. But still allowed Sally to wash her hair and help her dress in a clean gown. The one she'd been wearing for several days probably needed to be thrown away. When Olivia didn't see it after her bath, she was sure Sally had indeed thrown it out.

"How would you like your hair today, my lady?" Sally asked with a small smile.

Olivia shrugged. "It doesn't matter."

Sally sighed but didn't say anything. She brushed Olivia's hair until it shined, and twisted it back into a long braid which nearly touched her waist. Olivia had always had extremely thick hair and used to ask Sally to do some pretty intricate hairstyles to see if the thick locks could be tamed. Sally always succeeded; her hair would always shine and shimmer no matter the style. Olivia often received many compliments on her coiffure. One young lady in London begged to borrow Sally for one night to do her hair. Olivia had laughed, which made the girl furious.

"Thank you, Sally," she mumbled.

"A tray was sent to your mother's bedchamber for your afternoon tea. Would you like me to have it taken elsewhere? Maybe the library?" Sally asked hopefully.

Olivia gave her a weak smile. "Thank you, I'll stay with mother."

Sally's face drooped slightly. "Is there anything else you need, my lady?" she asked, her jovial tone dimmed.

Olivia shook her head and watched as her maid left the room, her shoulders slumped in defeat. A pang of guilt washed over Olivia but she quickly pushed the feelings aside. Looking at her reflection in the mirror, she frowned. She looked as pale as her mother currently was, and dark circles rimmed her eyes. She thought she'd lost a little weight, and the shape of her cheekbones and the loose fit of her gown confirmed her suspicion. She ran a hand across her middle and felt a darkness wash over her as she considered all of the things that had happened lately.

Shuffling her way back to her mother's room, Olivia wasn't surprised to find Charles sitting in a chair waiting for her; the tray of food before him.

"Come sit down, Olivia," he said quietly. "You need to eat."

Olivia took a deep breath before walking to the chair beside her brother. "I don't want anything, Charles."

He shook his head. "Livvie, I *need* you to eat. Your maid said she isn't sure when was the last time you tried. Fasting won't help mother or father, it will only make you weak," he pleaded. "I can't have you sick as well, please eat."

She looked up at her brother. He too had dark circles under his eyes and hadn't shaved in a couple of days, so a fairly good amount of facial hair peppered his face and chin. His clothing was crumpled, and she could smell he hadn't bothered to bathe either.

"I'll eat when you take care of yourself," she said waving her hand up and down to accentuate his attire. "You can't insist I do something when you're worse."

Charles sighed and leaned forward resting his elbows on his knees then dropped his face into his hands. "I'm fine, Olivia. My well-being isn't the problem right now, it's your refusal to eat and sleep," he said, angrily. "You do nothing but pace this bedroom and sulk. You aren't helping anybody Olivia; you're making it harder."

She glared at him. "How can you say such things about me when you look worse than I do?" she yelled. "You can't have it both ways, Charles. Either take care of yourself, or leave me be."

He inhaled sharply before standing abruptly. "Just eat, Olivia. I can't deal with anything else right now," he said, his voice barely audible. He gave her one final look and walked swiftly from the room.

Olivia threw her cup against the wall, her tea spilling onto the floor, the cup shattering. She put a hand over her mouth and screamed, trying to muffle the sound. Her anger had built and had been close to breaking for a while. Charles's attack pushed her over the edge. She pushed the tray away with a growl before going to her mother's side and laying down next to her.

"Please wake up, Mama," she begged quietly, burying her face into the blankets. "I need you."

She heard light footsteps coming into the room to clean up her mess. She didn't look up but heard the retreating footsteps of the servant and the click of the door closing a few minutes later. She turned her head away from the tear-soaked blanket and stared at the window again. She listened to her mother's slow, ragged breathing and felt her weak heartbeat. The bandages were the only thing showing she was fighting for her life and not simply sleeping. Hearing her mother's labored breathing was chilling and filled her with fear and despair.

When the man brought her parents' carriage to a stop in front of the house, Olivia had assumed her parents had finally arrived. They had been expected hours earlier, and their lateness had made her anxious. She feared something happened while they were on their way home from London, delaying their arrival. Maybe the carriage had broken a wheel, or a horse had been injured. Never would she have imagined they had been shot.

Since their arrival, all Olivia's thoughts and nightmares were filled with visions of her parents' lifeless bodies. One of the footmen had also been shot but survived. He told Charles they had been making good time and were scheduled to arrive early. When they were only a couple of miles from the town of

Tollerton, they were ambushed by four armed men on horseback. The footmen, along with the coachman, all fired on the highwaymen and did everything they could to protect the marquess and marchioness. Olivia and Charles were told a couple of days later, one of the highwaymen had been shot but was able to ride away. When the men left, the surviving footman tried to get to the carriage but fainted from his wound.

Olivia replayed the attack over and over in her mind, but couldn't figure out what the highwaymen wanted. Although they'd taken her mother's jewelry and her father's purse, it wasn't enough to warrant her parents attack. Thanks to the quick arrival of the farmer, the trunks hadn't been touched, and the nervous horses were left alone. She hoped when her parents awoke, she and Charles would get a better understanding of why they had been shot.

Walking toward the tray of food she had left untouched, she took a small biscuit, slathered it in red jam and slowly let the sweet treat satisfy her need for food. Her stomach grumbled, so she took another.

There, she thought, *I ate something. Maybe now everyone will leave me in peace.*

Olivia heard a rumble outside and walked to the window in time to see a distant flash of lightning. After a few more strikes, the gloomy clouds seemed to tire of carrying their heavy burden, and water poured from the sky and clattered into the window. Puddles formed immediately on the roadway, draining down the slope toward the grassy knoll on the far side of the pathway. She watched the torrent for several minutes before closing her eyes and listening to the howling of the wind as it roared thru the treetops. Storms like this had always fascinated her. Olivia loved to see the quick changes of the weather and the beauty left in its wake. Today it did nothing but add to her despondency.

She felt a tickle on her neck and touched a wisp of hair which had come loose from her braid. She rubbed it between her fingers and sighed heavily. She was going to need to find a way to help her brother. With the downpour happening outside, she knew it would hurt the newly planted crops. Charles would have to be gone most of the day tomorrow trying to assess the damage. She had no idea how he could remain so calm, and he surprised her with the attention he gave not only to their parent's recovery, but to her as well. After taking care of everyone else, he would turn around and care for the estate, tenants, and servants.

A few nights earlier, hoping to retrieve a book from the library, she'd happened upon him. He was sitting with his arms across the top of his desk, his forehead resting on his curled fingers. She could see his shoulders rising and falling and knew he was crying.

The sight shocked her. She couldn't remember a time in her life when her brother had cried. He had always been strong. She had silently watched him for a moment, wondering if she should go comfort him. Instead, she moved past the study and into the library giving him privacy. He found her an hour later, still trying to locate a book interesting enough to keep the nightmares she'd been having far away.

He had pulled her into a tight embrace and held her. She didn't realize until this moment, as she stepped away from reality and watched the raging storm outside, that it had been his way of seeking comfort from her. She felt guilt edge its way into her heart. She hadn't provided him any of her strength. In all honesty, she didn't think she had any to give, but she could have tried.

Another rumble reached her ears, but this time the sound was different. Barely visible through the torrential downpour, was a carriage pulling up the drive. The horse's breathing was easily visible from where she stood, which was three stories above the ground. The poor coachman was huddled into a ball, wrapped in a leather coat.

Who would make their coachmen take them out in this? She wondered, but as the carriage turned so the side was facing her, she gasped. The large stately traveling coach held the family seal of the Earl of Pembrooke. She heard the butler, Lewis, calling out to the coachman and other footmen who were on horseback behind them. Lord and Lady Pembrooke stepped into the rain and hurried up the steps into the house. Olivia was about to turn away when a third person jumped out into the rain and ran into her home.

She felt her heart flip. The one man she did not wish to see while in her current state, was now in her house. Even from a distance and through the pouring rain, Lord Hanley looked as handsome as the last time she'd seen him. She heard footsteps in the hallway coming in her direction and unconsciously touched her chestnut-colored braid and ran a hand down her gown. Turning toward the door as the steps slowed, she waited for the tap on the door.

"My lady, Lord Barton requests you to join him in the front parlor. Lord and Lady Pembrooke and Lord Hanley have arrived," Lewis said, eyeing her wearily.

Lewis wasn't your typical butler. He didn't seem as old as one would expect of someone in his position. He was tall with a medium build and not overly plump. He was strong and seemed capable of handling himself in almost any situation.

He was more like a second father instead of a servant. He had, on more than one occasion, saved her from one scrape or another, and never said anything to her parents. She knew it was because of Lewis she had never had a switch taken to her backside. Her governess would have loved nothing more after the many pranks Olivia had played on her.

"My lady?" Lewis questioned, walking toward her. "If you'd rather not see your guests at this time, I can inform them you have retired for the evening."

Olivia laid a hand on his arm. "You are so good to me, even when I don't deserve it." He grinned and she felt her shoulders slump slightly before returning her posture to a more ladylike stance. "Please inform my brother I will join them shortly."

He eyed her for a brief moment before bowing and retreating down the hall to deliver her message. Olivia wondered why a footman had not delivered the message but figured her butler used it as an excuse to check on her.

She walked to her mother's dressing table and held a candle close so she could see her reflection. She frowned at her appearance, but shrugged it off, knowing she could do nothing to change it. She gave her mother a final glance, sighed, then tried to smile before leaving to join her brother and their guests.

Alicia Rivoli

Four

William watched the door carefully, waiting for Lady Olivia to enter the room. He had heard the butler tell Charles his sister would be down in a few minutes. While they waited, William's mind continued to drift to the pain and horror this family had experienced over the last week. William had suggested on the journey to Nottinghamshire that they shouldn't bother Charles and Lady Olivia with a bunch of questions. His mother had waived him off, insisting they wouldn't mind.

The journey had been smooth, with very little to slow them down. They'd stayed at a small inn called the Dragon's Rose the night before, and William was impressed at how well kept the establishment was. The proprietor served a very delicious lamb stew and hot rolls, which was delivered to their private dining room. The beds were soft and warm, so he had no trouble falling into a deep sleep. He had dozed off in the carriage a couple of times the day before, but last night was the first full night's sleep he'd enjoyed in a while.

The darkening skies as the storm blew in, slowed their progress, but his mother insisted they continue. William felt terrible for their driver, Mr. Pierce, and the armed guards his father had hired. The men were sopping wet when they finally pulled up the drive to Elmwood Manor.

Charles had immediately invited Mr. Pierce and the other hired men to warm themselves with a hot cup of tea and some cakes in the kitchen. He also offered them rooms to allow them rest before their journey back to London in the morning. Father thanked him profusely for his gracious offer and had sent the hired men to the kitchens with one of the Elmwood footmen as a guide.

When he heard light footsteps in the corridor, William's heart sped up. He had no idea why he suddenly felt nervous. Lady Olivia was lovely and witty, but the feelings he was having now were foreign to him. When she walked into the room, William nearly gasped aloud. He had no idea how someone could change so much in so short an amount of time. She looked exhausted, with pale cheeks, and dark lines beneath her eyes. Her dress hung loosely off her petite frame, and she walked sluggishly as though she were too tired to move.

"My lord, my lady," she said in a bleak tone, before turning her gaze toward William. "Lord Hanley, welcome to Elmwood Manor." She gave a wobbly curtsy and a very small smile. "We are pleased you have come."

William didn't think she looked pleased about anything. She appeared so weak, that as she moved about the room, he stood ready to catch her in case she fell.

"Lady Olivia," William's father said. "I hope you're feeling well."

It seemed his father had seen the same bleary-eyed young woman he had. William looked at Charles who shrugged, but he could see the strain of worry in his eyes.

"I'm well," she said, sitting down in a chair near her brother.

"Olivia," his mother exclaimed, "have you been taking care of yourself?"

Leave it to his mother to come right out and ask the question on everyone's mind. He waited for Lady Olivia to answer and watched her forced smile drop away. It was replaced by a look of…complete fear. He wasn't entirely sure what the look was, but he knew he didn't like it.

"I have done what was necessary. My focus has been on my mother and father," she snapped, then took a deep breath. "Charles has already lectured me on my appearance and instructed I need to remember to eat," she said.

His mother placed her hand on her heart, her eyes wide and posture stiff when she looked over at Charles, clearly shocked by Olivia's outburst. Charles's head drooped, his chin nearly touching his chest in shame. He shook his head in disapproval.

"Lady Pembrooke," Lady Olivia said in a calm voice, "I must apologize for my short reply and my appearance. I appreciate your concern. I've had a very long week and my emotions are a little out of control."

His mother's lip quivered as she quickly moved to Lady Olivia and pulled her up from the chair into a motherly embrace. William watched the exchange, cocking his head slightly and narrowing his eyes. She wasn't looking at him; she wasn't looking at anything. Watching her gaze shift around the room, William noticed something he hadn't before; Lady Olivia's bright blue eyes, which he had grown accustomed to, were hollow and blank. His heart broke.

Charles cleared his throat. "I'm sure you're tired from your journey and wish to get settled. Your letter arrived this morning informing us of your visit, so your rooms have already been prepared." He stood and moved slowly toward his sister and offered her his arm.

"Please excuse us," Charles said with a bow. "I would like to take my sister to get some rest."

From the corner of his eye, William saw Lady Olivia glare at her brother. Something about the exchange had upset her even more than she already was. Lady Olivia curtsied, and he barely had time to bow in return before her brother swept her from the room.

"George," his mother said, her voice shaky, "what has happened to her?"

William's father rose and embraced his wife. "I don't know dear," he whispered. "I just don't know."

"William," his father called from over his wife's shoulder. "Why don't you go get situated."

William suspected his father and mother needed a moment alone, so he bowed to his parents, kissed his mother's cheek, and left the room. Closing the door quietly behind him. He sat down on the bottom step of the stairwell and rubbed his forehead with his fingertips.

"Can I get you anything, my lord?" Lewis said, bringing William's attention to the man.

William shook his head. "Thank you, Lewis, but I'm well for now."

The butler bowed and retreated around the corner and out of sight.

"Sorry about Olivia," Charles said from behind him.

William turned his head, so he could see his friend and gave him a knowing smile.

"I've done everything I can think of to get her to eat and sleep, but she refuses. Watching my mother and father in their sick beds is difficult, but watching Olivia die inside has been worse," he said, dropping to sit next to William on the stairs.

"When is the last time she ate anything at all?" William asked, staring at his friend.

Charles shrugged. "Her maid thinks she finally ate a couple of biscuits this afternoon, which is the only thing of real significance. She doesn't sleep in her bed, but stays at our parent's bedside day and night," Charles said with a deep sigh. "I don't know what else to do aside from tying her up and forcing her to eat."

William chuckled. "I don't have a sister, but I'm pretty sure it would not go well."

Charles gave a light smile. "At least she would be alive. Instead, she's a ghost in her own home."

William raised an eyebrow in question. "A ghost?"

Charles nodded. "She doesn't speak to anyone, rarely leaves the west wing of the house, and when she does, she avoids places where she knows anyone will be. She sits in the dark corner of a room hoping no one notices her and ignores direct questions."

"My mother will know what to do," William said with more confidence than he felt.

"I appreciate you saying so, but I think having our parents awake and well is the only thing that will bring her back," Charles mumbled.

William sat silently for a few minutes, then turned to Charles. "Isn't she a decent rider? I seem to remember her hanging around the stables when she was younger."

Charles nodded. "More than decent. She outrides me every time. People have begun seeking her out, offering to pay her if she'll train their horses." He shook his head. "She refuses, of course, saying she wishes to keep to her own stables."

"Do you think she would join me for a ride around the estate?" William asked, thinking that might bring Olivia out of her stupor.

Charles blew his breath out in a huff. "By all means. Whatever you think will bring her back from wherever her mind has gone, I give you leave to try. I've attempted to get her to ride, to play her piano forte, to help Mr. Smith in her garden, everything I know she loves. She only glares at me and tells me to leave her be." Charles's voice was low, and William could hear the stress behind his words. "Maybe you'll have better luck than I."

William gave him a half-smile. "Anything?" he teased, trying to get a smile from his friend.

"Anything within the limits of propriety," Charles answered, holding back a chuckle. "Although I have a beautiful set of dueling pistols which haven't been used in a while."

William laughed and shook his head. "I'll try to remember."

Charles smiled gratefully and clasped William's hand. "Thank you. I was running out of patience with her, and it will be nice not to worry about her for a while."

Charles stood, and with a nod of appreciation, excused himself and walked back the way he had come. William's thoughts had quickly turned back to Lady Olivia and how he could possibly get her to agree to come for a ride with him. He remembered watching her with her father when she was younger. She would ride around the paddock for hours at the time, but his young mind didn't comprehend whether or not she enjoyed it. He also didn't know what garden Charles was talking about; he only knew of the small one out back. It was beautiful for sure, but he couldn't recall anything special about it.

He pushed himself up from the ground and retreated to his room. He always loved the room he was given during his stays here. It had a large four-poster bed, a nice writing desk, and a good-sized wardrobe. The pale blue walls and matching drapes made him feel like he was outside enjoying a clear summer sky. His favorite part, however, was the view outside his window. It overlooked a small courtyard full of different stone statues and a few fountains. He could even hear the trickle of the water while he slept.

"Sam?" William asked as he entered the room. "I plan to go riding tomorrow morning, can you make sure all of my clothing and boots are prepared?"

Sam moved from the wardrobe with a pile of white shirts draped over his arm. "Of course. I'm also preparing your attire for tonight's dinner. I've been instructed it won't be a formal occasion, so I pressed the light-colored trousers and dark jacket. Will that suffice?"

William nodded, not looking at his valet. "Whatever you think best."

The calling of birds and the splattering of rain on his window, drew his attention back to the world outside and his mind wandered to Lady Olivia. How could he help her? Would the ride tomorrow even be something she wished to do? He would kill whoever did this to her family if they ever found them. He couldn't stand seeing his friends so distraught.

Sam raised an eyebrow in question. "You seem distracted. Is everything well with Lord and Lady Elmwood? Or Lady Olivia? Is she enjoying your company?"

William rolled his eyes. "Just make sure everything is ready. I'm going to go see if there is anything the family needs."

Sam laughed loudly. "Whatever you wish, my lord."

William shook his head as his valet went to work. He needed to have the man properly trained to adhere to his station. His cheeky comments and teasing would be enough to drive a person mad. William smiled. He knew, even though Sam was young and naïve, he would never change the way he was. William enjoyed having him as a friend too much. He was also one of the few servants who could be trusted not to divulge in gossip.

Thinking it would be a good time to pay his respects and see if he could help in some way, he sought directions to Lord and Lady Elmwood's chambers from a nearby servant. Although he would deny it if asked, he also wanted to see Lady Olivia again. Her demeanor had changed so much in so short a time, he was concerned she may lose herself in her turmoil. Charles had said she rarely left her mother's side, so he knew she would be in the sickroom.

William came to the large door of the marchioness's bedchamber standing partially open. He heard his mother's soft voice speaking to someone else in the room, and his heart broke as he recognized Lady Olivia's taciturn response. She sounded as dejected now as she had in the drawing-room. Somehow, he had to get her to smile again. He wanted to see her smile and to return from her melancholy so she could be happy. He hated seeing her in such a state.

He tapped lightly and entered. The two women turned to look at him and his mother flashed him a pained smile. Lady Olivia on the other hand looked away quickly and moved closer to her mother's bedside.

"William," his mother spoke softly, "what a nice surprise."

He could tell his mother had been crying. She was devastated by Lord and Lady Elmwood's current situation, and he knew she wanted to help. William could see the countess felt helpless since there wasn't a lot she could do but sit by their bedside. Lady Olivia didn't look up, so he decided to focus on the marchioness wrapped tightly in blankets. Lady Elmwood had large bandages sticking out under her chin and her pale skin looked sallow. Her maid had attempted to keep her mistress' hair tidy, but it stuck out in every direction.

"I came to say hello," he said, forcing his eyes to look away from the prone woman in front of him. "Is there anything I can do to help?"

"That is very sweet, William," his mother answered. "I believe Olivia has everything under control for now and the doctor has been taking very good care of Francis and Catherine."

He turned to Lady Olivia who kept her head down. In the dim candlelight, she looked even more sickly than she had in the parlor. He walked over to where she stood and took her hand in his. She shot a wearied glance at him but didn't pull away.

She reminded him of a frightened animal who would run away at the smallest of sounds. "Is there anything you need?" he asked quietly.

She shook her head.

He pulled her hand to his lips and placed a gentle kiss on the back, hoping it would be a show of support and kindness. He felt her take a sharp breath before she quickly pulled her hand from his grasp.

"Thank you, my lord," she said curtly. "I appreciate the offer, but I am well."

He nodded. "Would you accompany me on a ride around the estate in the morning?" he asked in a hopeful tone. "If I recall, you enjoyed the activity as a young girl."

Anger flashed in her eyes. "Did my brother put you up to this?" she snapped.

His eyes grew wide, and he shook his head. "No, my lady." He took a step back, "I would love to have you join me and thought the fresh air would be a refreshing change."

Her eyes seemed to soften, and she gave him a small smile. "I don't think I should leave my mother right now, but thank you."

"Olivia," his mother said softly. "I know you are concerned for your mother's well-being, but you need to take care of your own needs as well. If you continue as you are, you're going to become too ill to be of much help."

William cringed when Lady Olivia glared at his mother. He watched the emotions flicking across her face. She was trying to figure out the best way to escape this situation, but William wasn't going to make it easy for her. He wanted her to come with him, so instead of coming to her aid, he waited patiently.

She inhaled a deep breath and let it out slowly. "I appreciate your concern, Lady Pembrooke, but I'm not going to leave my mother."

William felt himself stiffen. Her words didn't come out in the angry tone he had anticipated, but he could see she was trying to remain calm. His mother's shoulders sagged and her head lowered. Lady Olivia's words hadn't been what either of them had hoped.

"Olivia," Charles said from the open doorway. "You need to get outside. Your maid will have your riding habit prepared so you can go with William in the morning." She opened her mouth to object, but Charles held up a hand to stop her. "No, Olivia, I don't want to hear your excuses, you're going."

Lady Olivia's eyes narrowed and the air around the room seemed to sizzle with the energy of her ire. She looked at her brother, her glare turning murderous and William absent-mindedly took a small step away from her. Charles stood his ground, waiting for his sister to either make some sort of excuse or start screaming. After several long silent moments, she gave one nod and stormed from the room. Charles collapsed into a nearby chair and laid his head back. William's mother hurried to his side and laid a hand on his shoulder, trying to comfort him.

"I'm sorry you were here for that," he mumbled. "It wasn't my intention to confront her."

William's mother patted his hand lovingly. "We know, dear; we understand. I hope our presence isn't creating more hardships for your family."

He shook his head quickly. "No, my lady," he commented as he put his hand on top of hers. "We are grateful you have come, even though Olivia is unable to realize it."

William looked toward the door Lady Olivia had stormed out of, a deep frown tugging on his lips. He couldn't imagine what she was going through, and he had made it worse by asking her to go for a ride. He could tell she wasn't thrilled about the idea, but he was happy Charles insisted she go. William truly believed a little fresh air would be good for her.

"I think I'm going to prepare for dinner," William said, kissing his mother's cheek. He turned to his friend. "Charles, can I get you anything?"

Charles didn't look at him but shook his head. William's mother tipped her head toward the open door, indicating she wished to speak to him. He followed her, slowly closing the door behind him.

His mother looked up and down the hall, before turning to him. "I'm concerned about Charles and Olivia. She's reacting to her parent's injuries both emotionally and physically. Charles has taken on the responsibility of a marquess as well as trying to care for his parents and sister," she said, linking her arm into the crook of her son's elbow and walking a little further down the hall. "Until his parents recover, we need to make sure Olivia and the house are looked after. Charles has enough to worry about. Your father will help with the estate, but somehow you and I need to keep Olivia from slipping even further away into her own mind."

William didn't understand why she was telling him this. They'd already discussed what they were going to do on the journey from London. He knew his mother was worried about Lady Olivia's health and Charles's as well, but he wasn't sure what else he could do to help.

"I asked Lady Olivia to join me on a ride tomorrow for the sole purpose of helping her," he explained. "Charles and I discussed it shortly before I found you. He thinks if we can get her mind on something that makes her happy, she'll return to her normal self."

"I understand, William, and I'm pleased with your attempt to help her. But how she is feeling right now isn't my main concern," she said sadly. "I'm afraid what will happen if their parents don't survive. What type of emotional toll will it cause Olivia? How much more of a strain will be put on her and Charles's relationship?"

His mother kissed his cheek and returned to the marchioness's chambers. William contemplated his mother's words as he walked back to his room. He could feel his body wearing down from exhaustion. Even with the rest he had at the inn, his body was still tired from the manhunt. His parents explained to Charles what had been done so far to find the men responsible. Now that they knew one man had been injured, it would help narrow things down a little.

William was grateful to find his room empty. He wanted a few moments of peace and quiet to try and get his thoughts in order. Lady Olivia's well-being was becoming increasingly more important to him. William wanted her to be happy. He needed to see her beautiful smile return and be caught in her bright blue-eyed gaze. Something inside of him broke at the sight of her today. No one should ever have to experience the pain she and her brother were experiencing.

With great effort, he was able to remove his boots, sighing in relief when his feet were able to move around freely. He rubbed his hands up and down his thighs, then stood and moved to the window. The storm which had nearly washed them off the road had moved on, replaced by a serene sunset. The surrounding wisps of clouds were tainted by purple, orange, and red colors, which shot in different directions. Although the sky was growing darker, there was still plenty of light left on the horizon.

Movement outside drew his attention to the many statues below. The ground was saturated with mud and water, but Lady Olivia walked slowly in and out of the art. When she reached the end of the row, she turned and did it all over again. Looking down at his bare feet, he cursed under his breath. He hurried to where he had left his uncomfortable black boots, and with great effort, was able to get them on without assistance. He felt like an invalid when Sam helped him with something as simple as putting on a shoe, but it was like trying to squeeze a round peg into a tiny square hole.

He checked out the window again and when he saw she was still walking among the statues, hurried from the room. As he was about to throw open the door leading out into the gardens, Lewis blocked his path.

"It's still rather cold, my lord," he said kindly. "Would you like your jacket and gloves?"

William nodded. Putting on his warmer items of clothing, he ran out the door. The garden was well-manicured and the path which led around each statue was well worn. A conservatory stood at the back of the house near a smaller barn where he could hear the sound of yapping dogs. He knew it was Charles's prized hounds, and it made him smile. His friend had developed a fascination with the animals at a young age. He shifted his body and saw smoke billowing out of an open door. He assumed the door led to the kitchen as a delicious smell raided his senses, confirming the cook was making something delightful.

The beginning of summer brought a plethora of newly budding leaves to the area. A large grouping of multi-colored hollyhocks stood in the center of the garden, changing the scene from winter drab to promising beauty. A bird call pulled his eyes in the opposite direction where he saw Lady Olivia sitting on a bench at the end of the path.

She'd wrapped a shawl around her shoulders, had no bonnet on, and her hair had slipped from her braid and floated wildly in the breeze. He smiled to himself as he wondered if her hair was as soft as he imagined.

"Lord Hanley?" Lady Olivia called in surprise when she spotted him.

William glanced at her and smiled when she curtsied. He gave a quick bow before walking to her side.

"What are you doing here?" she asked.

"Well, I saw this young lady walking in the cold and thought she might want company," he looked at her and smiled as a blush rushed to her cheeks. "May I?" He said, offering her his arm.

She stared up at him. William could see she was trying to determine if he had come with an agenda. After a few seconds, she took it and walked silently beside him. He watched her profile while she looked out over the garden. Seeing her so weighed down by worry and grief, he knew he needed to find a way to bring back her smile.

"I'm sorry," she said, "I'm afraid I'm not good company today."

He patted her hand. "I blame the cold," he teased.

She gave a soft laugh and smiled weakly at him. Normally, he would have loved to have seen it, but there was so much pain in her eyes, it made him stop their stroll.

"Lady Olivia?" he asked, turning her to face him, but the words he meant to say froze in his throat. Her blue eyes had turned a soft grey, with lighter blue bordering the edges. He was taken aback by their sheer beauty.

"Yes?" she answered, causing him to blink several times to clear his mind.

"I know you're not looking forward to our ride in the morning, but I do believe it will be good to get some sunshine," he said, hoping she wouldn't take offense.

She studied him for a few moments, then dropped her head. "I know everyone is trying to help me, and I should be more grateful, but I feel only anger." A tear streaked down her cheek and she quickly wiped it away with the back of her hand. "I'm hopeful, however, that everyone's persistence will somehow take away the pain."

"But you are unsure," he stated.

She nodded and turned her attention back to the path in front of them, her shoulders sagging from the stress she was feeling. He decided to try and change the subject, thinking if he took her mind off her worries, it might help her.

"Lady Olivia," he began. "I must admit I am quite terrible at distinguishing one flower from the next. Would you be so kind as to show me some of your favorites?"

She smiled, and William wanted to jump for joy. It wasn't a forced smile or a half-smile, but a beautiful bright smile which made his heart skip.

"With the cold and storms, there aren't many which have bloomed yet. But my favorite flower, well one of them, is right around the corner," she said pointing to a curve in the path which led to the other side of the house.

"That sounds intriguing," he responded. "If it's one of your favorites, I know it must be beautiful."

Her cheeks pinkened slightly, making him smile inside. The reaction he had from the simple blush was rather unnerving, but he thoroughly enjoyed the coloring on her cheeks. She led him down the path and around the corner. There were no statues in this part of the garden. Instead, row upon row of hedgerows and bushes stretched to the far end of the pathways.

A thoughtful expression crossed her face as she looked out over the plants. Holding out her fingers, she brushed the tips of the greenery as she guided him down the path. "I love lavender and lilacs. The aroma is calming, and the purple of the petals is my favorite color." She pointed out a green plant with full dark purple blooms further up the path. "I was worried the colder spring would prevent them from blooming this year, but they seem to be thriving."

As they drew closer to the large array of purple flowers, a sweet fragrance enveloped him, and he recognized something familiar in the scent. He searched his thoughts and watched as Lady Olivia crossed in front of him to take one of the blooms into her outstretched hand. She lifted the blossoms to her nose and took a deep long breath. When she turned back to him, a large smile lit her face, and he felt his heart stutter. She lowered her eyes to the ground as a breeze brushed by, sending tendrils of chestnut-colored hair swirling around her face. Again, the scent pulsed through his senses; it was maddening. Her eyes met his for the briefest of moments and something clicked.

"You wear this scent, do you not?" he asked, nodding his head in the direction of the lilacs. It probably wasn't appropriate to mention it, but he found he couldn't help himself.

She grinned and a small dimple formed. "My father bought me a bottle of the fragrance while we were in London," she said. "I'm surprised you noticed."

"My lady, to not recognize the smell of a beautiful woman would be scandalous," he teased in mock humiliation.

He was rewarded with a shy laugh from her. She was stunning, and he was thrilled to see her smile return. Knowing it would likely disappear when she returned to the house, he wanted to enjoy it as long as he was able. He returned her smile, and she blushed. Lacing her arm back through his, she guided him further along the lane. They walked past the intoxicating aroma of the blooming lilacs, and he knew he would never forget they were one of Lady Olivia's favorite flowers. The familiar scent of the perfume, the purple color of the blooms, all brought to mind the image of a beautiful young woman in a butterfly mask and shimmering gown. He could see some long strands of chestnut-colored hair that had escaped her braid and were blowing freely in the breeze.

"Lord Hanley, what are your plans for the summer? Are you returning to London?" she asked, changing the subject.

He cleared his throat, hoping to clear the images flashing through his mind. "I won't be returning to London until the Little Season. I had planned to return to Pembrooke Estates with my parents for a few months. My mother has been begging me to visit for some time," he answered, looking at her out of the corner of his eye. "However, I understand your mother has invited us to stay at Elmwood for a few weeks. I planned on joining my parents here in Nottinghamshire before making my way to London in the autumn."

She smiled. "I'd forgotten. My mother was so excited to send the invitation. You would have thought she was inviting the Prince Regent himself." She giggled and turned her gaze back to him. "Were you planning on returning to London for the little Season?" she asked.

Her curiosity of his plans intrigued him. "I hadn't thought about it. My mother seemed to be planning something upon our return home, but I couldn't get her to tell me what."

Lady Olivia smiled broadly and gave a little laugh. "She refused to tell you?"

He nodded. "She can be quite secretive when she wants to be. I have a feeling she was planning a large house party or ball. Something lavish to welcome back those returning to the countryside, but I never got the chance to get into it further with her."

"Did she scold you for your questions?" she asked him, her eyes growing brighter.

"My questions?" he asked, taking note of the new glimmer in her gaze. "You mean about her plans?" She nodded and he shook his head. "We were interrupted before I could get her to tell me."

"What was the interruption?" she asked, before turning her gaze back to the path ahead of them. "I'm terribly sorry, I shouldn't be so forward. It's none of my business. Please forget I asked."

He wondered what made her change so quickly but shrugged it off. "I don't mind at all. I'm happy to answer any of your questions."

She looked up at him through her lashes, her bluish-grey eyes causing his mind to go blank temporarily. It was almost as if, for a moment, she was back to the woman he knew in London; the bright, vivacious debutante who caught the attention of every gentleman in the room. He wondered if the change had something to do with the flowers and the garden surrounding them, or if it were something else entirely. She blinked several times, then returned her attention to the plants and trees. They came to a large stone fountain surrounded by a few matching benches. Wanting to spend a little more time in her company, he led her to the one nearest them.

"Would you like to sit for a moment?" His words came out quieter than he wanted, but she didn't seem to notice.

She maneuvered her gown around her and sat so close to the edge, that when William sat down it left a good deal of distance between them. He turned his body toward her.

"Excuse me, my lady," a footman said, his approach interrupting the moment between them. Lady Olivia turned her face up to him, and the smile William had tried so desperately to find, disappeared.

She shot to her feet. "Yes?" she questioned, fear replacing any remaining joy.

"Lord Barton asks that you and Lord Hanley join him in the drawing-room," he said, bowing.

She nodded frantically. "Is everything alright?" she asked.

William could see uncertainty in her expression, and it turned his stomach.

The footman spoke confidently. "I believe the doctor has news of your parents' recovery, my lady."

Lady Olivia stumbled over her dress as she hurried back towards the house. William strode forward to catch up to her. Once he did, he took her arm, and placed it through his own. "Please, let me escort you."

She glanced up at him and William could see the color of her eyes had again turned dark. The lightness of the last half an hour was gone. Replaced by the same fear he had seen in her since the moment he and his parents had arrived.

As they stepped back into the house, Olivia rushed forward, releasing William's arm and pulling her skirts up as they reached the bottom of the stairs. William gawked at the sight as he noticed for the first time that Lady Olivia was completely barefoot; her pale-colored skin and the hem of her skirt covered in mud from the saturated ground outside. His breath caught in his throat. He knew he should turn and look away but found himself unable to. Only after her skirts fell back over her feet at the top of the stairs, was he able to move again. He shook his head, following behind her two steps at a time. He reached the doors to the drawing-room right as she disappeared inside.

"Livvie," Charles said, standing to greet her. "Dr. Campbell wishes to speak with us."

William looked at a short man standing near his mother. He was younger than William imagined he would be. He was tall, with dark hair, and wore the typical dress of a physician; a black coat, white shirt, and holding a leather medical bag in his gloved hand.

"Of course," she said, turning to face the man.

The doctor's eyes showed kindness as he looked at Lady Olivia. William didn't know why, but he felt a slight twinge of jealousy course through him. He knew the doctor had been visiting the estate often to care for Lord and Lady Elmwood, but his own reaction to the doctor was unjustifiable. Neither he nor the doctor had any claim to Lady Olivia.

"My lady," Dr. Campbell said, moving toward her and bowing over her hand.

Lady Olivia looked at him with a false sense of happiness and gave him a brief curtsy. William turned to watch the exchange and caught his mother's glare from the corner of his eye. He stared at her in question, but she waved him off.

"Dr. Campbell," Charles said. "May I introduce, Lord William Hanley. William, this is Doctor Michael Campbell."

The doctor bowed his head. "My lord."

William gave the man a quick nod. "A pleasure to meet you, sir."

"Now," Charles said, turning everyone's attention back to him. "What do you wish to tell us, doctor?"

All eyes turned to the physician. "I checked the progress of Lord and Lady Elmwood's recovery," the doctor explained. "I believe Lady Elmwood will wake soon and be able to remain so without the assistance of so much laudanum. She seems much recovered. Her complexion is beginning to retain some color, which is a fantastic sign."

William cocked an eyebrow. He had thought Lady Elmwood was rather pale earlier, but he kept that thought to himself. How could she have looked any lighter than she was? he wondered.

"Lord Elmwood," the doctor continued in a somber tone, "is still in an unknown state. I've kept a rather vigil watch over his care. But he has yet to make any real progress. I'm hoping we will know more in a few days."

Everyone in the room seemed to be holding their breath, hoping for better news. At the doctor's words about Lord Elmwood the looks of hope came crumbling to the ground.

"Do you think my mother will make a full recovery?" Lady Olivia asked, sounding hopeful.

The doctor nodded. "Although, it is hard to say for sure until she is fully awake. But yes, I do believe she will."

William saw a visible sigh of relief, not only from Lady Olivia, but all others in the room.

"Thank you, Dr. Campbell," William's father said, shaking the man's hand. "Do you think there is anything we can do to help their recovery?"

He shook his head. "It's all up to the patients, I believe," he answered. "If you'll excuse me, I would like to check on Lord and Lady Elmwood once more before I return home for a few hours."

Charles shook the doctor's hand and the others bid farewell. William watched the doctor's eyes linger a little longer than necessary on Lady Olivia. What could only be described as jealousy, pricked at his conscience. He quickly shoved it aside. He had no reason to feel such things. She was the little sister of one of his closest friends, not anything more. At least that's what he kept telling himself. The vision of her bare feet and ankles popped into his mind, and he smiled to himself. She had to have been cold walking outside without any stockings or shoes, but she made no indication she had been.

"William?" his mother said in concern.

He realized the doctor had gone and he was staring at the empty doorway. His mother must have been talking to him, but he had been so caught up in his own thoughts he hadn't heard a word.

"I'm sorry, mother," he said, grinning sheepishly. "My mind was elsewhere. What did you say?"

She narrowed one eye and watched him carefully like he was hiding some special secret. "I asked if you were already dressed for dinner?"

He shook his head. "No, I went for a walk instead. I'll go change."

She nodded. "Is something wrong?" she asked before he turned away.

William's lips raised at the corners. "Nothing at all, mother, only lost in thought."

She watched him carefully and he heard his father chuckle at her side. "I believe the boy is doing fine, dear," he said. "Let's let the lad return to his room."

She opened her mouth, but then closed it and nodded. "Of course, apologies William."

William kissed her cheek and hurried from the room. He realized Charles and Lady Olivia must have followed the doctor because they were nowhere to be seen.

When William finally retired for the night, he thought about checking on Lord and Lady Elmwood but decided he didn't wish to intrude. He drifted to sleep rather quickly and awoke to a room still shrouded in darkness.

"Lord Hanley?" Sam called from the doorway.

William rubbed his eyes and looked to the lone candle and the face of his man servant. "What is it, Sam?" he asked, rubbing his eyes.

"My lord, Lady Elmwood is awake and speaking coherently for the first time since the attack," Sam said softly.

William shot up from his bed. "How long ago?"

"About an hour. The entire house is in an uproar," he explained, moving to William's dressing room and leaving the candle on the table.

"I need to go see if there's anything I can…" William began but was cut short as Sam hurried from the dressing room with an armful of clothing. William's lips curled. "You always seem to know my thoughts," he teased.

Sam shrugged. "I assumed you'd want to be there for Lady Olivia," he laughed.

William's mouth gaped open. "What are you talking about?"

"Nothing, my lord," Sam said, still laughing as he helped William dress, his eyes twinkling in merriment.

"Sam, I don't…" William started to say, but was cut off by his valet.

Sam held up one hand and chuckled. "Calm down. I'm only teasing you."

He glared at his valet. "I should sack you; you know that?"

Sam continued to laugh. Once the last boot was in place, his valet shoved William from the room, urging him to move quickly.

William's mind reeled. He hoped Lady Elmwood would have more information about her attacker so the investigation would lead somewhere. He hurried down the hall and turned toward the family's rooms, colliding with someone.

"I'm so…" he began, but froze before he could complete the thought. Lady Olivia was glaring at him from the floor slowly moving to her backside. she folded her arms over her chest in annoyance. "Lady Olivia!"

She raised an eyebrow. "In a hurry, are we?"

He reached down and assisted her to her feet. Surprised at the light teasing tone she presented. "I'm so sorry, my lady. Are you injured?"

She shook her head and rubbed a hand down her gown. "Only my pride."

He covered his face with his hand. "Truly, I'm so sorry. I'd heard your mother was awake and wanted to see if there was anything I can do. Apparently, I should have stayed in bed."

She chuckled, the sound sending William's heart into a frenzy. "Lord Hanley," she teased, "if it was the first time you had knocked me down, I might be offended. But, seeing as you used to purposely push me down, I'll take an accident any time."

He groaned. He'd forgotten about his follies as a youth. "I was young and rather daft; you must accept my apologies."

She smiled and shrugged one shoulder. "I guess it all depends on you, now doesn't it." She gave him a wink and walked away; leaving him standing in the hall, alone and confused.

What the blazes had just happened? Was that the same woman he'd spoken to earlier? William wondered. He watched as Lady Olivia turned the corner into her mother's room, and he felt a smile pull at his lips. He had no idea what she'd meant, but he found he was quite excited to figure it out.

Five

Olivia sat in the garden and stared out at the birds flitting around the small grove of trees. She'd come here three straight days. When Sally roused her the night her mother woke, she was sure it was a dream. When she arrived to her mother's rooms, Olivia had been thrilled to see her sitting up and speaking. For a moment it was as if nothing had even happened. Olivia had nearly crumbled in relief. She'd hurried over and thrown her arms around her mother's neck and cried. Her mother laid her head against Olivia's and attempted to calm her.

"It's alright, my dear," she'd told Olivia. "Everything is going to be alright."

Olivia was shocked at how weak her mother sounded. Luckily, she'd since grown stronger. She'd taken over Olivia's chair and sat with her husband as often as she could. Her mother had also been eating more solid meals. Olivia was happy she didn't have to keep bouncing from one room to the next now that her mother was on the mend. She hoped having her mother at her father's side would help him recover quicker. But so far, there was no change in his symptoms. He would wake briefly every few hours, which gave Charles or Dr. Campbell the opportunity to force him to drink some water or broth. Then, they would give him another dose of laudanum. The doses were helping to keep her father from being in agonizing pain. But even though he woke up, he never uttered more than a few groans.

Olivia's thoughts kept returning to the night her mother was able to wake fully. She smiled as the memories flooded back to her. She had left to get some fresh towels when she was knocked, rather forcefully, to the ground. She'd looked up into the shocked face of Lord Hanley. He looked so distraught, she'd almost laughed out loud. Instead, she decided to tease and taunt him a little. Watching him squirm under her glare was almost too much. She'd told him her acceptance of his apology for knocking her down and his childhood antics would depend entirely on him. She had to leave quickly following the remark so she wouldn't burst into laughter, an emotion that had been stifled since her parents' attack. Now she was teasing William, and she knew he had no idea what she was talking about. But she was enjoying watching him try to figure it out. She'd been so caught up with her antics, she'd forgotten to retrieve the towels she had left to retrieve. Charles eyed her questioningly when she'd returned empty handed.

Having her mother awake had finally begun to help her feel more herself and pulled her from the darkened state of mind she had been in. She was still deeply concerned for her father's health and prayed daily he would make a full recovery. However, all she wanted to do now was find ways to make Lord Hanley question everything. She knew she shouldn't enjoy taunting him. He made it so easy it would have been a shame not to have a little fun. It also helped relieve some of her worries and let the tension in her body relax.

The promised ride with Lord Hanley had been postponed for a few days after her mother woke because of the rain, but after her walk in the garden this morning, she was ready to let the wind blow through her hair and leave the world of stress behind her. She made her way to the stables and began rubbing down her mare. She'd come out, unbeknownst to her brother or other members of the staff, performing the task every morning since her mother woke. She had missed her horses, and the calm that came as she spent time out of doors had been good for her.

She asked Henry, the stable master that had worked for their family for ten years, to ready the mount she had chosen for Lord Hanley. The dapple-grey stallion, whom her brother had purchased a few months earlier, was tall and strong and had a dark grey mane and tail. His heavily muscled body revealed the strength, and in certain light, the horse's coloring looked blue rather than grey, so she'd named him Blue. He was a magnificent creature.

Olivia had risen early and worked tirelessly with the animal in a mostly empty Hyde Park while in London before Charles sent him back to the estate. She wanted to make sure Blue would be able to handle a rider. Training horses was something she loved doing, and she had become so proficient, others begged her to train theirs. She had declined, deciding instead to put aside her hobbies for a short time and learn to become a lady and join society. Horse training was definitely not on *La Belle Assemblée's* list of approved accomplishments for young ladies. Olivia's father, seeing her talent and wishing to help it grow, vehemently pressured her to continue. But she only worked with the family horses, *after* her training on the proper behavior of ladies had been completed for the day.

She heard a shuffle of feet and paused in her ministrations to Blue. She turned and found Lord Hanley watching her from the doorway. He was leaning against the frame of the entryway, his arms crossed over his chest and his ankles overlapped as well. She smiled and heat rushed to her cheeks. Teasing her friend had changed over the last few days and turned into more of a desire to see him smile. Every time he did, she would blush. She hated blushing, but no matter how much she attempted to teach herself to stop, it only became worse.

"Are you finally going to allow me to ride today?" he teased. He pushed from the wall and walked toward her.

She turned her attention back to her horse. *Yes, this is going to be extremely enjoyable.* She thought to herself, knowing Lord Hanley had no idea what she was planning.

Lady Olivia led her horse to the mounting block and deftly lifted herself into the saddle. William watched her in awe. She would never be predictable, which he found he liked. The women he'd been acquainted with in London always insisted a groom assist them into their saddles.

"Is something wrong?" Lady Olivia asked him, her expression curious.

William realized he had been caught staring at her and shifted uncomfortably. "Not at all, my lady. I was only admiring your mare."

She smiled and patted the light brown horse on the neck. "She's one of my favorites. I haven't been able to ride her for several months because I was in London." Her eyes beamed as she spoke of her horse, and it made William's heart speed up.

"I have Sweet Pea as well," she said pointing to a sorrel mare in the last stall. "She brought me here from London."

William approached her and reached his hand out to the mare she was on, scratching the horse's nose. "What's her name?"

She smiled again, her cheeks flashing a deep red. "Uh...Buttercup."

William laughed. "What makes you say it like that?"

Her lips twitched as she lowered her head, not meeting William's gaze. "I named her several years ago when I was much younger. Buttercup is almost seventeen now, so her name is a little juvenile."

He chuckled. "It suits her."

"Here's your horse, my lord," Henry said, handing him the reins.

"Thank you, Henry," William replied. "I believe you or a groom will need to accompany Lady Olivia and me. Can you make sure another horse is prepared for whomever you decide to send?"

Henry nodded. "Already done, sir. I'll be following behind in case there's a need for me."

William quickly pulled himself into the saddle, following Lady Olivia into the early morning light. As the sun began to rise over the horizon, the sky turned all sorts of bright colors.

Lady Olivia watched the sunrise, pure admiration on her face. "Isn't it beautiful?" she questioned, not turning to look at him. "My father used to tell me the sunrise and sunset were God's personal masterpieces."

William couldn't take his eyes off of the beautiful woman next to him. The intense emotions he was feeling for Lady Olivia had begun to scare him. He knew she was a beautiful woman, and he enjoyed her company, but something else was happening to him he couldn't explain.

"I believe your father has it right, it's very beautiful," he said, not taking his eyes from her.

Their eyes met, and she took what sounded like an unsteady breath. William wondered if maybe he had the same effect on her as she had on him.

She shook her head, giggling quietly to herself. "You're absurd," she said in a slightly teasing tone.

William laughed out loud. "How can I be absurd? You asked me if I was enjoying the beauty of the morning, and I answered."

Her blush returned, and she narrowed her eyes at him, mischief twinkling within. Before William could say a word, she winked at him and kicked her horse in the sides. Buttercup immediately took off down the path, leaving him behind.

Henry chuckled from behind William. "You best keep up, my lord. That horse of hers is quite the runner, even in her older age."

Lady Olivia's wink had caught him completely off guard. He kicked Blue into a gallop, excited at the idea of a race. William was certain he could catch Lady Olivia, no matter how fast her horse was. When he'd nearly caught up with her, Lady Olivia looked at him, her smile lighting her face. Her pale blue eyes, which seemed to be changing colors along with the sunrise, captivated him.

"Let's see how fast Blue is," she grinned, and leaning forward, lowered her body over Buttercup's neck.

The mare, which had been going quite fast before, looked to almost be flying as her legs only briefly met the ground. William heard Lady Olivia laugh as she left him behind once more. William shook his head and loosened his grip on the reins, giving Blue his head so the animal could run freely. The horse immediately obliged and followed Buttercup. Lady Olivia looked back once before turning and disappearing from sight when she crested a hill.

When William came to where he had last seen her, he saw her approaching a thick cropping of trees in the distance. He heard her tell Buttercup to stop and the horse instantly obeyed as she came to a sliding halt, dirt spraying the ground in front of them into the air. Lady Olivia kicked her leg free from the pummel and slid quickly to the ground. She looked back as William drew closer, and with a mischievous grin, he watched as she picked up her skirts and raced into the trees.

He couldn't believe what he was seeing. This woman was a gift. It was as if she were a little girl, playing a game of tag or hide and seek. The change in only the last few days was astounding. Her mother's recovery had given her new life. Lady Olivia was a different person out here, and he found her even more attractive than before. Pulling Blue to a stop, which wasn't nearly as impressive as Buttercups sliding performance, he jumped from his saddle. Throwing the reins over a branch he yelled back at Henry to take care of the horses then followed behind Lady Olivia. He knew he shouldn't be alone with her, especially in a forest; he didn't wish to ruin her reputation or to lose her trust. But he didn't care. In that moment, all he was thinking about was having fun with this wild adventurer.

William looked into the darkened forest, took a deep breath, and hurried after her. He had no idea which way she'd gone, but after a few steps, he found a well-used path and decided to follow it. He could hear the roar of water up ahead, and with each stride he took, it grew louder. He searched the trees and saw a small clearing not too far ahead of him. Speeding toward it, he burst through the trees, stumbling in shock at the sight before him.

A beautiful cascading waterfall plummeted into a raging river directly in front of Lady Olivia. The sound, which until this point had been muted by the trees, was deafening. She stood facing the water, her back turned toward him. Her riding hat was thrown onto a nearby tree trunk, as loose strands of long brown hair fluttered freely around her. Her arms were outstretched at her sides, as she titled back her head and closed her eyes.

William couldn't take his eyes off her. It was possibly the most stunning sight he had ever seen and could have been a painting hanging in one of the most prestigious art galleries in the country. His heartbeat quickened, whether from the exertion of his run or the scene filling his vision, he didn't know.

She turned and her blue eyes found his. They stared at one another for several moments before a smile crossed her face and she dropped her gaze. He stepped to her side and she leaned closer, making William's breath catch. "This is my sanctuary," she said, raising her voice, so it could be heard over the noise of the waterfall.

Lady Olivia took slow deliberate breaths, her entire countenance changing before William's eyes. Not wanting to be caught staring at her, he turned to watch the water tumble down the rocky cliff and crash into the river below. From the corner of his eye, he noticed she was watching him coyly through her lashes.

"I can see why you enjoy this," he said, trying to get the vision of her earlier antics from his mind.

She smiled. "It really is something, isn't it?"

He was finding it more and more difficult to take his eyes from her. He had no idea why it had taken him so long to notice how intriguing, smart, and witty she was. The more he learned about her the more he wanted to know.

She cocked her head to the side, her eyes moving back and forth across his face. Her smile fell almost instantly. "I'm sorry," she said, "I should not have brought you here. It only made things worse."

He raised an eyebrow. "Made what worse?"

She sighed heavily and rubbed her temples but didn't speak.

"Lady Olivia…" he stopped at the look she gave him, his mouth still agape.

"Olivia," she said with a shy smile.

"Olivia," her name came from his mouth in a whisper. He returned her smile. "I'm not sure what you think you made worse by bringing me here, but I couldn't disagree more. It's amazing."

She sighed and backed up a little toward the water. "My father used to bring me here after a long day of riding around the estate. He would have our cook pack a blanket and food, and we would sit at the edge of the clearing having a picnic while we watched the waterfall. He would tell me stories, making us both laugh until we had tears rolling down our cheeks. It became my sanctuary, a place I visit often when I feel the need to be close to my father."

A tear fell down her cheek, and she quickly wiped it away. Her chin dropped to her chest, and her hands covered her face as a sob ripped from her chest. "What if he never gets to bring me here again?"

"Olivia," he said quietly, reaching up and pulling her hands down. "Please don't cry." He handed her a handkerchief, and she took it silently.

"No one else in my family, at least, not anyone I know of, has ever been here. He always told me it was a place which held magic powers; a place where anything can happen," she explained, a far-off look on her face. "When my parents were first brought home after the attack, a part of me wished I could bring him here, and maybe it would help him heal. I knew, of course, I was being ridiculous," she shrugged. "But, I would have done anything to have them both well again. Now Mama is feeling better and I'm hoping she can bring my father back to us." Her face was unreadable as William watched her. "I felt strongly this morning I needed to show you this place. For some reason, I wanted you to see it, but I see now we shouldn't have come here."

He reached for her hand and kissed her knuckles. "Coming here shouldn't be a burden, Olivia, it's a place with good memories and should continue to be. Don't let anything or anyone keep you from coming here."

"Lord Hanley…"

"William," he interrupted, "please, call me William."

She smiled. "William, I…" she stopped and turned her head back toward the horses, listening.

Seconds later, Henry burst through the trees, his chest heaving heavily as his breaths came deep and long. "My lady," he wheezed and pointed toward the manor. "Your father…"

He didn't get another word out before Olivia raced through the trees toward her horse. By the time William had caught up to her, she was nearly out of the forest. He saw another groom nearby, waiting for Henry to return. He must have been the one to let Henry know something was amiss. William hurried behind her as she looked around for a way to mount her horse. Without thinking, William moved to her side, grabbed her around the waist, and lifted her easily into the saddle. He paused only for a moment when she inhaled at his touch. Her eyes met his, but instead of waiting, she kicked her horse into a gallop. By the time William mounted his horse, Olivia was halfway across the expansive property, disappearing and reappearing as she and her mare flew up and over each hillside.

William urged Blue to follow, knowing he would never catch up to Olivia. Her horse was much quicker than his, but he wasn't too far behind. Instead of heading for the stable, she turned her mare toward the front of the home and again slid to a stop. Before Buttercup had fully ceased moving, Olivia slipped from her back and hurried inside before anyone could help her.

William took the stairs two at a time and watched Olivia's skirts round the corner as she rushed into her father's bedchamber. He followed her inside and his heart stopped as he heard Lady Elmwood's nearly broken voice. "He...he's gone," she sobbed.

Watching Olivia collapse in agony would be burned into William's memory for the rest of his life. He tried to catch her before her knees hit the floor, but her body crumpled so quickly he didn't get to her in time. He reached beneath her and lifted her into his arms. He held her against him, wishing he could do something to take away her pain. She buried her face into his chest and her body shook violently with deep sobs. He set her down at her mother's side and Olivia immediately laid her head in Lady Elmwood's lap. William saw Charles on the opposite side of the bed, his head bent over his father, crying on the man's lifeless shoulder.

William watched the scene before him for several moments. The entire staff gathered outside the doorway and joined the Bartons' grief. James, Lord Elmwood's valet, was in a dark corner of the room, and William could see him attempting to hold back his own emotions.

"I need you to send word to Lord and Lady Pembrooke. They took a carriage into town," William said to a nearby footman.

"Yes, my lord. I'll go myself," the man answered quietly.

He looked at the remaining staff and decided the family should have time to grieve in private. He ushered everyone, including James, into the hallway before returning to Lord Elmwood's bedside.

He bent low and laid a hand softly on Olivia's shoulder as she wept. "I'm here if you need anything," he said quietly. She didn't move or react to his touch.

William walked from the room, closing the door, and followed the tearful servants away from Lord Elmwood's bedchamber. Entering the library, he made his way to the window and stared blankly outside. The sunny day had turned grey as storm clouds moved over Elmwood Manor, almost like the world knew a good man had left this earth. William listened to the wind blowing through the trees, as they swayed back and forth. A tear fell down his cheek and he brushed it away. He would not lose his emotions, not now. He needed to be strong for Olivia, Charles, and Lady Elmwood. They would need whatever help he could offer.

He sat in an overstuffed leather armchair and dropped his head in his hands, rubbing his forehead. Olivia had just lost her father. She had lost the man who had taken her to a magical waterfall, made her laugh, taught her to ride, and loved her unconditionally. William was at a complete loss as to how to help her. He wanted to be the one to pick up the pieces of her heart and help her put it back together. But he knew such an arrangement wasn't an option. He had no claim on Olivia. He was her friend and wasn't sure his help would be welcomed by her. Pain pulsed through him, a deep emotional pain which he had never experienced.

The door to the library flew open and his mother and father rushed to his side. He didn't look up at them. He couldn't let them see his eyes full of unshed tears.

"William," his mother whispered in a mournful tone. "Is it true? Has Francis passed?"

William could do nothing but nod.

She gasped and sat in the chair beside him, taking one of his hands in her own. His father put a hand on William's shoulder, and they sat together quietly mourning the loss of their friend. The quiet tears of his mother as she cried into her handkerchief were the only sounds to be heard.

The storm outside released its fury and a deluge of rain fell from the sky, as howling winds and bursts of lightning filled the sky. It fit the anguish looming throughout the manor.

"I…I think I'll go comfort…Catherine," William's mother said an hour later as she tried to control her sobs.

"I'll go with you dear," his father said, patting William's shoulder. "Why don't you have some tea delivered to the family, William?"

William laid a hand on atop his father's and nodded. As he heard his parents leave, he stood and pulled the bell for a servant before returning to watch out the window. Water poured down the glass in rivulets, which reminded him of the tears being shed throughout the home. The vision of Olivia in agonizing pain flashed through his mind and he dropped onto the small window seat as he waited for a maid. He asked for the tea, then he retreated down the hall toward Olivia and her family. She had remained near her mother; her tears replaced by a look of emptiness which crushed William from the inside and broke his heart.

Six

Forty-eight hours later the families walked together along the gravel path outside the cemetery, Olivia holding on to William's arm for support. Lord Elmwood's funeral had been well attended, and the graveside service had been emotionally taxing on everyone.

Olivia had dressed in a deep black gown with black lace, and wore a matching veil to cover her face. William couldn't see her eyes, but they had been red and swollen since her father's death. His worry for her increased when she wouldn't respond to anyone when asked a question. He tried his best to understand her grief, but he'd never lost a parent.

Olivia only stared ahead stoically, ignoring the world around her and never saying a word.

William assisted Lady Elmwood, Olivia, and his mother inside the carriage before taking a seat opposite them, followed by Charles and William's father. Olivia lifted the veil from her face and flipped it over her head. William frowned, the pale coloring on her cheeks and the dark circles under her eyes had become worse. He reached for her hand to offer comfort, but she pulled away and avoided his gaze. He sighed. The silence was deafening, and he didn't know how to help her.

A small luncheon was held at Elmwood Manor in honor of the late marquess. Olivia refused any food offered and kept entirely to herself. After an hour, she excused herself and walked somberly from the room. William watched her go, not sure what else he could do. He had tried consoling her, asked if she wanted to go for a ride or walk, he even tried sitting beside her while she cried. Nothing he did made a difference.

"She's hurting son," his father said sadly. "She needs time to grieve."

"How do I help her, father? I have tried everything I can think of." William rubbed his hands up and down his legs. "What should I do?"

"Give her time," was all his father said before moving to join his wife and Lady Elmwood at the other end of the room.

William glanced at Charles, who had been doing his best to maintain a strong presence in the household. As the new Marquess of Elmwood, Charles understood he needed to act the part, no matter his grief. But William could see how deep his friend's pain and worry truly ran. William walked toward him and shook Charles's hand, giving him an apologetic smile.

"I'm sorry, my friend," William murmured, placing his hand on his friend's shoulder.

"Thank you. I don't know what we would have done if your family hadn't been here. Mother and Olivia need your family's presence while they mourn the loss of father," Charles said, his voice raw and deep with anguish.

"Is there anything I can do for you?" William asked Charles.

"Take care of my sister. I'm worried she'll become lost in her grief." Charles answered when he looked up at William.

"Of course." William replied, looking around the room to see if Olivia had returned. When he didn't see her, he turned toward the door and felt a pull in that direction. He needed to find Olivia. Not because Charles asked him to. He wanted to let her know she could lean on him so he could take away at least some of her pain. He checked the public rooms before hearing music. Hurrying toward the sound, he found Olivia sitting before the piano forte, her fingers pressing down one key at a time. William slowly made his way to her and stood beside her.

"How are you feeling?" he asked, hoping she would open up to him.

She stared over the top of the instrument; her eyes hollow. She didn't respond but continued to play the same note repeatedly.

"Olivia?" he asked taking her hands in his. "Please, talk to me."

Silence.

He sighed. "I know you're hurting. I can help if you'll allow it. Tell me what I can do."

No emotion crossed her face, no words left her lips. She stared ahead at nothing. It was like she had died inside; like she couldn't break free of the cage holding her captive.

William put a hand on her cheek, and finally, she looked up at him. He nearly gasped at what he saw. The cheerful expression he'd grown to love, had lost all light and was replaced by pain, suffering, and anger. William instinctively moved his hand and took a small step away from her when her eyes darkened.

"Olivia?" he questioned.

She narrowed her eyes and glared at him. "Leave! Just get out of here, and leave me be! I don't want you here!" She flipped back toward the piano forte ignoring him.

William took a deep breath, her words cut through him like a knife. He took another slow step away wanting to be there for her, but also, to give her the space she demanded. "Olivia, please let me help you."

Nothing.

He dropped his head, and after one last look, shuffled from the music room, his heart breaking for a different reason than before. The single monotone sound from the piano forte echoed throughout the corridor. William shut the door and walked away, unable to listen any longer.

"Don't take it too personally," Charles said sadly, startling William. "She hasn't spoken to anyone, not even our mother. I tried to hug her at the funeral, and she stumbled back like I had burned her."

"I know she's hurting, but why is she shutting herself off from everyone? Why won't she allow us to help her, to ease some of her burdens?" William asked, his voice only a whisper.

Charles shrugged. "I've never seen her like this before, and neither has our mother. You saw her when both our mother and father were ill. I never thought I'd see anything worse, but Olivia seems to have broken in ways which may take a long time to heal. She has always been the strong one between the two of us. But this," he said pointing to the music room with his head, "has shattered her entirely."

William looked back at the music room. He let his shoulders fall and rolled his neck to relieve the tension which had built over the last couple of days. Charles's eyes were on the closed door of the room, his own pain showing on his face.

"How are you doing, Charles?" William asked.

He shrugged one shoulder. "I don't know. I know my mother and sister need me to be strong, but I don't know if I can. I'm beyond terrified and I have no idea what I'm supposed to do. I'm not ready to be a marquess, William. I'm not ready for such responsibility."

William didn't know how to respond. He hadn't thought of what he would do if his father passed away. He had plenty of training to be the next Earl of Pembrooke but had never really thought if he were ready to take on the title.

"My father and I will help you get comfortable with your new position," William responded, saying the only thing which came to mind.

Charles's entire body seemed to droop under the pressure of all that was now expected of him. He shrugged his shoulders and fidgeted with the sleeve of his black jacket.

"How's your mother?" William asked, trying to take Charles's mind away from the idea of being a marquess.

"She's alright. The doctor told her she needed to stay in bed and rest. Her injuries haven't had a chance to heal completely, and he's afraid they might get infected if she isn't careful," Charles explained. "He also believes my father's death was from an ailment of the heart. He thinks the injuries were too much for his body to overcome."

William had heard about Lord Elmwood's possible cause of death the night before, but it still felt like a fresh wound which needed to heal. It was still very difficult for him to imagine Lord Elmwood not in the home. It seemed surreal.

"Lady Pembrooke has taken her to her room to rest," Charles said. "Your mother has been a blessing to her, you know. Having Lady Pembrooke here has helped my mother bear this loss."

William inhaled, then released the air which built in his lungs. "Maybe there is something my family can do to help Lady Olivia smile again."

Charles looked again at the door separating them from his sister. "If you figure out how to get through to her, please let me know. I hate seeing her like this."

William nodded. "I'll keep trying."

Olivia knew she was being selfish. She knew she wasn't the only person in her family who was hurting from the loss of her father. No one seemed to understand that all of this pain and suffering was possibly because of her. She had rejected Lord Greenly and if he were somehow involved, then her father died because of her. Lord Greenly had been furious when she rejected him, but was he angry enough that he would kill her parents? Lord Pembrooke had explained they had already investigated him, but she couldn't shake the feeling that this was all her fault. What was worse, she had left her father's side to go ride with William and didn't get a chance to say goodbye.

Charles tried to convince her she was being ridiculous when she had confided in him after her parents were brought home after being shot. He told her there was nothing she could have done to cause this, but she knew he was wrong. Burying her face in her pillow, she released a sob just as her stomach growled in hunger. She couldn't remember the last time she had eaten anything. Charles said she was causing their mother to worry, and if she didn't join them all for afternoon tea, he would drag her to the table and force her to eat. His words grieved her. It wasn't her intention to cause any more grief for anyone, but she wanted to be alone.

Knowing she had no other option she left her room and moved slowly down the hall toward the drawing-room where she knew her family would be. Pushing open the door, she made her way to her mother's side. She knew her mother needed assistance with nearly everything, but seeing her many injuries reminded Olivia too much of everything they had experienced over the last few weeks. Her father was gone and it sent a pang of emotion through her. She felt herself stumble as she sat near her mother.

"How are you feeling, dear," Lady Pembrooke asked in a soft voice.

Olivia's lips raised in a small half-hearted smile. "A little better, thank you."

She could see the distrust in Charles gaze, but he didn't refute her claim. She could do this. Olivia could put on a show to help her mother and brother heal.

Lady Pembrooke put a hand over Olivia's and gave her a reassuring nod of encouragement. "Would you like something to eat?"

She looked to Lady Pembrooke, then to Charles who glared at her. "Yes, please," she said quietly.

Before Charles or anyone else could move, William walked to a table which had been laid with different types of snacks and grabbed a little of everything, and handed it to her. Their eyes met, and the side of his mouth rose in a gesture of understanding.

A feeling of remorse flowed through her, but she pushed it aside. She didn't want his pity; she didn't want anyone's pity. Even after all she'd done over the last several days for both of her parents, Olivia lost the only man who truly pushed her to become better than the *ton* demanded her to be.

Although Olivia was grateful her mother was recovering, she didn't know how she was supposed to put on a happy face and move on without her father? She had split her time evenly between her parents' bedchambers, making sure they both had her attention and love. Shaking the anger from her thoughts, Olivia thanked William, before making a point to let everyone see she was eating. The food tasted good in her mouth, but she felt queasy with every bite.

When she glanced at her mother, who was watching her carefully, Olivia tried to offer a warm smile. She leaned her head on her mother's uninjured arm to both offer and receive comfort. She felt her mother lay her cheek on top of her head, but Olivia didn't dare look at her again. She knew seeing the pain in her mother's eyes would make her guilt worse than it already was.

Olivia knew William was watching her as she sat trying to control her emotions, and it was making her want to squirm in her seat. The fidgeting caused one of her hair pins to loosen and a thick curl tumbled down the back of her neck, making her cringe. Her stomach fluttered at the thought of what she must look like, but she pushed it aside. She didn't care. She didn't care what anyone thought of her.

She'd enjoyed William's attentions while in London, but having him in her home during the most difficult time of her life had drained her joy. She didn't dare look in his direction again. She knew what she would see, and she wasn't in the mood to deal with his *understanding* stares. He didn't understand, and he never would. Her anger was returning, and she didn't try and stop it.

"Mother," Charles said, "when you are ready to return to your room to rest, please let me know and I'll assist you."

She nodded. "Actually, I believe I am ready now. I am feeling rather tired."

Charles quickly moved to his mother's side and helped her to her feet and out the door. Olivia watched them go, her mother's shoulders sagged and her steps were slow. Olivia didn't know if it was caused by the grief over the loss of her husband or the pain from her injuries. As soon as they were out of sight, Olivia knew she wanted to go back to her room rather than sit and pretend like everything was fine.

"I should probably go as well," Olivia said, rising from her seat. "Please excuse me."

"Lady Olivia?" William called as she tried to retreat.

She froze, trying to put the smile back on her face before turning toward him. "Yes, my lord?" she said in forced politeness, but he didn't seem to notice.

"Can I entice you to join me for a stroll in the garden before dinner?" he asked, watching her carefully.

She took a deep breath to calm the anxious fluttering of her heart. She felt the tears inching their way forward, wishing for an escape, but she wouldn't let anyone see her cry again.

"If you don't mind, my lord, maybe tomorrow would be better. I really am quite tired." She watched the disappointment flash in his eyes.

"Of course, my lady," he said, taking her hand in his and pressing a gentle kiss on her fingers. "Until tomorrow then."

Olivia curtsied and hurried away, the exhaustion from all that had happened taking its toll. As soon as she reached her room, she could no longer hold the tears and they rolled freely down her cheeks. She threw herself onto her bed, hoping sleep would overtake the raw emotions she was feeling. The last thing she remembered before falling asleep was William's pained expression in the music room.

Seven

One Year Later

William pulled at his cravat as the carriage pulled into the drive of Elmwood Manor. He hadn't been back here since Lord Elmwood's death, nor had he seen any of its occupants for months. Sweat rolled down his neck and along his back at the thought of returning to a place which held so much heartache. When the carriage came to a stop and a footman opened the door, William descended before offering his hand to assist his mother.

"Welcome back to Elmwood, Lady Pembrooke," Charles's voice boomed over the quiet of the day. "We are pleased you were able to join us."

William's mother smiled and hit Charles softly on the arm with her fan. "How many times over the years have I insisted you to call me Victoria?" she tittered.

"At least a dozen more, my lady," he said smiling and taking the countess's hand. He placed a brief kiss to the back, then bowed respectfully to William and his father.

"Hello, my boy," William's father said, clapping Charles on the shoulder and shaking his hand fiercely. "We're happy to be back."

The door of the house opened, and William's jaw dropped. Olivia stood on the top step, a bright smile on her face. She was wearing a pale-yellow day dress with a purple sash tied around her middle. Her dark chestnut hair was pulled up and curls fell freely down the side of her face and grazed her neck. The beauty of the woman left him utterly speechless. He could do nothing but stare as she walked toward them, her elegant stride even more alluring than the dress she wore.

"Lord and Lady Pembrooke," she said, her voice full of joy. "I'm so delighted you accepted the invitation to join us."

William's mother pulled Olivia into a tight hug and kissed her cheek. "It's so good to see you, my dear," she said, tears filling her eyes. "You look absolutely beautiful."

A pink blush steeled across her cheeks. "As do you."

"Olivia, what a joy to see you again," his father said, bowing to her.

"My lord," she grinned. "Thank you for coming."

He stepped up and placed a light kiss on her cheek and she smiled so warmly, William wondered how his father had earned so much of Olivia's affection.

"Victoria!" Lady Elmwood called, as she all but ran down the steps toward William's mother.

The two ladies hugged for a long moment before separating enough so Lady Elmwood could greet his father and himself. Both mothers had tears in their eyes as they walked arm in arm to the open door of the manor, his mother's green traveling gown muted by the black mourning clothes her friend still donned.

Lady Elmwood had never gained back the full use of her left arm, but she seemed to be in high spirits. William's father followed behind the two giddy friends, his walking stick twirling in his fingers as he ascended the stairs.

"William," Olivia greeted before dropping into a low curtsy.

The sound of her voice sent nervous chills through his body. The last time he saw her she had been in mourning. He and his parents stayed a fortnight following Lord Elmwood's passing the year before. While in residence, he only saw Olivia a handful of times and had spoken to her even less. She had shut herself in her room, only making an appearance at the occasional family dinner. She always sat by her mother, her head lowered to her plate and only answering questions specifically directed to her. She had smiled and laughed, when necessary, but William could tell it was forced. The joy never reached her eyes and he hated it.

"Lady Olivia," he said pulling her hand to his and kissing her knuckles as he bowed to her.

"Olivia," she said, watching him, a small smile on her mouth.

He grinned at her, pleased she still wished for him to call her by her given name.

"You look lovely," he said offering her his arm, which she took willingly.

Her cheeks blushed ever so slightly. "Thank you. I hope your journey was pleasant." Her eyes lit up as she smiled.

The warmth of her smile made William's heart beat wildly in his chest as he realized how much he had missed her. He had done all he could think of the year before to help Lady Olivia overcome her melancholy when her father died, but nothing he attempted had worked.

"You seem in high spirits this afternoon," he said. "It suits you."

He nearly laughed as her blush darkened her cheeks and she demurely dropped her gaze from his face.

They walked into the front parlor. Tea and an assorted array of finger sandwiches had been placed in the center of the room. Olivia released his arm and handed him a teacup full of a warm liquid, placing a biscuit on the small plate alongside it. He could see she was holding back a laugh, and he chuckled.

Flashes of memory from a family dinner in London during her first Season made him smile. He and his parents had visited Elmwood House often. During one of their visits, William desperately tried to get Olivia to tell him what had happened at the theatre the night before. He hadn't been able to attend, but some of his friends had told him Lady Olivia was surrounded almost the entire evening. One gentleman stormed from their box during one of the intermissions, and no one had any idea why. It intrigued him. After pleading with her for some time to share her secret, he looked to Charles for help, but his friend only smiled.

"Good luck, William, my sister is very good at keeping her secrets," he grinned. "When we were children, she discovered a way to sneak biscuits from the kitchen. To this very day, I still don't know how she managed it. Any time I tried, Cook hit me with her spoon," he laughed at the memory.

"Didn't you bury her spoons in the garden?" Olivia chuckled. "I have never seen Cook so flustered. She looked around the kitchen for hours before figuring out you were the one who had taken them."

Charles laughed loudly at the memory, making everyone else in the room join in. "I think it may have been one of the scariest moments of my life," he said, still laughing. "I still have no idea how she figured out it was me who hid them."

Olivia turned bright red and covered her mouth with her hand, trying to stifle her laughter, but William recognized her attempt.

"I believe, Charles, your sister has another secret," he tossed his head in her direction, a huge smile lighting his face.

Charles gasped. "YOU!" he laughed. "I should have known you would tell her."

Olivia laughed until her sides ached. "Of course I did, dear brother. How else was I going to sneak a biscuit?" the entire room filled with laughter.

The memory was one William hadn't thought of in some time, but he could tell Olivia was thinking of it. He decided to play along. He had wondered how she would be when they arrived, and so far, he liked what he saw. He had a difficult time leaving last summer, and he told himself it was because the Barton's needed his help. Looking at the woman across from him, he knew he was lying to himself.

"Am I to assume your cook will be here with a spoon at any moment and insist I stole this?" he teased, pleased when she released a rather joyful laugh, it seemed to make the room even more cheerful.

"Only if you allow her to see it," she said with a playful grin. "So, you better eat it quickly."

He smiled and raised an eyebrow at her when she gave him a playful grin. Something inside him warmed at the sight, and the feeling caught him completely off guard. Lady Elmwood asked her daughter a question, so William excused himself and moved to join Charles.

"Amazing, isn't it?" Charles said, startling William out of his thoughts.

He turned to look at his friend, confused. "What is?"

He nodded pointedly at his sister. "To see her so happy. When you and your family were here before..." he let the sentence fade without finishing it. William knew Charles didn't wish to talk about his father.

"It is indeed amazing," he said. "How long has she been like this? It was nearly impossible to pull a smile from her the last time I was here."

He shrugged. "My mother suggested we host this house party a few months ago after the London Season ended. Until that point, Olivia had been very slowly starting to return to us," he explained. "At first she thought the house party would be a horrible idea. She complained constantly about having people in our home, continuously bringing up the fact we would only just be coming out of mourning."

William turned his gaze back to Olivia. "So what changed?"

Charles looked at him and dropped his gaze to the floor, smiling. "My mother suggested we invite your family."

William stared at him waiting for his friend to continue, but Charles didn't say anything further. "Why would that have caused such a change? We were here for several weeks last summer and she didn't seem happy then," William said as confusion filled his every thought.

Charles chuckled. "I would think it obvious," he said. "Olivia has missed you."

William's mouth dropped open and he stared wide-eyed at his friend, but he couldn't seem to find a single word to say. Charles laughed quite loudly, the eyes of everyone in the room turned to them and William barely had the sense to close his mouth.

"Are you quite alright?" Lady Elmwood asked Charles, a hint of laughter in her voice.

"Indeed, mother," he said, still laughing. "It's nothing."

She raised an eyebrow suspiciously before turning back to her friend. William noticed Olivia was watching him, but he couldn't figure out the look she was giving him. She looked pleased, but there was something else, something he very much wanted to discover. It was a searing look which could easily bring any man to his knees. It had very nearly done as much to him. Something was very different about the woman he was seeing. He had been captivated by her the last few years, but when they last parted, William was sure Olivia would never speak to him again.

"Believe me yet?" Charles whispered under his breath, still watching William with a satisfied grin on his face.

William turned and shook his head. Charles's smile grew. "I highly doubt that I am the reason," William said, leaning against the wall, hoping it would mask his complete undoing.

Charles laughed again, slapping William on the shoulder. "You'll see," he said, before walking off to greet William's father.

William turned his gaze back to Olivia who was listening intently to something his mother had said. She chuckled before responding with a flip of her wrist in the air. He wished he could hear their conversation. The animation in her face, along with the smiles and laughter, confused him. He was pleased she had overcome some of her grief. It gave him hope they might continue as they had been in London a year earlier. He knew she wasn't completely healed, and she may never fully get over the loss of her father. It was understandable. When she laughed again, William was no longer able to stand and watch her from a distance. He approached the ladies somewhat cautiously and asked if he could join them. His mother smiled and pointed to the chair near Olivia. He swallowed hard. Why the idea of sitting near her made him nervous, he couldn't say, but all the same, he was.

"Olivia?" his mother inquired after he'd sat in the offered chair. "Your mother tells me you have a beautiful rose garden on the east side of the manor you tend yourself. Is this correct? Do you have a talent for such things?"

Olivia blushed a deep pink and lowered her head shyly. "My rose garden is quite lovely, and yes, I do tend to them. But our gardener does the majority of the work. I simply help water them when needed, or I prune them on occasion," she answered. "I would love to show them to you whilst you are here."

His mother smiled brightly. "I believe I should like that very much. Do you have a favorite flower in your garden?"

"She likes lilacs," William said, immediately realizing he had spoken out loud and his cheeks warmed slightly.

His mother and Lady Elmwood both eyed him curiously, but when he looked at Olivia, she smiled and turned her gaze to her hands folded in her lap.

"Lilacs?" his mother said, watching him with narrowed eyes.

"They indeed are my favorite, my lady," Olivia said rescuing him from the matrons' stares. "Lord Hanley was gracious enough to walk me about part of my garden during your last visit, and I had the pleasure of pointing them out to him. I was disappointed circumstances didn't allow me to give you all a tour of the rest of the garden."

"Livvie dear, why don't you take Lord Hanley to your rose garden and show him what you have been working on. I'm sure he would love to see them." Lady Elmwood said conspiratorially, a glint of pleasure in her eye when she looked at William's mother.

Olivia looked at him. "Actually…"

He braced himself for another rejection like she had done last year.

"Lord Hanley does owe me a walk in the gardens."

He stared at her in obvious shock. He couldn't remember ever telling her he would take her for a stroll in the garden after her rejection. Did she wish to renew the relationship between them? He stood and offered her his arm, wanting to see where this *walk* would lead them. He wondered if, away from her mother and Charles, she would revert back to what he remembered when his family had left Elmwood Manor.

He felt her trembling hand slip into his arm, and he eagerly walked her toward the doors.

"Olivia, darling," her mother called. "Make sure Sally goes as well, or a footman."

She nodded and smiled. "Of course, Mama."

She continued walking and they found her maid already waiting for them outside the parlor. William found it odd, but maybe this is where her maid stayed in case her mistress needed her for some reason.

"Sally?" she turned toward the young lady. "Do you remember Lord Hanley?"

William was taken aback at being introduced to Olivia's maid. He wondered if the two shared a relationship similar to the one he had with Sam, or if Olivia introduced all the servants in this manner.

Sally curtsied. "Of course, my lady. My lord," she said with a curtsy in his direction before handing Olivia her bonnet.

Olivia twisted the ribbons of her bonnet under her chin, quickly securing it as Lewis opened the door leading outside. They walked in silence for several minutes, then rounded the side of the house and into the same well-manicured garden they had walked in a year ago. She turned around and looked in every direction before quickly untying the bonnet and tossed it back to her maid. Sally then stepped back enough to give her mistress a fair amount of privacy. He stared at her and she laughed.

"Mother insists I wear this thing outside, but I would much rather feel the warm sun on my skin. I'm afraid I will be a freckled mess and my mother will be extremely disappointed in my abhorrent behavior," Olivia explained with a shrug, barely holding back her laugh. She turned quickly in his direction. "Don't you dare tell her I took it off, she'll never let me out of doors again!"

"I wouldn't dream of it." He laughed at the pretty glare on her face. "Promise."

She raised her eyebrow and narrowed her eyes at him. "I trust you, but don't make me regret it."

He laughed and patted her arm inside the crook of his elbow. "I too enjoy the sunshine, so your secret is safe." He winked.

She took a few more small steps before speaking again. "I am truly happy to see you. I was afraid after our parting last summer, you wouldn't wish to come."

William couldn't forget the cold dismissal she gave him as his family prepared to leave Elmwood. She'd ignored him for two weeks, and he had hoped she would come and wish them a happy journey. When she finally came out of the house, he had breathed a sigh of relief. She had given his mother and father a hug, but only gave him a very brisk curtsy before running back inside without a word or single glance in his direction.

He had spent the last year worried about her well-being, wondering if she was well. William's mother had shared some of the letters Lady Elmwood had sent, especially when they mentioned Lady Olivia, but it never seemed like enough to settle his heart. Now the smell of her lilac perfume was intoxicating to his senses. Everything about her was perfect as the sun shone down on her, highlighting her chestnut-colored curls.

"William," she said, stopping to look at him. "I must apologize for my behavior before. Even in my grief, I should never have treated you the way I did."

William opened his mouth to speak, but before he could utter a single word, she placed her fingers on his lips, affectively silencing him.

"Please," she said, looking over her shoulder at her maid, who William had forgotten followed them. The young maid had turned her back to them as she stared off into the distance. "I must do this." She gave him a small smile and took a long deep breath then released it. She removed her fingers and let her hand fall back to her side.

"The loss of my father," she paused as her voice shook slightly and took another breath before continuing, "broke me. I was filled with a darkness which took over my every emotion; my very being. I tried to be happy, tried to pretend I wasn't dying inside. In truth, the only thing I truly wanted was to slip into a dark room and never leave."

She put her arm back in his and pulled him back along the path. "It wasn't until after your family left that I realized all I had done. The realization pulled me even deeper into the dark recesses of my mind. I walked around the house like a ghost for months. I avoided my mother and brother, and every other person who came to the house."

She looked down and sighed. "I hurt everywhere. I had lost my father. The man who loved me no matter what, and made me smile on my darkest of days. Adding to my pain, I felt I had also lost my heart. Six months after my father died, my brother suggested we go to London for the Season. I refused immediately. The last place I wanted to go was the city where I would be expected to attend balls, and soirees, listen to the horrid gossips and pretend I was happy, all while in half-mourning.

Charles tried for weeks to convince me. He even tried to bribe me with another horse, but I wouldn't give in," she said, giving him a weak smile. "A few days before Charles had to be in London to take my father's seat in parliament, my mother brought up the idea of having a summer house party. Needless to say, I wasn't happy, but she refused to listen. She started the invitations and pulled me into the planning and details until I thought I was going to lose my mind more than I already had."

Olivia looked out over her garden, then stopped and sat on a bench near a tall hedgerow leading to a part of the garden he hadn't been to. She moved to the edge of the bench and he sat beside her, turning his body so she knew she had his full attention. Her eyes seemed to bore into his own as they sat in silence for several seconds.

She looked away, her voice a touch quieter than before. "Two months ago, I finally asked my mother who she had invited to the party. I wanted to make sure I had a place to hide if needed."

He chuckled and she smiled in return.

"She handed me the guest list. To my utter surprise, when I saw your family on the guest list, I smiled, something I hadn't done in a very long time. My heart filled with happiness as I realized I would finally get the chance to apologize."

Olivia looked up at him, a mischievous glint in her eyes. "Blue was also very upset with me, you see," she said. "I had run off his rider, and he still hasn't forgiven me."

They both laughed. "Well, I'm sure he'll forgive you if I join you on one of your rides while I am here," he said. "But I make no guarantees."

"Yes," she said. "I'm sure you're correct."

She stood and walked a few steps away from him, then whirled back around to face him, her blue eyes sparkling in the sunshine. "I don't know if you'll ever be able to forgive me for my actions, but I am truly sorry."

William approached her and pulled her hand to his lips. "I never blamed you. I understand you needed time. I had only hoped we were still welcome here… that I was still welcome."

Olivia looked up at him, and he froze. She studied him in such a way that made his entire body tingled with excitement. She smiled, and so quickly he barely realized what was happening, she raised onto the tips of her toes and kissed his cheek. His heart sped up at the touch of her lips on his skin and the sweet fragrance of lilacs. He stared at her and she lowered her eyes shyly.

"Sorry, my lady," Sally interjected, her words thick with regret as she broke the moment. "Your brother is coming up the path."

Olivia cleared her throat and placed an unsteady hand on her stomach. "Thank you, Sally."

William turned around and waited for Charles to reach them, disappointed at his friend's timing.

Charles smiled when he approached, looking between Olivia and William. "I was sent to tell you Mr. Colfelt has arrived."

"You were sent?" Olivia said, one brow raised in question. "Why not a footman?"

Charles only shrugged.

William looked at him confused. "Mr. Colfelt is here?"

Olivia smiled and said, "I knew you and Mr. Colfelt were friends, so I included him in our party. I hope it's alright."

He tilted his head down and looked at her. "I am certain you have made the man's entire year." He laughed. "Being invited to the home of a marquess probably sent the poor man into fits of hysteria."

"Poor Mr. Colfelt," she said placing a hand lightly over her mouth to stifle her laugh.

Charles beamed. "Am I truly so frightening?"

Olivia shook her head and rolled her eyes. "Charles, we should go greet our guest. It's rude to keep him waiting," she scolded, still quietly tittering to herself.

William offered her his arm. "Shall we?"

She nodded, and in a hopeful tone said, "we will have to continue our walk another time."

"I would love nothing more."

Eight

Olivia's heart still hadn't settled from her and William's walk. She'd forgotten what his simple touch did to her. Her body had prickled with excitement and happiness engulfed her. The months they were apart made her realize how much she loved being around him. He made her smile and laugh, and to her horror, blush. She had missed him.

Mr. Colfelt was exactly as she remembered when she walked into the drawing-room on William's arm. The poor man looked terrified to be in the home of a peer. His face had drained of all color, and he stood rigidly across the room. They greeted one another warmly and after a few minutes of teasing from both William and Charles, Mr. Colfelt was doing much better. They remained in the drawing-room for the next few hours before Olivia excused herself to prepare for dinner. They were expecting a few other guests to arrive tomorrow. A young woman, whose company Charles had enjoyed while in London for the Season, was among them. Olivia hadn't met the lady and found it curious her brother was so nervous about her arrival.

Charles had known he needed to go to London for the Season to perform his parliamentary duties and he met the young lady while attending the theatre. He said she was the most beautiful creature he had ever seen. Olivia had thought it only a passing fancy, but the more he talked about the lovely Miss Lyla Abbot, the more Olivia wished to meet her. Charles talked of little else after he'd arrived a week earlier to help prepare for the party. He'd even talked mother into throwing a ball, which she was reluctant to do. When Charles suggested her dearest friend, Lady Pembrooke, could help with the planning, it had been settled.

Olivia ordered a new gown from London for the occasion, but it wouldn't arrive for a few more days. The ball would be held at the end of the week, so the modiste hadn't a lot of time to make it. She assured Olivia and her mother the dress would be ready. Tonight, she was dressed in a pale pink evening gown with a shear overlay, a ruby necklace, and matching pink slippers. Sally had done wonders with Olivia's mop of curls, styling it atop her head in ringlets, allowing small soft curls to frame her face. She'd finished off the toilette with a pink ribbon lined with small white flowers.

Olivia's stomach twisted itself into knots and she had to take several deep breaths to calm her nerves before she walked down the grand staircase. The wooden floor below the steps gleamed with candlelight and shadows danced along the walls like tiny ghosts. It reminded her of being a ghost in her own home for almost a year. Her thoughts turned to her father, and she touched the red gemstone hanging around her neck. She rubbed the smooth surface between her fingers as she tried to control her emotions. Her father had given the jewels to her on the eve of her coming-out ball. He'd wrapped them in a black-velvet-lined box, explaining they had been what her grandmother wore to her own wedding. Olivia loved the gift. When he placed them around her neck, tears were on the verge of falling down her father's cheeks.

"You look exactly like her," he said emotionally, causing her to wipe a tear from her cheek. "Did you know my mother is the reason for your hair color?" He only paused for a moment, touching a curl resting against Olivia's chin before continuing. "Your grandmother's hair was a lovely shade of brown in the summer. In the winter it changed to a more copper color, and some told her she had streaks of red hiding amongst the strands at certain times of the year. Your hair does the same thing."

"Mother told me I was more like her than either of you," she said, earning her a loving smile and a tight hug.

Olivia wiped her cheek, the memories of her father had caused tears to fall, and she had promised herself she wouldn't cry tonight. She took slow even steps as she descended the stairway, listening to the light fabric of her dress gliding along behind her. The guests were seated in the parlor, but she paused before walking to the door to put a smile on her face.

Lewis bowed low and winked before opening the door, causing a whoosh of air to ruffle the light curls around her face. Olivia inhaled and walked into the room. Her mother stood near the window with Lady Pembrooke, Charles was in the center of the room with Mr. Colfelt looking over a piece of parchment, and William stood with his back toward her, talking to his father. Lord Pembrooke looked over his son's shoulder and said something to William. He turned to look at her, making her breath catch in her throat.

"Lady Olivia," Lord Pembrooke said as the two men joined her. "What a lovely gown."

She smiled. "Thank you, my lord."

"Isn't Lady Olivia stunning in her gown this evening?" William's father asked him, slapping his son on the back.

"Very," William said, his eyes never leaving her own as he kissed the back of her hand.

"We were just discussing the ball, Olivia," Lady Pembrooke said as she approached them. "Your mother said you ordered a new gown for the event. Is it the same color as this one?" she asked, running her hand up and down in the air to point out her dress.

Olivia shook her head. "No, my lady."

Lady Pembrooke tilted her head to the side. "What color gown did you order?"

"Mother," William said, all eyes moving to him. "Let's leave details of the ball for another time."

His mother looked at him enquiringly. "Whatever for?"

He walked to his mother's side and kissed her softly on the cheek. "Because knowing the details takes all the fun out of it for the gentleman," he teased, wagging his eyebrows at her.

"Oh William, stop it," she laughed heartily. "You are such a tease."

Olivia watched the exchange, and it filled her with warmth. William truly loved his mother, no one could deny it. His sweetness to her brought on other feelings inside herself; a longing she couldn't escape if she tried. The man had stolen her heart from her chest and locked it up, forever keeping it with him.

She realized this fact halfway through her first Season while attending a small dinner party. He had spent the entire night in her company, teasing and complimenting her. He made her laugh and smile far too much for a lady of the *ton*, and when he looked at her, her legs wobbled slightly. That night, standing in their friends small drawing-room, she knew she'd fallen in love with Lord William Hanley. But after her treatment of him during their last visit to Elmwood, she didn't know if he returned her feelings.

Their walk in the garden earlier did wonders for the loneliness she'd been feeling. When they had to part ways, she instantly missed him. She hadn't seen him for a year, but as soon as he stepped out of the carriage, a piece of her heart had returned to her. A piece she hadn't realized was missing until the moment his eyes met hers.

"Olivia?" her mother asked. "Did you hear me?"

Olivia turned her head to look at her mother. "I'm sorry, Mama, my thoughts were elsewhere."

"I asked if you were able to show Lord Hanley the rose garden?" she repeated, her eyes boring into her like she was trying to discover a secret.

"I'm afraid we didn't get very far," she said. "Mr. Colfelt arrived, and we came to greet him."

"Hmm," her mother said suspiciously. "Will you take him tomorrow?"

Olivia cleared her throat, not entirely sure she liked where this was headed. "Only if he wishes it, Mama."

"Of course, he wishes it," Lady Pembrooke said with a regal air. "Why would he not?"

"He may wish to spend time with his friend, Mr. Colfelt. Or take a ride around the estate," Olivia said frantically, trying to steer the conversation to one putting less attention on herself. She was beginning to panic and knew her face had turned red.

"Mother," William said, eyeing her and moving to block Olivia from their mother's stares. "I have already talked with

Lady Olivia. She will show me the gardens after we return from our ride. She would like to show Mr. Colfelt the grounds as well, and I must admit, I am anxious to ride Blue again."

Olivia sighed in relief, he had saved her, again. He glanced back and winked at her. She smiled warmly in return.

"William has told me so much about your grey dapple, Lady Olivia. I find myself quite anxious to see him in person." The jovial tone in Mr. Colfelt's words lightened her anxiety further, and she began to relax.

Lewis announced dinner, turning all attention to the dining room.

"I would love to escort you to your seat if you'll allow me," William said, giving her a very proper bow.

Olivia gave him an elegant curtsy. "Nothing would please me more, my lord."

He offered her his arm, and she placed her hand in the crook of his elbow. A tingle from the simple touch spread through her fingertips, shooting through her body until it reached her toes.

He smiled at her. "You do look lovely tonight. The gown is perfect on you," he said quietly so only she could hear him.

She blushed and took a breath to try and calm her pounding heart. "Thank you. My maid considers herself quite the fashion expert."

Lord Hanley chuckled. "Spends a lot of time on St. James' Street, does she? Or does she prefer to peruse *La Belle Assemblée* to find the latest fashionable coiffure and gown ensembles?"

Olivia laughed. "William, do you read *La Belle Assemblée*? It really is quite the thing you know."

"My dear, that is a secret I will never divulge," he laughed and the smile on his face and the term of endearment he'd used, making her stomach flutter.

He pulled out her chair, then took the seat next to her as was appropriate.

She faced him. "That would be quite the scandal, would it not? A gentleman being caught reading a ladies fashion plate." She tsked. "Very ungentlemanly if you ask me."

"Ah, yes, but not if said gentleman's secret was never revealed," his eyes looked at her with pleading, but full of humor.

She leaned closer to him, and he to her. "I would say your secret is safe with me, but it wouldn't be entirely true."

His laugh brought every eye toward them, making her blush again. She'd almost forgotten there were others in the room.

"What are you two laughing at?" Lady Pembrooke asked with a small smile of her own.

"Lady Olivia was telling me about her maid's love of *La Belle Assemblée*." He laughed again, bringing his mother's chuckle to the surface.

"*La Belle Assemblée?*" his mother smiled. "Is this true my dear? Does your abigail enjoy the periodical?"

Olivia smiled. "No. Your son is, I'm afraid, a terrible tease. He would of course never admit to it, but he said *he* was the one who enjoyed the articles."

The entire room laughed. William gave her a look which could make any lady swoon.

He leaned slightly closer to her. "You," he said smiling, shaking his head in laughter, "are a minx."

She giggled and turned to her plate, unable to reply. She thoroughly enjoyed flirting with William, but it was very difficult to focus on her dinner when he kept glancing over at her.

"Olivia?" her mother asked. "Will you play for us tonight?"

Olivia gave her mother a small smile. "If it's what you wish," she said, daring a brief glance at William who sat to her right. The look he was giving her sent a sense of thrill to her very core, making her feel giddy.

"I was blessed to be able to hear you play in London, my lady," Mr. Colfelt said, kindly. "What shall we be graced with this evening?"

Olivia had always been proud of her skills on the pianoforte. She loved how the songs she played could match her moods. When she felt down, playing almost always lifted her spirits. She'd tried to soothe the pain of her father's death with the piano many times but found it difficult to play. She'd never experienced a time when music hadn't helped her, and when it failed, her despondency deepened. She wasn't a prodigy by any means, but she was pleased with the talent God had given her.

She wiped her mouth with her napkin and placed it in her lap. "I enjoy all types of music, but my favorite is determined by how I'm feeling when I sit and play."

Her words sparked something inside him, and she felt herself fidgeting under his gaze. "What do you think you shall play for us this evening?"

She swallowed, why was she suddenly nervous again? He hadn't asked her anything she couldn't answer, but for some reason, his scrutiny made her uncomfortable. Maybe she was only out of practice in society. This was the first time she had been around anyone other than her family in a year.

"Lady Olivia?" he asked, bringing her attention back to him. "Do you know what you'll play this evening? I only ask because Lord Hanley is also quite the instrumentalist."

Olivia heard William's sharp intake of breath from the seat next to her and she smiled mischievously. "Is he really?" she asked, enjoying the attention shifting to someone besides herself. For some reason, she loved that William had become uncomfortable with the conversation. "Lord Hanley, is this true?"

He sighed. "I wouldn't call my ability a gift, more like torture for all those unlucky enough to hear it."

She laughed, her mood lighter at his confession. "What instrument do you play?"

He shifted to face her more fully, glaring at his friend behind her. "I'm afraid I am very *untalented* at playing the guitar."

Mr. Colfelt's booming laugh echoed around the room. "Don't let him fool you, my lady, Hanley is a gifted guitarist."

"William, are you going to play for us as well?" his mother asked hopefully. "It has been so long since I have heard you play."

He sighed in resignation and nodded his agreement. Olivia had never looked forward to anything more in her life. She hadn't heard many people play the guitar but loved the way it sounded.

"Lady Olivia," he asked, "you wouldn't happen to have a guitar in your music room, would you?"

She could see he was pleading for her to say no. Her smile grew, and not because she was excited to hear him play, but because she indeed had a guitar. When she was younger, she had convinced her mother and father to buy one for her because she was determined to learn to play. When she had been practicing for only a few days, she developed sores on her fingertips and never touched it again. It had been collecting dust in the music room for several years. Charles picked it up now and again, strumming its strings, but nothing more had been done with it.

"Yes, I do," she said with a wicked grin. She held back a laugh when she noticed his eyes contained a mixture of surprise and pleasure. "You may need to tune the strings to make it sound right. I'm afraid it hasn't been used for some time."

He smiled brightly at her. "It's settled then. We shall all suffer tonight with my horrid musical ability, but Lady Olivia will save us with her talents."

Lady Pembrooke clapped her hands in joy. "This is so exciting. William has such talent on the instrument."

"Mother," William said looking at her, "the only way tonight will have any success is if I trip on the way to the music room and render myself unable to play."

The room erupted in laughter, and his mother swatted the air. "Nonsense."

As soon as the gentleman had rejoined them after they had enjoyed their after dinner port, the group made their way to the music room. Olivia felt tightness in her chest as her fear started settling in her. She placed a hand on her stomach, willing the twisting and turning to cease.

"Olivia," her mother said, sitting in a nearby chair, "would you like to start?"

She nodded. "Any requests?" she asked. Her nerves were starting to affect her ability to breathe.

"Whatever you like, my dear," her mother said. "Everything you play is lovely."

She grabbed a few pieces from her small collection and began playing. She started with the Mozart piece she had been working on the day William and his parents joined them for afternoon tea in London. She moved to a few more upbeat songs before finishing with a slower more melodic piece she had written on her own. She received ample applause after her last piece and stood to curtsy.

"Lord Hanley," she said smiling. "I believe it's your turn to entertain us."

"Actually," William said, "if you play anything by Johann Sabastian Bach, we may be able to perform a duet?"

She laughed and raised an eyebrow in curiosity. "You have heard me play his music before. Which piece are you referring to?"

He looked around the music room and spotted the guitar in the corner. He walked over and seemed surprised at how beautiful the instrument was. It had a long neck with intricately carved patterns on the body. Its six strings were in good shape, but as he strummed a chord, the entire room cringed at the horrible tone. Olivia watched him in silence. He closed his eyes and held the guitar closer to his ear and twisted the pegs, continuing a variation of strumming and twisting until he had the pitch he wanted. She was suddenly breathless for a reason she didn't understand.

He hurried back to her and started digging through her many pieces of music. "How about this one? It's a beautiful piece."

She took the papers and looked over the notes, then glanced up at him in surprise. "Are you sure this is the piece you would like?"

He nodded with a large smile. She hadn't played Bach's Prelude 1 in C major in a while, but looking at the notes, she didn't find them too difficult. She didn't see a place in the music where he would play but decided not to ask him.

She sat at the pianoforte and placed the music on top before looking at William. He had pulled a chair near her and was sitting with the guitar on his lap, one leg propped up on a small stool.

"Ready?" he asked.

She nodded, and he turned his attention to his instrument. Olivia stretched her fingers, took a deep breath, and began the slow rhythmic music. The notes were familiar, and she was able to play them easily. Her fingers flowed over the keys and a sense of peace filled her.

After a few measures, William began playing. He had no sheet music but played his piece completely from memory. Olivia found she was rather impressed by his abilities. The music he started was unfamiliar but seemed to fit perfectly with hers as he continued to play. The tune rang through the room like a lullaby, sending goosebumps down her arms and neck. The air around her stilled as she continued to play the music in front of her. When they approached the middle of the piece, William turned the slow lullaby into a tender melody, pulling emotions from every corner of the room. She felt a tear fall down her cheek and wiped it away on her shoulder. As she approached the ending of her song, he slowed with a few dramatic notes, ending as she played the final measure.

She lifted her hands slowly off the keys, not daring to look at him. The room was silent. Olivia knew no one had expected something so emotional and beautiful. She could hear a few sniffles, and it made her feel less alone knowing now she wasn't the only one to cry. She dared a glance at William, and noticed he was watching her. He gave her a sly smile and put the guitar against the side of the piano forte before walking to her side. He didn't say a word as he handed her a handkerchief and held it out for her. She dabbed at her eyes and let him help her up.

He leaned his head toward her, his breath tickling her ear. "Curtsy to your fans," he teased in a whisper.

She did as she was told, and he bowed. Lord Pembrooke stood and started applauding, showing his obvious approval of their duet. The others joined in and a blush rushed to her cheeks. She lowered her head and smiled.

"Beautiful," Mr. Colfelt said, walking up to where she and William stood. "Who knew you had it in you?"

William shook his friend's hand. "It only sounded the way it did because of this young lady. She is the true musical genius."

His pleasure at her playing made her blush again. The number of times she found herself blushing since his arrival was bordering on the side of ridiculous. She needed to pull herself together.

"Olivia, my dear," her mother said hugging her tightly and dabbing her eyes with her own handkerchief. "You both sounded wonderful." She pulled back, looking Olivia in the eye as she smiled lovingly at her.

"Thank you, Mama, but I have to give the credit to Lord Hanley," she said smiling at him when he glanced at her after hearing his name. "Where did you learn that particular arrangement, my lord?"

This time he blushed, which gave her an odd sensation of pleasure to see the roles reversed.

"I heard the piece by Bach during a musicale. While I was sitting there listening, the melody came into my thoughts," he explained after a few seconds of silence. "I couldn't shake it. I returned to my rooms in London, pulled out my guitar, and played." He shrugged as if this sort of thing was completely common.

Olivia stood in stunned silence; this man had no end to his surprises.

"It just came to you?" she asked, shocked at his revelation. "While at a musicale?"

He laughed, "Is it so hard to imagine?"

She could hear the teasing tone of his words, and she smiled.

"William," his mother called, pulling his attention from Olivia. "I knew you played, but that was beyond anything I have heard before. Why haven't you played for us previously? We have held plenty of musicales and parties at Pembrooke House in London, as well as our estate in the country."

He shook his head. "I had no reason to play before now." His eyes darted to Olivia for a split second before returning to his mother. "Lady Olivia's skills at the piano forte gave me no choice."

His mother beamed at him. "You must play it again after all the other guests arrive tomorrow. It will be one of the highlights, I think."

He shook his head. "It was a one-time thing."

Disappointment rushed over Olivia. She was thinking the same as Lady Pembrooke, something so beautiful had to be shared.

"Of course, you will play it again," his mother pleaded. "How could you not?"

He shrugged his shoulders. "Sorry, mother."

She glared at him. "We will discuss this matter later."

Olivia raised a hand to her mouth to block her grin. William noticed her movement and gave her a half-smile.

"After something so stunningly beautiful, I do believe I need to retire for the evening." Olivia's mother said. "There has been too much excitement this evening for me."

Olivia grinned, and hugged her mother. "Good night, Mama."

She patted Olivia's cheek when she pulled back. "So beautiful, my darling. Your father would have enjoyed it immensely."

Olivia froze, staring at her mother. She rarely said anything about her father. Olivia blinked back tears and smiled as her mother left the room on Charles' arm.

"Oh, and Olivia," she called as she poked her head back around the corner. "When you return from your ride in the morning, come see me."

Olivia nodded, wondering what her mother could want to see her so early in the morning for.

"I think I shall retire as well," Lady Pembrooke said. "Come, George."

Lord Pembrooke strode to his wife's side, and with a bow, excused them both. William stood talking with Mr. Colfelt so she thought maybe she could slip out unnoticed if she moved quietly. She had so many things going through her mind, too many emotions she didn't know if she was in control of yet.

William's head snapped in her direction the instant she moved, and he smiled. "Excuse me Colfelt, I must speak with, Lady Olivia."

Mr. Colfelt took his leave with a quick bow, leaving the door open for propriety. William stepped toward her and took both her hands in his and kissed each before letting their hands fall, still intertwined, in front of them.

He looked into her eyes, trapping her in his gaze. "Thank you for accompanying me," he said, his voice low and quiet. "I love to hear you play."

Her heart pounded and she wondered if he could feel it as he held onto her hands. She swallowed. "Did you really compose the piece you played tonight?" she asked, urging her heart to calm down.

He chuckled and nodded. "I did. Actually, it was at the very musicale I saw you during your first London Season."

She cocked her head at him. "I don't remember anyone playing Bach that night," she said, trying to think back. "Who played it?"

He shrugged. "I honestly have no idea."

His brown eyes were mesmerizing as he watched her. His thumb had begun rubbing small circles on the back of her hand, the sensation crumbling her resolve to keep her distance throughout the evening. She smiled, knowing she had lost the battle the moment she saw him in the drawing-room before dinner.

"What are you smiling at?" he asked, grinning at her.

She shook her head. "I am only surprised you composed the piece; it was one of the most beautiful songs I have ever heard."

Her face heated as he gave her a coy smile. "What if I told you, I wrote it for you?" he asked. He took a step closer to her and pulled her hands back toward his mouth. She gave a little gasp when he flipped them over so they were facing him and gently kissed the inside of each wrist before releasing them and moved his hand to her face. He lifted her chin, and moved another step closer, stroking her cheek and down her jaw. Her hands moved to his chest where she could feel his heart beating as quick as her own. She knew she should push him away, knew they shouldn't be this close, but her body refused to do anything but stare at him. When his eyes shifted to her lips, she took a small step back, but he gently pulled her back to him.

He leaned back down toward her and whispered quietly in her ear. "Can I join you on your ride in the morning?"

She tried to clear the fog clouding her judgement. "You already told everyone I was taking you and Mr. Colfelt around the estate in the morning."

She couldn't decipher the look he was giving her. It was an intense gaze making her feel slightly self-conscious, but at the same time made her want to press her mouth to his and never let him go.

"Yes, but I never actually asked your permission." His voice sounded husky, making her shiver.

She leaned her head toward him and quickly placed a kiss on his cheek before hurrying to the door. "I would love to race you again in the morning," she teased. "Good night, William."

He smiled at her, humor in his eyes at her words but he hadn't moved from where she left him. She groaned inwardly, nodding at the footman standing by the music room doors with a barely contained grin on his face. She should have known they weren't truly alone and that a servant would have been close by to keep watch.

Olivia wanted to rush back to William, but she knew if she did, she wouldn't be able to make herself leave again. She had heard William hurry forward to stop her after he'd finally snapped out of his trance, but she ran down the hall and out of sight

Alicia Rivoli

Nine

What was he doing? How could he put her in such a situation? William pushed his fingers through his hair and paced back and forth in front of his bed. He didn't know what had taken over him. The pull he had been feeling toward her since the afternoon tea in London four years earlier, seemed to have taken control. The dress she had chosen for the evening, the simple flowers in her hair, the blush on her cheeks when she saw he was watching her, all captivated him completely. He groaned and stopped pacing to look out his window at the darkness. The sounds of bellowing hounds echoed around the courtyard, but he didn't want to think what they could be barking at. He wanted to figure out his own mind and how he had lost complete control of it.

He thought back to their duet and the tears falling down her cheeks while they played. It had touched him deeply to know she liked the song. He had planned of telling her he had written it for her, but now he thought about the reason for the piece, he realized it was true. The melody flowed through his thoughts the moment he saw her at the musicale and he couldn't get it out of his mind, so he'd worked on it in his rooms.

An image of the afternoon tea where he'd first seen her since he and Charles had gone to school, popped into his thoughts. She was even more beautiful now than she had been at fifteen. Her hair had darkened slightly from the dark blonde he remembered, but her eyes were still the same vivid blue. Looking into them tonight while she was so close to him, he realized they had specks of green and brown around the edges.

He tried to think back to the reason which led him to nearly kissing her, and smiled. She had tried to leave after his parents, and when he approached her the smell of lilacs had overthrown his resolve to only wish her a good evening. In less than twenty-four hours since returning to Elmwood Manor, Olivia had pulled him back into her web, and he found he was rather enjoying it. He pulled his hand down his face, the rough texture of his unshaven cheeks scratching against his palm. He needed to sleep.

He undressed without calling Sam, throwing his clothing on the back of the chair near the fireplace. He climbed into bed, and after what felt like hours, drifted off with visions of Olivia's eyes boring into his own, and the remembrance of her pink lips gently touching his cheek.

William felt Sam shake him awake after what felt to him was only a few minutes. He was exhausted. His body ached from tossing and turning all night.

"Are you alright?" Sam asked him, throwing the discarded clothing across his arm.

William heaved a sigh. "She's going to kill me," he said in exasperation.

Sam stopped trying to magically will the wrinkles from William's clothing and stared at him. "Who is going to kill you?" he asked with concern.

William threw his legs over the side of the bed and walked to the basin of warm water Sam had already prepared. He splashed his face several times and rubbed it dry with a towel. Sam hadn't moved, which told William he would wait all day for an answer if he needed to.

"Lady Olivia Barton," he said with a drawn-out breath, moving to where Sam could help him shave and prepare to go riding.

He gave William a knowing look. "Ah yes, the spell of a beautiful woman is every man's downfall."

William chuckled. "You speak the truth, my friend. She has me entirely enchanted."

Sam laughed before helping William. When he was dressed in his riding attire, Sam gave him a look of pity.

"Don't look at me like that," William laughed, grabbing his hat off the bed. "I already know I'm doomed."

Sam let out a bellowing laugh. "You haven't even begun yet."

William stared at him in dismay. "What?"

"Oh no, my lord. Your troubles are only beginning, I'm afraid," he said, laughing as he disappeared into the room adjacent to William's.

William groaned. He was never going to get another good night's sleep if Lady Olivia kept smiling and teasing him. He hurried down the maze of hallways before turning to the right and taking the stairs two at a time to the front door.

Lewis was already waiting. "Lady Olivia requested you and Mr. Colfelt join her in the stables as soon as you are ready, my lord."

William had forgotten Robert was supposed to join them and turned to go find his friend but saw he was already coming down the stairs.

"I hope you haven't been waiting long," he said. "I had trouble with my boots this morning."

William smiled and gave a little laugh. "It only feels like forever."

Robert grinned widely and slapped him on the back. "You have known Lady Olivia for years. Why is she unraveling you now?" he asked as they left the house and headed for the stables.

William dropped his head and tried to think of an answer to his question. "I have no idea," he finally said, "and it's making me crazy."

Robert said nothing but looked at William in humored apology.

When he heard Olivia's voice coming from the open door of the stables, he wondered if he should turn back and hide for the remainder of his family's visit, but he forced his legs to keep moving. From the corner of his eye, he saw Robert shaking his head and suppressing a laugh.

Robert entered the stables, and with a deep breath, William followed.

"Good morning, gentleman," Olivia said, approaching them with Buttercup close behind her.

William's heart pulled in his chest, and he swallowed. *Lud, she's beautiful,* he thought as he watched her draw nearer.

She smiled when their eyes met, and he froze. *What is wrong with me?* He wondered.

"Good morning, my lady," Robert said, smiling and bowing over her hand. "I trust you slept well."

She nodded. "Yes, thank you."

"Lady Olivia," William said, the words feeling foreign after using her given name so often as of late. "Robert and I are pleased you have agreed to ride with us around the estate this morning."

She smiled and lowered her head shyly before looking back at him. The intensity in which she stared at him quickened his breathing. He cleared his throat; grateful Robert was between Olivia and himself.

"Truly," she said, addressing both men, "the pleasure is mine." She inhaled a small breath. "Henry has prepared your horses." She pointed to Blue and Robert's tall black horse, Amadeus.

William took the reins from Henry and watched as Olivia led her mare to the mounting blocks and lifted herself up, sitting gracefully into the seat of the saddle. She adjusted her skirts, so they laid carefully over her boots and down the horse's side. Buttercup danced a little under her, but she didn't seem to notice. William quickly flipped himself up onto Blue's back and the three of them set off around the marquess's land.

Robert rode a few paces behind them with a stable boy who had been asked to accompany them. They talked quietly, and William heard him ask the young boy about his family. He'd always liked Robert's friendly manner. Station didn't matter when it came to whom he spoke with. He treated every person he came across with respect and kindness.

"Did you sleep well?" Olivia's voice startled him after the silence of the morning.

He nudged his horse to get into step with her mare and turned toward her as much as he could.

"I did, thank you." His tongue was beginning to feel heavy in his mouth the longer he looked at her. The rare chill of the summer morning air made her cheeks and the tip of her nose pink. It brightened her eyes even more than normal.

"It's a beautiful morning," she said, turning her head to look out at the rolling green hills and fields of crops. "I especially love the mist as it rises from the trees."

William followed her gaze and knew why she liked the scene so much. It shifted and moved with the breeze, pushing this way and that, shining in the light of the rising sun.

"The rainbows which are created when the sun's light hits the water droplets, are my favorite," she said, a stillness to her tone. "Much like it does at the waterfall."

He watched her and when she looked at him, he smiled. "I remember the waterfall, it was a rose among the thistles."

She cocked her head to one side. "I don't believe I have heard the term before, what does it mean?"

His horse began to grow impatient at their slow pace, and he took a moment to get him settled before answering her. "It means even though the land around us is beautiful, like the purple tips of a thistle, the waterfall is a rose." His heart fluttered as she smiled at him. "The rose is one of the most beautiful flowers."

"One?" she said inquisitively. "Do you have a favorite flower, William?" her smile was teasing and light.

He thought about the first time she had walked with him in the gardens outside her home and pointed out all the flowers growing around them. Her eyes lit up as she explained each one and how they attained their names.

"Recently," he said, a playful tone to his voice, "it's the beauty of the lilac which draws my attention."

His words were rewarded with a deep stunning blush against her already pink cheeks. She dropped her gaze away from him, a small smile pulling at the corner of her lips.

"And why is that?" she asked, not turning fully to face him.

William shrugged and gave her a clever grin. "I would think it rather obvious," he teased.

She giggled. "You'll have to be a bit more specific, I'm afraid," she said, smiling. "There are many qualities to the lilac which are enticing."

He laughed. "Yes, I agree. But the aroma of the lilac is…" he paused and glanced at her as she watched him. "Rather alluring when surrounded by so much beauty."

She watched him, another light blush rushing to her cheeks, but she didn't turn away. He wanted to reach out to her, to touch the curl which had slipped from beneath her hat, but resisted.

After several minutes of silence, she looked back at Robert and the stable hand. "Mr. Colfelt?" she called over her shoulder.

Robert joined them on her other side, and William felt a twinge of jealousy, but he shook the thoughts away. He was being ridiculous.

"Yes, my lady?" Robert answered, matching their pace.

"Mr. Colfelt, I don't know if you are aware or not," she said, and William wondered at the humor he heard in her words. "But Lord Hanley is a terrible racer." She laughed when she heard his chuckle behind her. "I wonder if you would have better luck?"

Robert's grin amusingly stretched across his face at the mention of a challenge.

"Don't do it, Robert," William called. "She cheats."

She guffawed and turned to face him. "I do not cheat," she said, her hand on her chest like she had been wounded by his words. "It isn't my fault you can't keep up." She winked at him then looked at the path in front of her and smiled. "Don't worry, William, Mr. Colfelt won't tell anyone you were beat by a woman."

The two men burst into laughter.

"Shall we make it interesting then?" William said, still laughing.

She shrugged her shoulder. "I guess you'll have to catch me to make the terms." She clucked at her horse, and Buttercup didn't hesitate. The animal bolted down the path, away from them.

"I will say this," Robert called as they both kicked their horses to follow, "you'll never be bored."

William smiled at his words. "Now do you understand my dilemma."

Olivia was ahead of them by some distance by the time William was able to get Blue into a full gallop. Her skirts were flipping up and over her horse's back, and her chestnut hair had slipped from its confines beneath her hat, whipping wildly around her. He could hear her laughter as he and Robert drew closer, but William knew from their last race, Buttercup had more in her.

"This isn't even the mares top speed! Watch!" he called to his friend over the crashing of their horses' hooves against the earth.

He kicked Blue and pulled alongside Olivia. She looked over at him, and she flashed him a beautiful heart-stopping smile before Buttercup picked up speed and pulled further away from him. She glanced back once and gave him what she probably had thought was an innocent challenge with her smile, but it was anything but innocent. His entire frame shivered as he tried to get his breathing and heart rate back to their normal levels.

"You were right, William," Robert called shaking his head, laughing. "She cheats. I can't think of a single man in England who wouldn't falter at the smile she flashed at you."

William chuckled and grinned at his friend. "Neither can I," he said with a shake of his head.

William turned to look ahead where Olivia had gone and chased after her when he saw she had slowed and was moving at an easier pace. When he and Robert pulled their horses alongside her, she was breathing heavily, and the joy she exuded showed in every inch of her face as she beamed at him. She slowed Buttercup to a walk and rubbed the mare's neck, whispering something to her horse William couldn't hear.

She glanced at him from beneath her lashes as she raised back to full posture, her hand still rubbing her horse's neck affectionately.

"William was right, my lady," Robert said, drawing her gaze to him and away from William. "You cheat."

She snickered. "I beg your pardon, but I do *not* cheat."

William chuckled. "Oh, yes you do," he teased. "You always fail to mention Buttercup is a racehorse, and as such, we have no chance to outrun her."

She smiled brightly. "Like I said the last time we raced and you lost," she said between breaths. "You never asked if

Buttercup could run. Besides, you already knew what you were up against."

She had everything right. He had known Buttercup was a racehorse, and he would lose, but she was wrong on one aspect of her logic. When it came to Olivia Barton, he had no idea what he was up against, but he knew without a doubt he had lost before the race began.

"Yes," he said, "but poor Colfelt had no idea. I believe you have wounded him quite severely."

She turned her head toward his friend and batted her eyelashes in obvious exaggeration. "I'm terribly sorry, Mr. Colfelt."

William raised an eyebrow at her, wondering about her overly sweet tone as she apologized unnecessarily.

"Whatever for, my lady?" Robert asked, apparently having the same thought as William.

She tilted her head back to William for only a moment before she started giggling again. "Lord Hanley kept a vital piece of information from you before we began this race." She continued laughing, trying desperately to control herself.

"What information did I not receive?" he eyed William with humored suspicion.

"I have never lost," she said, in a forced serious tone.

William and Robert both erupted into uncontrolled laughter, startling the horses. The three of them teased each other for the rest of their ride. Olivia seemed to be free of all worry and stress. Her eyes were bright and every time she smiled at him, he melted inside. He didn't know if he had ever seen her so unrestrained. Not in her home, or at any of the events during her Season in

London. Something had changed over the last year, and he secretly hoped he was the one to have caused it.

They returned to the house and were able to change in time to have breakfast. The house was alive with activity as servants went from room to room preparing for the arrival of the other guests. William hadn't asked how many people were going to be in attendance, but from the looks of it, it was going to be a large group. Olivia hurried to her mother. They bent their heads over a piece of paper, talking animatedly, but quiet.

William watched for a few minutes before he retreated and made his way to the library. He hadn't been here long, but he knew he needed some space. His mind was already whirring from this morning's ride, and he felt helpless to control his growing attachment to Lady Olivia. Simply being in the same room as her unmistakably shook him.

His feelings for Olivia had always been nothing but friendship for as long as he could remember. However, sometime after the afternoon tea, they changed and grew stronger with each interaction. He found it difficult being away from her, became jealous when she talked to other gentlemen, and when she was with him, his heart went wild inside his chest. When he looked at her, he no longer saw *Charles's little sister*. Instead, he noticed a striking young woman he was beginning to think he cared deeply for.

He pushed the doors to the library open, and walked to a large chair in the corner, plopping down unceremoniously. He tilted his head back and closed his eyes, breathing slow and deep.

He willed himself to relax, needing to organize his thoughts and figure out what he was going to do. Time slowed and his body became heavy as he drifted in and out of consciousness.

"The chair by the window is much more comfortable. If you plan on falling asleep, I highly recommend you switch seats."

William's eyes popped open and he rose from his chair as Olivia strode into the room. She had changed from her riding habit, and now wore a rather flattering morning dress in the perfect shade of light green. Her disheveled hair had been neatly pinned up and her cheeks were slightly flushed.

"I can leave you to your thoughts if you'd like," she said, leaning against the door frame of the library.

William smiled at her. "The chair by the window?" he said, pointing to the object in question.

She nodded. "It's my favorite place in this room."

He moved toward it and sat down. As his body sank deeply into the cushion, he sighed in pleasure.

"You're right," he said smiling. "This is more comfortable."

She returned his smiled and strode into the room with her hands tucked behind her back. The library was warm from the rising temperatures outside, and the sun peeked through the windowpanes, shimmering off the wooden floor. She perused the books, tracing her finger along each one until she found what she was looking for. William watched, entranced by her movements.

When she pulled the book from the shelf, he noticed it was an older book. The binding was coming apart and the book itself wasn't in the best condition.

"Do you like to read, William?" she asked tapping the book on her other hand.

"It depends on the book, but usually," he answered. "Why?"

She walked toward him and held the book out to him, he took it, interested as to why she wanted him to have this particular book. He turned it over in his hands and couldn't see a title anywhere on or within the book.

"Is there something you would like me to do with this book?" he asked, raising it and shaking it slightly.

"It was purchased by my great-grandfather's father. I'm told he bought it from a shop in Rome," she explained. "The problem, however, is I can't read it."

He eyed her suspiciously. "You can't read?"

She chuckled. "Yes, I can read," she said rolling her eyes. "I just can't read *that* book."

"Why?"

She shrugged but didn't say anything else.

Curious, he opened to the first page. It was yellowing from age, and the words were difficult to make out, but after a few moments, he thought it to be a book of poetry.

"Is it poetry?" he asked her, still carefully turning each page.

She smiled. "That was my initial thought as well," she said, walking back toward the door to the library. "I figured if you were going to be in here, you may as well have something to entertain you. Let me know if you find anything interesting," she said.

"Olivia?" he said, stopping her. She turned to face him and gave him a coy smile.

He swallowed. "Why this book?" he said, smiling. "This library is rather large and has books with comprehensible words in them. So, why did you choose this book?"

She batted her eyelashes and lowered her gaze, "I thought it would give you something to do. You seemed rather contemplative when I came in. But I couldn't tell if your thoughts were happy in nature, or if they were unpleasant," she explained. "Having a book like the one I gave you, may help you take your mind off of whatever you are thinking about and help you relax. Its contents are a mystery. I've only been able to find a few words here and there which were legible, maybe you'll have better luck."

She didn't wait for his response before leaving him to his thoughts. He watched the door for several seconds, but when she didn't come back, he turned his attention to the ratty old book in his hand. She had one thing completely wrong, he wasn't having unpleasant thoughts when she arrived, more the opposite. Like they had been for hours, his thoughts were completely taken over by her.

He squinted to see the words on the page. Like Olivia had explained, only a few words were legible. He found a page which had a few more words he could read and studied each sentence.

> *"can't speak—a subtle fire races inside—*
> *can't see— trembling takes ahold—dying*

He nearly choked as he read the words. It was definitely a book of poetry, and this particular poem, even with the words missing, seemed to explain exactly how he was feeling. Of course, he didn't feel like he was literally dying, but his resolve definitely was. He read the words again, and then again. Turning toward the door, he wondered why Olivia had chosen this specific book. It hadn't helped him relax or clear his thoughts at all but made him even more confused than before. He snapped it shut and put it back on the shelf before leaving the room, and its haunting words.

Ten

The carriages began arriving after luncheon. Since it was their first house party in well over a year, Olivia's mother wanted it to be well attended. Elmwood Manor could hold everyone she had invited, plus a few spare bedrooms in case unexpected visitors arrived. Olivia stood in the gravel drive, greeting each guest alongside her family. Charles and her mother provided the necessary introductions to some couples whom she didn't know well, like Mr. and Mrs. Bowman with their daughter, Miss Angela Bowman, whom Olivia thought a very lovely young woman with an exuberant smile and laugh. She heard Charles shift impatiently beside her and looked at him. She hadn't had much of an opportunity to talk to him since William had arrived, and she wondered why he was so anxious.

"Charles," she whispered, "are you alright? You seem nervous."

He looked down at her and gave her a half-smile. "I am nervous."

"But why?" she asked. "You have nothing to worry about."

"Olivia, this is my first house party as the Marquess of Elmwood. Mother has invited some very prominent members of the *ton* to help me gain their support," he explained. He faced her and took a deep shuttering breath. "I don't know if I'm ready for this Livvie."

She put her arm in his and laid her head on his shoulder. "You know father would be proud of you," her voice stuck a little, but she continued. "You have been a rock to both myself and Mama. You pulled our family together and have taken your responsibility as a member of the House of Lords to new levels. I have heard nothing but praise from those friends in London I have corresponded with the last few months."

He squeezed her fingers. "I hope you're correct."

"Besides, you and I both know the reason you aren't able to hold still," she smiled as he looked at her inquisitorially. "The real reason is because the carriage coming up the drive belongs to the Abbots."

He gaped at her, then laughed. "Little sisters are so nosy." A lighthearted reprimand behind his words, he said. "You better behave yourself, Livvie, none of your pranks."

She frowned in feigned shock. "I am afraid I have no idea what you are talking about."

He was about to reply, but the Abbots' carriage rolled to a stop in front of them. He gave Olivia one final narrowing of his eyes to repeat his statement for her to behave. She rolled her eyes, making him chuckle. The footman rushed forward and lowered the step. The door opened, and Mr. Abbot stepped down, greeting Charles. They exchanged quick pleasantries before Olivia's brother put his hand out to help the ladies alight.

A tall woman with a pointy chin, grey eyes, and streaks of grey running through her dark black hair, stepped out first. Olivia watched her closely. The woman was rather attractive, except she had a sour-looking scold which looked like a permanent feature on her face.

"Lord Elmwood," she squealed in delight, shocking Olivia with the unexpected exuberance the stern woman presented. "What an honor it is to be invited to your home."

"Mrs. Abbot," Charles said, bowing over the woman's hand. "I hope your journey was uneventful."

She waved her hand at him. "But of course it was," she drawled. "Everything was absolutely perfect. We are so thrilled to finally be able to see your lovely estate. Although, Nottinghamshire is rather far from London. Do you plan to stay in the country often?"

He smiled. "I plan on being where I am needed," he said smartly.

She grinned at him. "Indeed," she said as she turned toward Olivia's mother.

Charles turned his attention back to the carriage, and Olivia watched him swallow hard as a petite young lady took hold of his hand and stepped out. Olivia stared at the girl. She was so shockingly beautiful, Olivia felt bland in comparison. Miss Abbot's dark red hair was twisted atop her head in an elegant style one would find in a London ballroom, not exiting a carriage after a long journey. The light coloring of her skin and perfectly pink cheeks and lips gave her a very refined air. The young woman stood taller than her mother, but shorter than Olivia, and wore a long yellow traveling cloak which made her hair stand out even more. When she glanced at Charles, Olivia noticed Miss

Abbot had the most shocking shade of green eyes she'd ever seen.

"Miss Abbot," Charles said, bowing over her hand. "Welcome to Elmwood Manor."

She looked from him to the estate and smiled, her teeth white as snow. "It looks so lovely, my lord." Her voice was pleasant and kind, unlike her mother's higher-pitched tone, but Olivia remained on her guard. She'd witnessed what the debutantes of the *ton* did to rich titled men, and her brother fell into that category as a young marquess.

Charles cleared his throat. "Mr. Abbot, Mrs. Abbot, Miss Abbot, may I present my mother, the Dowager Marchioness of Elmwood, and my sister, Lady Olivia Barton.

Both ladies dipped into elegant curtsies and the man bowed. "We are pleased to be included in your party, Lady Elmwood," Mrs. Abbot said gently.

"We are happy you were able to accept our invitation," her mother said kindly. "Olivia and I look forward to getting to know you better."

Charles led the party back to the house, Miss Abbot attached to his arm, cooing at his every word. Olivia eyed the back of their guest's heads and narrowed her eyes.

I will have to keep a very close eye on them, she thought, her suspicion at their intentions to her brother growing more and more alarming with each step.

The drawing-room was full of people when they arrived. The Duke and Duchess of Morton were talking with Lord and Lady Pembrooke, and the Earl and Countess of Greystone had struck up a conversation with a couple she couldn't recall the names of. She searched the room, not knowing what she was looking for until her eyes fell on William. He and Mr. Colfelt had their backs to her and were talking to the two daughters of the duke and duchess, Miranda and Catherine. Olivia had known the two girls for as long as she could remember and knew they were ladies of strong character, but it didn't stop her jealousy from rising.

William must have sensed her watching him because he turned and looked right at her, smiling warmly. Her stomach leapt to her throat. She had completely embarrassed herself on their ride this morning. Her flirting had been absurd. She teased him mercilessly and laughed far too much. But she couldn't stop herself. He had a way of getting her to drop her guard, and she didn't realize until later what repercussions her actions could bring. She issued the challenge of the race only so she could try and get herself back in control of her emotions, but it hadn't worked.

Her thoughts flashed to finding him in the library earlier. It was a shock when she saw him sitting back in the chair, his eyes closed and one of his hands holding the side of his face with his elbow on the arm of the chair. She watched him for some time before deciding to speak. She should have turned and walked from the room to let him rest. For some reason, however, she couldn't get her feet to work with what her brain was telling them.

She had acted like a debutante her governess would have been proud to have trained. She flirted and eyed him bashfully, and for some unknown reason, she gave him a book she knew very well had almost no legible words except ones speaking of the pains of love. After Olivia left the library, she ran to her bedchamber. She had never done something so bold in all her life. She didn't know if she wanted him to understand the words in the book or be completely oblivious. She shook herself from her wanderings and brought her eyes back to the man.

He excused himself from the small group and walked toward her, his eyes never leaving hers. She watched him, her heart racing and her equilibrium out of sync with the rest of her body.

Why does he have to be so handsome? She thought as he closed the distance between them.

"Lady Olivia," he bowed and kissed her hand, lingering slightly longer than was appropriate. "Would you care to take a stroll around the room with me?"

She glanced around; she had no idea how they were going to take a *stroll*. The entire space from one wall to the next was full of her mother's guests. She watched as Charles introduced Miss Abbot to the duke and duchess, the poor girl's eyes grew so large, Olivia had to stifle a laugh. Realizing she was being quite rude; she turned her attention back to William. He stood waiting for her, a question in his gaze.

She stood and slipped her arm into his. "How do you propose we take this *stroll?*" she asked, her tone quiet. "Have you seen the number of people in this room?"

The corner of his mouth twitched ever so slightly as he led her around the perimeter of the room. "I assumed people would move out of the way for the sister of the marquess," he teased. "Like Moses and the Red Sea from the bible."

She giggled before covering her mouth to restrain herself. "Like Moses and the Red Sea? You are quite nonsensical"

He pulled her hand to his lips and kissed her fingertips. "Only when I'm with you."

There was no teasing in his tone or look, and it made Olivia blush. "You really need to stop doing that," she whispered.

He looked at her confused. "Doing what?"

She refrained from smiling, realizing she could toy with him a little, and possibly, make him a little nervous. She wanted him to believe he'd truly done something wrong. She had no idea why the idea held so much fascination, but she didn't wait to think it through all the way. She shook her head, refusing to answer him. Not because she didn't want to, but because she knew if she opened her mouth to speak, she would laugh and ruin the whole act.

"You won't tell me what I have done?" he asked, his tone playful.

She shook her head again, and he laughed. "How am I to stop doing something if I don't know what it is I have done?"

She looked at him, his dark eyes full of mischief, and they captivated her. She quickly looked away, her face burning. She knew immediately her plan had backfired. He could make her extremely nervous, and from what she could tell she had done nothing to make him uneasy.

"That," she managed to say after a moment.

He smiled. "You'll have to be a bit more specific. I'm a little daft you see, it drives Colfelt crazy."

She couldn't help it any longer, she laughed and turned to look at him. She realized her mistake a little too late and found herself standing much too close to him. She took a step back. "Don't be absurd," she said, trying to convince her heart it needed to stop pounding so hard.

She saw something flicker in his eyes, as he watched her, but she couldn't describe what it was. Something had changed. The humor had left, and he looked at her with such longing, it made her mind race and legs go weak.

"What must I stop doing?" he whispered, not taking his eyes from hers.

She forced herself to return to his side and keep walking. Her body was trembling, and she felt slightly dizzy. She tried to shake it off, knowing full well it was impossible. "Making me blush," she finally said.

He didn't laugh. "That, my lady," he whispered. "I cannot do."

She felt the heat flush her cheeks, and he leaned closer to her.

"It is far too appealing," he muttered, his breath tickling her ear.

She swallowed, unsure if she could look at him.

"Lady Olivia!"

Olivia started and looked toward the voice which called her name. The duke and duchess were approaching her, and she quickly put on a forced smile. William's hand squeezed her fingers on his arm, and he winked at her.

"Good afternoon, Your Graces. What a pleasure to see you again," she said, her voice cracking a little. She cleared it quickly. "Have you been introduced to, Lord Hanley?"

They turned to William. "Why yes, we have."

"Your Graces," William said, bowing as they all exchanged the proper greetings.

"Have you been at Elmwood Manor long, Lord Hanley?" the duchess asked him in a soft voice.

Olivia remembered the duchess always being very soft-spoken. People often had to step closer in order to hear what she was saying. William did just that, and Olivia chuckled quietly.

"We arrived only yesterday, Your Grace," William answered.

The duke smiled at him. "How have you liked it here thus far?"

William didn't even hesitate before he answered. "Elmwood is a beautiful place. I always enjoy my stay here. This morning, Lady Olivia, was kind enough to take Mr. Colfelt and me for a ride around the countryside."

The duke looked impressed. "Lady Olivia, do you still enjoy riding? If I remember correctly, you were quite the horsewoman when you were younger."

Olivia felt herself relax. Horses were a safe topic and one she enjoyed. "Yes, Your Grace," she said. "It's still one of my favorite pastimes."

The duchess turned to her, and Olivia instinctively stepped closer. "Do you have many horses?" the duchess asked so quietly, Olivia still barely heard the question.

"I personally have two mares, Your Grace. But my brother has several if you and His Grace wish to ride whilst you are visiting. You are also welcome to ride Sweet Pea or Buttercup if you so choose."

The duke raised an eyebrow at her. "Sweet Pea and Buttercup? Those are memorable names for a horse, are they not, my dear?" he chuckled as he looked at his wife.

The duchess nodded but said nothing.

"Lady Olivia," the duke said. "Her Grace and I may take you up on your offer of riding if you don't mind coming along and showing us the estate." He took his wife's arm and placed it in the crook of his elbow. "But for now, we must visit the other guests."

Olivia and William said their goodbyes and watched as the duke and duchess moved elegantly toward another group of people.

She took a long slow breath, forgetting she wasn't alone. "Where were we, Lord Hanley?" she asked, trying to cover up how nervous she was when speaking with the duke and duchess. It was ridiculous really; she had known the man most of her life. He had never done anything to make her feel nervous and had been great friends with her father. Olivia appreciated His Grace's friendship even more after her father's passing. He had taken it upon himself to make sure Charles was properly introduced to other members of Parliament. Her Grace had also taken her mother under her wing when Lady Pembrooke wasn't available.

William took her arm and tucked it back into his, keeping his hand on her own. "I believe, my lady," he grinned impishly. "You were blushing."

She gaped at him. "You are evil," she giggled, a blush creeping up her neck.

The rest of the afternoon went by in a blur. Olivia had been tossed from one conversation to the next, and when it was time to dress for dinner, all she truly wanted was to go to bed. Her cheeks hurt from smiling so much. Dropping to the bed, she kicked off her shoes and fell backwards. Maybe she would have a tray brought up. She wouldn't truly be missed, would she? She groaned when Sally entered her room, her lavender gown, now freshly pressed, draped across her arm.

"I don't want to, Sally," she whined, covering her face with her pillow. "I hurt everywhere. Did you know cheeks can cramp?"

Sally laughed. "Yes, my lady, it has happened to me before."

Olivia shot up straight. "How did you make it stop?" she asked.

She shrugged. "I don't know. I can't remember."

Olivia threw her hands into the air. "Well, that's no help to me, is it?" she teased.

Sally moved to finish preparing everything she would need to help Olivia dress for the evening.

Olivia loved her lavender gown, and Sally had topped the ensemble off with lilac blossoms tucked into the twist of her coiffure, something she had never done before. She wondered why her maid had chosen lilacs in particular, but she shrugged it off. She could smell the beautiful scent as she descended the stairs to rejoin the party until dinner was announced. The small comfort made her quivering body slightly relax.

She stood outside the door for some time before entering. She wasn't sure she could smile anymore as a stray hair pin stabbed her behind her ear, making her head ache. She reached up and tried to push it back into place, but it was no use. She couldn't pull it out, because parts of her hair would come loose, but she also wasn't sure how long she could keep it where it was.

"Lady Olivia," Mr. Colfelt said from behind her. "That color looks lovely on you."

She turned to face him, wincing slightly. "Thank you, sir. Purple is my favorite color."

"Well," he said, "it's very becoming."

She rubbed the back of her ear with her finger. "Have you seen Lord Hanley this evening?"

He shook his head. "Not yet, but I'm sure you'll see him before I do."

She looked at him and tilted her head slightly. "What makes you say so?"

He chuckled. "Because you are the only person he looks for when he enters a room."

Her blush heated her cheeks and made her shiver. She couldn't think of how to respond, so she smiled and turned her head shyly. She wished she had a fan to hide behind. Her movements ended up being a mistake. The loose pin shifted and it pushed hard against her skin. She inhaled sharply; sure the pin was drawing blood.

"Are you feeling quite well, my lady?" Mr. Colfelt asked when Olivia threw her hand to the side of her head.

She nodded. "I am well, only a slight headache is all."

He watched her anxiously. "Are you sure? I can have someone assist you to your room if you wish."

Mr. Colfelt was a very sweet and kind man. Olivia would have to think of who at the party would enjoy his company.

"I am fine, but I thank you. It will pass soon enough," she said, not believing for a minute what she said was the truth.

"At least allow me to assist you to a chair," he said taking her arm without waiting for an answer. He escorted her to an open seat by the window.

"Thank you, Mr. Colfelt. How very kind of you." She smiled when he took the seat next to hers.

He watched her cautiously for a moment, before turning his eyes to the hot, overcrowded room. She pulled a fan from the hidden pocket of her gown and flipped it open, hoping desperately to cool off. The room was much too warm. She took several deep breaths and counted to ten, then repeated the step, but it wasn't helping.

"If you'll please excuse me," she said, rising from her seat. "I think I'm going to go get some air on the terrace."

She didn't wait for him to try and escort her there. She moved as quickly as she was able to the French doors leading outside. She twisted the knob and stepped out, sucking in the cool night air as she did. She leaned against the stone wall away from the crowded room and closed her eyes. Her breathing slowed, and her panic was starting to melt away. She had never minded crowds before, but since her father's passing and what had transpired to her afterwards, she found it difficult to be near too many people. She could still feel some of the darkness which had overpowered her for months, but she had slowly learned how to push it behind her and move on. It hadn't been easy by any means, but she was getting better.

"Olivia?" Charles asked, stepping out onto the terrace and moving toward her. "I saw you almost running to get out here, are you feeling alright?"

She nodded and gave him a forced smile. "Yes, I'm sorry. I started to feel too warm and needed some fresh air."

He stared at her, narrowing his eyes. "You're a terrible liar, Olivia. Always have been."

She looked at him and gave a small chuckle. "I am not."

He shrugged and leaned on the wall next to her. "Sorry, my dear sister, but I speak the truth."

She nudged him with her elbow. "Are you enjoying your guests?"

He seemed to understand her meaning and he smiled at her. "Very much. But what about you?" he said lifting his eyebrows in question.

She didn't know if he meant the guests in general, or a specific guest. "Everyone is quite pleasant. I especially loved talking with Miss Bowman." His eyes widened, and she laughed at his expression. "What?"

"Miss Bowman is very kind, but I don't know if I can take another story about her cat." He said with a sigh.

She burst out laughing. "She does love her cat, doesn't she?"

He looked at her in mock disgust. "I've never met someone so obsessed with their animal. What's worse, she said she would like to *gift* me one of the kittens her darling cat had blessed her home with," he said in feigned horror.

"Oh, what a lovely idea, Charles," she said in a serious tone. "I would love to have a kitten here. They are so incredibly adorable."

He stared at her. "You *want* a cat?"

She nodded. "Do you not think it would be the perfect thing?"

He grabbed her by the shoulders and looked at her. "I refuse to allow you to end up like Miss Bowman. I will not have a sister obsessed with her cat."

She laughed so hard, she snorted, which embarrassed her and caused her to laugh even louder.

"You must stop, Charles. Do not make me laugh." She wiped tears of amusement from her eyes and placed a hand over the protruding pin as it continued to shift and stick her.

"You are feeling unwell!" he growled. "Why wouldn't you tell me?"

She shook her head and winced. "It's not that," she said pointing to the place where her pin was stabbing her. "I have a pin from my hair which has become loose. Every time I move, it pricks me."

His eyes grew wide in shock. "Why haven't you gone to your maid and had her fix it?"

She shrugged. "I didn't want to leave our guests."

He shook his head. "No Olivia, you do not have to take the weight of this house party on your shoulders."

She stared at him in confusion. "What are you talking about?"

He pulled Olivia away from the outer stone wall and led her to the opposite doors on the balcony that would lead her away from the drawing-room and their waiting guests. "You have been trying to keep mother from feeling the pressure of this party for months. You have bounced from room to room, and from person to person all day. Not to mention, all you did *before* our guests arrived. You need to return to your bedchamber and have your maid fix your hair. If you feel well enough to join us after, then, by all means, please do. However, if you aren't feeling up to it, send for a tray and get some rest. I will take care of mother."

Olivia hugged him. "Thank you, Charles. You always were a balm to my misery."

He pushed her gently away from him. "Go," he ordered.

She hurried from the terrace and snuck inside, moving quickly through the dining room before any of the guests entered for dinner. The servants stopped their preparations and looked up as she approached, but she didn't stop. When Olivia reached her room, she dropped into a chair at her dressing table and reached up and yanked the offending pin from her head. Once the pin was removed, a lock of hair came loose and fell to her shoulders. Olivia sighed in instant relief and lightly touched the sore spot with her fingertips, massaging it to try and force the pain to stop. Her white glove had a light-red stain when she pulled her hand down, confirming her suspicion she had been bleeding.

Taking a long look at her hair in the looking glass, she frowned. Sally would have to start over in order to fix it. The simple pin she had wrenched from her head, had caused the entire twist to loosen. She could see several places where the pins were ready to fall, so with a sigh of resignation, she pulled each pin from her hair and let her thick chestnut-colored tresses tumble down her back. Her hair was sleek and shiny, and she could smell the lilacs now strewn out on the floor of her bedchamber. She picked them up and held them in her hands, smelling the lovely scent, before dropping them onto her dressing table.

Olivia stood and moved to the window. Clouds covered every bit of light, blanketing the earth in an austere darkness. She heard the whistling of the wind as it pushed its way into her room and shivered as a chill forced its way through any weakness the window contained. Even though summer had arrived, the temperatures were still much cooler than normal, and Olivia found herself aching for warmer weather. An owl screeched, and she shuddered involuntarily. Pulling the drapes closed, she grabbed a blanket from the chest, wrapping it around her shoulders. Whether or not she wanted to call for Sally and have her maid re-pin her hair, Olivia didn't know. She wasn't sure she wished to rejoin the party for dinner. All she truly sought was the warmth the covers on her bed provided.

Another blast of icy wind hit against the window, so Olivia moved closer to the fireplace to avoid the cold. Watching the flickering dance of the flames, the movement helped her body slip into a simple trance. The warmth pressed against the thick blanket and Olivia knew instantly that she wouldn't be returning to the party, no matter how much she wished to see William. She sighed and rang the bell to call her maid.

Sally arrived only moments later, a look of concern on her face as she saw the state of her mistress's coiffure. "My lady?"

"I'm sorry, Sally, I hope I didn't pull you from anything important," Olivia said, running a brush through her unruly hair.

"No, my lady," Sally replied. "Are you unwell?"

She shook her head. "Only tired. I believe I will turn in for the evening. Would you mind helping me out of my dress and then turning down my bed?"

Sally hurried to her side and began unfastening her gown. After only a few minutes, Olivia was in her nightgown, the bed had been prepared, and she was settled into the warmth of the covers.

"Can I get you anything else, my lady?" Sally said as she walked around the room and snuffed out all the candles except the one near Olivia's bed.

"Actually, would you mind bringing up a small tray of food and a cup of warm chocolate? I haven't eaten yet this evening." Olivia said, propping herself up and grabbing the book she had picked out from the library earlier when William hadn't been in the room.

Sally gave a small curtsy and hurried from the room. Olivia opened the book but found herself too distracted to get through even one page. Her mind was a whirlwind of thoughts, and almost every one of them was of Lord William Hanley. Sally returned and placed the tray on the bed.

"Sally?" Olivia called before her maid could leave. "I have written a note to my mother explaining my absence. Can you make sure they receive it?"

Sally nodded. Then with a final glance at her mistress, took the letter and retreated from the room.

Olivia closed her eyes and drank the warm cup of chocolate, sighing as it ran down her throat and settled in her stomach. The crackling of the fire and the sound of the howling wind quieted her mind. The more she focused on the sounds, the sleepier she became. She finished off her dinner then laid back against the soft pillows.

Olivia didn't know what time it was when she awoke, but the room was dark, the house was quiet, and she felt groggy and tired. She laid quietly, hoping if she didn't move around too much, her body would allow her to fall back to sleep. She tossed and turned, twisting herself in her covers then kicking them off completely. Her room was cold, and the fire was now nothing more than a few smoldering embers. Annoyed, she kicked her legs over the side of the bed and put on her dressing gown, tying the ribbon tightly around her waist.

She lit the candle by her bedside, and without thinking, left her room. She'd been having a dream of her father when she was startled awake, so she decided to go to the portrait gallery and spend some time with him. She moved silently through the house, not wishing to wake any of the guests. The last thing she wanted was for someone to see her so undone.

She came upon two large wooden doors with brass handles. She pulled one open and shivered as a cold breeze slipped under her night clothes and bit at her skin. Olivia walked to the window and pulled open the large heavy drapes, but it did little in the way of providing light. The clouds were thick and still refused to allow the light of the stars or moon to touch the earth.

Olivia held her candle up higher, lighting the faces of the portraits along the wall. She studied each one, seeing generations of marquess's and their families. She paused when she came to the portrait of her grandfather. He wore a white wig and dressed in all black. She had been told the painting had been commissioned shortly after her grandmother had passed, so he had been in mourning. Some men only wore a black band around their arm, but he had insisted on being in full mourning clothes for almost three years. His eyes were dark like her father's, but even in his advanced years, her grandfather's complexion had the same light coloring as she did.

Touching the golden frame, Olivia ran her fingertips along the intricate carvings and raised decorative wood. She moved down the line, smiling at her grandmother posing with Olivia's father and his brother who died after contracting measles shortly after the painting had been finished. He had only been four at the time, and her father six, but with the stories she had heard about Edmund, she felt like she knew him well. Her feet continued to carry her to the end of the hall where a large painting stood in the place of honor above the large fireplace. Her father stood tall and stately. He had dressed in his navy-blue coat, white shirt, and red waist coat. It was paired with tan knee-breeches and dark slippers. He had a silver sword strapped to his waist with one hand on the hilt, while the other hand sat on the back of a red velvet chair. He too was donning the powder white wig. There were other paintings of their family nearby, but this was one of Olivia's favorites.

She looked around the room and pushed a chair to a position where she could sit and memorize her father's features. She missed him every day and sitting with his portrait soothed some of the heartache.

"I miss you, Papa," she whispered to the stillness of the room. "I'm not sure I know how to live without you."

Her father stared down at her from his place on the mantle, and Olivia smiled. She tucked her legs up on the chair and covered them with the thick folds of her dressing gown to keep herself warmer. The wind couldn't be heard as clearly in this room. After a while, her legs begun to fall asleep, so she stood and moved them around. A tingling sensation ran through her toes as they began to feel normal again. She picked up her candle, smiled at her father, and left the room.

She had no destination in mind, but wandered through the house, eventually finding herself standing in the empty ballroom. Charles had ordered some work to be done on the floors and walls before the ball took place, but thanks to the poor weather and muddy conditions, the workers he'd hired, although almost done, were still finishing the final repairs. There were a few tin pails filled with tools and thick canvas piled up on the floor.

She moved to the center of the room and put the candle at her feet. The flickering flame caused dark shadows to dance along the walls like an apparition haunting a tower. She moved away from it, putting her hands out to her side like she had done so many times before, and she spun. Her hair flew around in circles making her smile. Twirling made her feel as if a huge burden was lifted from her shoulders. She wobbled a little when she stopped and tried to regain her steadiness. The room spun as the dizziness took hold of her. When she was unable to hold herself up any longer, she fell to the floor. Her laughter echoed around the empty room, sounding strange to her ears. She laid back and stared up at the crystal chandelier hanging above her.

When there were candles lit, the crystals sparkled and shined, casting bursts of reflecting light to move around the room. She remembered her first time dancing in this room. She was seven, and her mother had been preparing a ball for the neighborhood. Olivia had pleaded with her to allow her to join the fun, but her mother shook her head and told her she would have plenty of time for dancing when she was older.

The night of the ball she had her dinner in the nursery. When she finished and her nursemaid had gone to help her brother, Olivia snuck into the ballroom before any of the other guests had arrived and stood in stunned amazement at all the decorations and flowers lining every table and wall. She moved to the very center of the room and spun like she had done a moment ago. When she had become dizzy, she felt strong hands grab her and her father pulled her to him, hugging her tightly.

"You shouldn't be in here poppet," he said. "If your mother sees you, you know you'll get in trouble."

"I wanted to dance at the ball like you and Mama," she said, her lip jutting out in a pout.

He smiled lovingly at her and rested her against his hip as he moved to a large wooden music box near a window. A moment later, music rang through the room, and he set her down.

Bowing low, he put out a hand for her and with a deep silly voice said, "Lady Olivia, may I have this dance?"

She had giggled when he lifted her into his arms and held her close as he whirled her about the room. Her mother caught them, but instead of scolding her daughter, she joined in the dance.

Olivia would never forget it. She would never forget the feel of her father wrapping her in his arms in a tight embrace when she had fallen and ripped her favorite dress or skinned her knee while chasing Charles around the house. He encouraged her to get back on her horse when she had been thrown from its back and taught her to lead the horse with her legs, rather than the reins. He encouraged her to excel in every endeavor she tried, and when she failed at something, told her to hold her head high and keep trying.

The music box still sat in the same place near the window, but it hadn't worked since Charles accidentally knocked it over when they were playing hide and seek many years earlier. A tear slipped down Olivia's cheek, and she quickly wiped it away. Her father was with her every day in her heart, but in moments like this when she lay in the dark, alone, she wished more than anything her father was here to spin her around the dance floor again.

"I thought I would find you here."

Olivia turned to the door, her mother stood just inside, holding a candle and smiling. "What are you doing out of bed, Mama?" she asked, pulling herself up into a sitting position.

Her mother strode across the floor and before Olivia could say anything, lowered herself to sit by her daughter. She looked around the room, a slight smile touching her lips before settling her gaze on Olivia.

She smiled lovingly at her and patted her arm. "I used to find you in here so often when you were growing up." She laughed when Olivia stared at her mother in shock, and held up a hand to keep Olivia from saying anything. "When your father would leave for London to perform his duties as a marquess, you would run to your room and cry for a long time." She cleared her throat, pushing down the emotion Olivia heard breaking through. "One night, you refused to come to dinner and insisted you were tired and wanted to sleep. Later, after everyone had retired for the evening, you snuck from your bed, tiptoed down the halls, and came to this very room. Lewis found you in here, a blanket wrapped around your sleeping body. He easily lifted you from the floor and tucked you back into your bed."

Olivia smiled; she had no idea about any of this.

"After a while," her mother continued. "Lewis would wait for you to fall asleep in the middle of the floor after your father left. He did this for years before he told anyone. He probably would never have said anything if your governess hadn't gone to check on you in your room one night and found your bed empty." She grinned. "The poor woman panicked and hurried to my room to inform me that you'd gone missing. When we came to the bottom of the stairs, we found Lewis standing guard to the ballroom. He explained about your late night jaunts, assuring us that he would take you to bed once he was sure you were asleep."

Olivia's heart felt near to bursting and her eyes stung with unshed tears. She had thought her exploits to the ballroom had been unknown to everyone. She didn't remember ever going back to bed, but never really thought about how she ended up there.

"If you knew I was doing it, why didn't you stop me?" Olivia asked.

She simply raised a shoulder. "It was how you coped with your father being away, and I understood why you needed to do it."

She raised an eyebrow. "But..."

Her mother pressed a gentle kiss to her cheek. "Everyone has a way of dealing with pain, Olivia, yours is here in the ballroom." She sighed deeply and wiped a tear from her face, "After your father died, you used to come here every night and cry yourself to sleep. Lewis knew it would be inappropriate for him to carry you to your room himself, so Charles did."

She stared at her mother wide-eyed. "Charles carried me to bed?"

She nodded. "I never could understand how you didn't wake, but we figured you had exhausted yourself from crying. It took you several months to stop coming in here each night."

Olivia watched her mother carefully; both of their emotions were on the edge of breaking, and she really hadn't wanted to cry again.

"I don't know why I stopped. It felt like I didn't need to come here anymore," she said with a deep sigh.

Her mother nodded. "You were finally healing. Your grief will never fully be gone, but you had finally reached a point where you could sleep in your bed. You did much better after that. When I suggested the house party, and your initial shock wore off, you were excited and smiling. I finally had my little girl back," her mother said, tears falling down her cheeks before she could wipe them away.

Olivia reached over and pulled her mother into a tight embrace. "Thank you for telling me."

Her mother smiled and patted her back.

"None of this explains how you knew I would be in here tonight," she said curiously, pulling back to look her mother in the eyes.

She grinned. "Your heart is searching for answers, my dear. You are restless and need your father's comfort."

She stared at her mother in confusion and her mother kissed her on the cheek.

"Listen to your heart, Olivia, the answer is already there." Her mother stood. "The ballroom may bring you comfort now, but I think sometime in the near future you'll find something even better."

Olivia watched her mother walk out of the ballroom and the light from her candle disappeared. Her mind reeled with what her mother had told her. She had known all along Olivia came here to gain comfort when her father was away. She smiled at the thought of Lewis carrying her up the stairs to the nursery and tucking her back into bed. He had watched her and Charles grow up and had gotten them both out of more scrapes than she cared to admit. She would need to remember to thank him.

Her heart full and her emotions raw, but bearable, she made her way back to her room and curled up in her bed. It didn't take her long to drift into a dreamless sleep, her body finally relaxing after a very long day.

Alicia Rivoli

Eleven

William woke early. Even though Olivia had sent a note to her mother, he had been worried when she didn't come to dinner. Lady Elmwood had excused her Olivia's absence, explaining her daughter hadn't been feeling well and had retired for the evening. Robert had told him beforehand that Olivia had gone out to the terrace, but that he hadn't seen her since.

William quickly dressed before hurrying down to the stables. He hoped Olivia was well enough to come for a ride this morning. When he arrived, Buttercup and Sweet Pea were sitting in their stall. He found Henry to see if Olivia had been there yet this morning, but he shrugged and told him he hadn't seen her. He waited for close to half an hour before he had Blue saddled and left on his own.

The morning skies were grey and menacing, indicating there would most likely be a storm soon. He kicked Blue into a gallop and rode hard and fast, wanting to clear his mind. By the time he returned to the stables, his horse was dripping with sweat and breathing heavy. He unsaddled the horse before returning him to his stall. He grabbed a brush from the shelf, slowly moved it along the horse's back and neck, wiping the sweat and dirt from his coat. When he finished, William got a bucket of oats and poured some into Blue's trough along with a sheaf of hay. After the workout they had this morning, the horse definitely deserved the extra treat.

"How'd he do for you today, my lord?" Henry asked, taking the brush William had been using and began scaping the loose hair from the bristles.

William rubbed his hand down the horse's long face until he got to the tip of his soft nose. He had always been fascinated by the nose of a horse being so incredibly soft.

"He's a brilliant piece of horse flesh," William finally answered. "I believe I'm going to try and convince Lord Elmwood to sell him to me."

Henry chuckled. "You'll have a hard time doing so, my lord. Ol' Blue is one of his lordships favorites. He and his father bought him the year before last. It was the first horse Lord Elmwood purchased on his own, and he is mighty proud of him."

William could understand his friend's attachment to Blue. He truly was magnificent. He shrugged. "I think I'll still try. I've grown quite fond of him myself."

William shook the stable master's hand and returned to the house. Sam was waiting for him when he got to his bedchamber.

"Would you like a hot bath this morning?" he asked William.

William nodded. "Yes, thank you."

Twenty minutes later he was alone in the hot water. He leaned back and closed his eyes, enjoying the soothing sensation the water was providing to his sore muscles. When the water grew cold, he dressed and prepared for the day then made his way to the breakfast room. The door stood ajar and he wanted to run the remaining distance when he heard a familiar feminine laugh.

"Olivia," he mumbled to himself, before taking the last few strides into the room.

Olivia sat at the table near the Abbots. She was deep in conversation with Miss Abbot, and when the lady said something to her, Olivia giggled. He'd only taken one step when she noticed him enter the room. She focused her mesmerizing gaze on him and flashed him a flirtatious smile before returning her attention to Miss Abbot. Relief washed over him as he saw how happy she was. He grabbed a few items from the table laden with meats, cheeses, fruit, and pastries.

"Good morning, Lord Hanley," Olivia said from directly behind him.

He spun around, quickly adjusting his grip on his plate to keep it from flying from his fingers.

She bit her lips to hold back a laugh. "I'm terribly sorry if I startled you, my lord," she teased, a look of humor in her bright blue eyes.

He chuckled and dropped his head. "Apologies, my thoughts were elsewhere, my lady," he said, trying to sort through his feelings. "I assure you, I'm not usually quite so jumpy."

She laughed. "It really was quite entertaining."

He grinned widely, his heart nearly leaping from his chest when the sweet smell of lilacs reached his senses. "Are we to have a battle of wits this morning, my lady?"

She looked at him with a raised brow. "Aren't you tired of losing our battles?"

He threw his head back and laughed heartily. "I believe, my lady, our games have only just begun."

Olivia shook her head and shrugged. "If you insist," she said, mischief in her expression. "But I feel terribly horrid when you lose."

"Lady Olivia?" a female voice called, interrupting. "Lord Elmwood tells me you have a beautiful garden. Would you mind giving us a tour?" Miss Abbot asked, smiling.

"I would love to," Olivia said. "How about I take everyone after breakfast?"

Miss Abbot nodded in agreement, then turned her attention to Charles who'd arrived only a few seconds after William.

"Would you care to join us, Lord Hanley?" Olivia asked.

"I can't think of anything I would enjoy more," he said, holding his arm to her so he could escort her to a chair.

They sat together, talking for a long time. They discussed the weather, politics, and her horses. Every time they discussed her two mares, her eyes would light up in excitement. She would speak animatedly as she told him stories of childhood riding lessons and the challenges they presented her. Her enthusiasm was contagious. The longer she discussed the animals, the livelier her stories.

"My father didn't care if it was raining," she said, explaining a difficult day she had training Buttercup. "He told me to get back on and to never give up. I'd already been unseated multiple times and covered from head to toe in mud, but I successfully learned to get Buttercup where I wanted with only the use of my legs. Mother was furious with him when we got back to the house and she saw my ruined riding habit, but I did it all again the next day."

"So, Buttercup isn't only a racehorse, you also successfully trained her with different commands. This allows you to now ride without the use of a bridle?" he asked, impressed by her knowledge of horses.

Olivia nodded with a large smile. "It's one of the reasons I try to ride every morning. I am constantly training her and brushing up on what I've already taught her."

"But not this morning," he said, watching her closely for any sign of distress.

She shook her head, her smile never faltering. "I'm afraid I slept later than usual, so I didn't make it out today."

"Even if you missed today, your skills are quite impressive," he said, his own smile matching hers. "I'm not sure I've ever met a more accomplished lady in all my life."

She turned red at his compliment and he laughed. "I told you it was too alluring to stop."

William laughed when Olivia gawked at him. He could see the specks of green and brown around the edge of her eyes and struggled to look away from her.

"Olivia, are you ready?" Charles asked, breaking the connection between William and Olivia.

She stood quickly and nodded. "Certainly."

Olivia took William's arm, and they led the small group into the gardens. The skies were still grey, and the wind had picked up substantially since his earlier ride. Olivia didn't seem to notice. She led them through the path she'd shown him earlier, her face bright with excitement as she pointed out various types of flowers.

When they reached a large stone wall covered almost entirely in ivy, they turned again and walked toward a small gate blocking the path a short distance away. They walked silently, no one speaking as Olivia continued to point out different plants and their many uses. She turned to face her captivated audience when they reached the gate, her eyes shining with pleasure.

"This area is my favorite part of the garden," she paused and looked at the gate. "Mr. Smith, our gardener, has been working tirelessly with me to get it to where it is now."

Charles cleared his throat, and William watched as his lips twitched at his sister's excitement. He obviously knew how passionate she was when it came to her flowers. William smiled and mentally told himself he would make sure she had fresh flowers in her room every morning while staying here.

He heard the squeal of hinges as Olivia pushed the gate open, then she stepped aside to allow Charles, Miss Abbot, Robert, and Miss Bowman to enter the gate, disappearing from view. He heard the audible gasps from the ladies and his interest continued to grow. Olivia put a hand on William's arm, stopping him before he could mollify his curiosity. He turned toward her and noticed her look of hesitancy.

"Would you mind doing me a favor?" She asked, a light pink hue touching her cheeks.

He smiled. She was rarely nervous. "Of course," he said. "Anything you wish."

Olivia smiled, making his stomach flip pleasantly. "Will you close your eyes?"

He laughed. "You don't want me to see your garden?" He knew it wasn't what she had meant, but the opportunity to tease her had been too great.

She giggled and put her hands on her hips. "You are the most absurd man," Olivia said. "Just close your eyes."

William smiled but did as she asked. He felt her fingers intertwine with his as she pulled him forward. "Don't look yet," she said, giddiness filling her words. "A few more steps."

She put a hand on his shoulder and turned him in a different direction but left her other hand in his.

"Okay," she said quietly. "You can look."

He opened his eyes slowly, wanting to draw out the moment as long as possible. When his eyes finally focused, his mouth dropped open. They stood beneath an iron trellis which lined the pathways in each direction. It reminded him of a tunnel. Each frame was covered in roses of every shape, size, and color. There had to be thousands of beautiful flowers surrounding them. How he hadn't seen this garden before now, he didn't know. He turned to look at her and froze in place. Olivia was standing very close to him, glowing with excitement while looking over her garden. It took his breath away and he mentally had to shake himself out of a stupor.

"Olivia," he said hoarsely. "This is amazing."

Her smile widened at his praise. "I'm so glad you like it," she whispered. It was as if the slightest noise would ruin the magic encircling them.

He cleared his throat and took a step toward her, but she pulled back a little and led him further down a path and away from the sounds of the other guests, who had turned down a separate path, leaving William alone with Olivia. He wondered why they were going off on their own, but was too captivated by the lady to care overly much.

"I want to show you my favorite part of this particular section of the garden," she said, looking at him over her shoulder as they walked.

"There's more?" he asked, completely enthralled by the woman holding his hand.

Olivia chuckled but didn't say anything.

He followed behind, loving their intertwined fingers and grateful for a few minutes alone. They made their way further into the maze of flowers, his amazement growing with each step.

It must have taken years to do this, he thought to himself.

She stopped in front of a large marble statue, which William noticed, was a likeness of her father.

"This," Olivia said, her voice cracking as she tried to hold back her tears. "Is the best part."

He looked at the statue standing majestically in the center of her garden, completely surrounded by roses. The sound of a trickling fountain nearby adding to the ambiance. He didn't speak; he knew he didn't need to. He had a strong desire to pull her close to him and wrap her in his arms, but instead put linked his fingers behind his back and sighed.

"Olivia," William said quietly, but she wouldn't look at him. She took a few steps away and touched a hand to the cold stone. He came up behind her and placed his hands on her shoulders, turning her to face him. Lifting Olivia's chin so he could look into her eyes, William's heart lurched in his chest. Tears were slowly falling down her cheeks, and he knew she was desperately trying to control them.

"I know you miss your father," he said, grabbing her hands. He lifted them to his lips and placed a gentle kiss on each, wishing neither of them were wearing gloves. He lowered her shaking fingers to his chest and held Olivia's hands against him. "You have done a fantastic job of providing a place to honor him."

She gave him a faint smile but lowered her eyes to the ground.

"I come here often to sit and listen. I find the scent of the roses, sounds of the water, and the presence of my father's likeness to be soothing," Olivia explained, releasing a shaky sigh. She looked back up at him, and her eyes locked with his. "I miss him dearly. There isn't a day I don't think of him."

William gently stroked her cheek. "I know," he said softly.

He watched her eyes fill with tears again, and she shifted to turn away from him. William drew her back against him and Olivia grabbed the lapels of his jacket, burying her face into his chest. The emotions she had experienced over the last year seemed to catch up to her. He held her tenderly and rubbed her back, laying his cheek on top of her head. He felt her relax in his arms, and after several minutes, Olivia's tears slowed, before stopping all together.

"I'm sorry," she muttered so quietly William wondered if she was even speaking to him. "I didn't plan on ruining your cravat."

He chuckled quietly. "Believe me, I don't mind in the least."

Pulling back slightly, Olivia stared at him, her eyes full of an intense emotion William didn't recognize. She stood up on her tip toes and kissed him softly on the cheek, surprising him.

"Thank you," she said quietly. "I can't tell you how much it means to me that you came back after I was so horrible." She lowered her head and stepped back.

William grabbed her wrist and tugged her into his arms. "I will always come back to you."

William's heart pounded as goosebumps raced down his arms when he felt Olivia's gloved fingers trail along his jacket and up to his cheek. The sounds of the other guests nearby became nothing but a buzzing sound as Olivia tilted her face upward. She raised up on her toes and pressed her lips to his. For a brief second, William had been too shocked to move and then realization dawned. He placed a hand at the back of her neck and pulled Olivia closer to him, his other hand finding the small of her back. Wrapping her arms around his neck, Olivia intensified their connection. Her lips felt soft on his own. Shivers of pleasure moved down his entire body as she ran her fingers thru his hair and along his neck. With a sigh, Olivia tilted her head so she could kiss William more fervently. When they finally drew apart, both were gasping to catch their breath.

William put his forehead against hers. "That was a welcome surprise," he said, breathlessly.

Olivia laughed quietly. "For both of us," she said, her words coming out as affected as his own had been.

William leaned down and lightly kissed her again. "I love this garden," he said when he moved slightly away.

Olivia laughed. "I thought you might." She shifted in his arms and put a little more distance between them. "But I do think we need to leave before my brother sends someone after us. I'm surprised we've been left alone as long as we have."

William moaned but knew she was right. His fears weren't of them being caught. He was more concerned that he would take her in his arms again and be unable to let her go. He nodded, then took her hand and put it in the crook of his arm, leading her back the way they had come and toward the sounds of people speaking in low tones. They found the others not far from where he and Olivia had been, and he pushed out a silent sigh of relief. Olivia moved to Miss Abbot and Charles's side. Miss Bowman slowed her pace, and walked slowly behind them. William's skin tingled from Olivia's earlier touch, and he felt empty without her at his side.

The group walked through the garden, Olivia stopping now and then to adjust her flowers on a trellis, or to explain something she'd noticed. William and Robert walked behind the others, watching them ooh and ahh over one color of rose and then another.

"So," Robert whispered, nudging William with his shoulder. "How was your time with Lady Olivia?"

William's lips twitched into a small smile. "I honestly can't believe she created all of this," he said, pointing to the flowers above their heads.

Robert laughed. "I think you're lucky Charles's attention is otherwise engaged, or he may have noticed your prolonged absence. Although, a duel would have truly made this house party memorable."

William eyed his friend suspiciously before returning his attention to Miss Abbot, listening as she asked Olivia questions about a particular rose.

William knew Robert was right about Charles. They were fortunate her brother had been more or less oblivious to William and Olivia's absence. Now that his thoughts had time to clear of Olivia's ability to hold him captive, William was very grateful to not have drawn Charles's suspicion and put a strain on their friendship.

William would need to thank Miss Abbot one day for her unknowing assistance in keeping Olivia's brother distracted. However, as he thought back to Roberts words, as innocent as they were, William didn't actually know what had happened between himself and Olivia. All he knew was his heart was completely and utterly hers.

Robert chuckled quietly at William's silence. "It's about time," he said. "Watching you two tip-toe around one another was getting hard to watch."

William stared at his friend with wide eyes. "We weren't tip-toeing around one another. And, besides, Charles already told me he wished for a union between our families."

"William, Charles may have wanted a union, but I don't think he meant for you to become so familiar with his sister in her garden," Robert laughed. "If he didn't notice the smile on both your faces when you walked up, I'd count your blessings. It was the only proof I needed to know your relationship had pushed past the boundaries of a mere friendship. Eventually, Charles will realize what's happened," he said, smiling brightly at his friend. "What he does then is anyone's guess."

William's mouth gaped open in surprise. He'd thought he had masked his feelings quite well. He shook his head. "You are such a great friend," he chuckled, but couldn't get Roberts' words from his mind. William had suspected Olivia had a partiality to him and the kiss they had shared only confirmed it. The question he had to ask himself now, was what he planned to do about this new step in his and Olivia's relationship.

A flash of lightning ripped through the sky, causing the group to pause in their leisurely stroll. In a matter of seconds, the clouds released their fury, pouring rain down on the group. The girls squealed and laughed as they all ran for the house. Lewis must have seen them coming, because the door swung open and allowed the group to burst into the entryway. They were laughing and dripping water all over the floor. Lewis raised an eyebrow and sighed at them before moving to call someone to clean up the mess they'd created.

William looked over at Olivia and noticed the spark in her eyes.

"I think we should go change before we catch a cold," Olivia said as she put her dripping coat on a hook near the door. "I also don't believe Lewis will be too happy if we stand here any longer," she laughed before hurrying up the stairs towards her room. William followed the others up their stairs as they all retreated to their chambers to change into warm, dry, clothing. When he entered his bedchamber, Sam was standing in the middle of the room, his arms folded across his chest.

"Do you intentionally find mud to scuff up your boots so I have more work to do?" his valet asked.

William chuckled. "Sorry, we got caught in the deluge outside."

He cocked an eyebrow. "We?" he asked as he waited for William to sit down.

"Yes, we," William answered, gripping the sides of the chair as his valet yanked his filthy boots from his feet. "I was with Lord Elmwood and his sister. She showed a group of us around her garden, but I don't need to explain myself to you." He laughed when Sam glared at him.

He changed his clothes quickly, then hurried to the library to find his parents, deciding it was time to enlist their advice on his and Olivia's attachment. His father was sitting on a settee reading a book next to his mother who was working on her embroidery. William smiled at the idealistic scene before him. He had always admired his parents' obvious love for one another.

"How's your book?" he asked his father, taking a seat opposite them.

"A little plain, to be honest. It's a book discussing land management. The topics the author points out are no longer seen as the best way to get the most out of your crops," he explained, closing the book and setting it on the table. "Did you have a good morning?"

William looked at his mother, who was biting her lips to hold back a smile. She seemed to already know what he came to discuss and was clearly pleased. He eyed her suspiciously.

"I had a fantastic morning," William said, unable to hold back his own smile, despite his wariness of his mother. "Have you seen Lady Olivia's garden?"

His mother nodded. "She has a real talent for such things. I have never seen another quite like it."

"I have no idea where they found seeds and the knowledge to grow so many different varieties. I don't think even the Prince Regent himself has a garden so fine," his father replied. "Now, a book explaining her methods to get those roses to grow, I wouldn't mind reading."

William chuckled. "I have to admit I agree with you, father. I'm positive there isn't another garden in the entire country like Lady Olivia's."

His mother narrowed her eyes. "This isn't why you came in here," she said with a short pause. "Is it?"

William smiled. "No, I want to know how you feel about Lady Olivia?" he asked calmly.

"You want to know how we feel about Lady Olivia?" his father asked quizzically. "Why? Has something changed?"

William shook his head. "Not really," he answered with a shrug of his shoulders. "I've been spending more time with her and wanted to know how you felt about her."

His mother eyed him suspiciously. "William," she replied. "We adore the entire family. Olivia has many accomplishments, is stunningly beautiful, and loves her family. We think very highly of her and don't have anything negative to say about her."

William smiled. "Her many talents have been surprising. The only things I haven't seen her do is needle work and drawing."

"She also speaks multiple languages," his father told him. "Italian and French, I believe."

William stared at him. "Of course she does," he laughed. "I would never have doubted it."

"Why are you asking us these questions, William?" his mother asked, skirting around any more small talk. "Is there something you aren't telling us?"

"Not yet," William answered. "I'm very captivated by her and find I desire her company above any other lady. But I'm still trying to determine not only my feelings, but hers as well."

"You know son, your mother and Catherine have been planning yours and Olivia's wedding since you were eight years old," his father said, laughing when William gave him a look of shock. "Did you think stopping in for tea all those years ago was an accident?"

William stared at them both but found he couldn't say a word. He had no idea any of this had been going on.

"We arranged for tea at Francis and Catherine's to see if you and Olivia would be a good match," his mother explained. "It was clear you enjoyed her company that day, but we couldn't be sure she caught your eye on any other level than friendship."

"But how…" his mother held up a hand to stop William before he could say anything further.

"We did everything we could to try and bring you together, but too many things got in the way. It was at the first musicale of her Season when Catherine and I knew you both would suit. You rarely looked anywhere else but at her when she was in the room. Catherine told me Olivia was the same," a sad look washed over her face.

"Then, last year when Francis was killed, we didn't know what was going to happen. Olivia closed off her heart to everyone, even her own family. Catherine said it wasn't until recently Olivia would go walk in her garden or get on her horse."

William had known she had been in a dark place, but learning exactly how bad, even after they had left, brought up his anger at the men who took away her joy, and her father. William and his father had continued their search for Lord Elmwood's attacker for months, but never had another lead. William even watched Lord Greenly himself for quite some time to see if he could determine if the man was involved. But other than the viscount being a snake and a cad, he couldn't find any involvement.

"Charles began worrying obsessively. He was even considering bringing in a doctor to see if there was anything they could do to help her," William's mother continued. "Catherine, of course, refused. She didn't wish to put her daughter through any more pain and knew the doctor could have her sent to an asylum if he thought her case warranted it. She wasn't going to take the chance. Catherine wrote to me, and she and I came up with the idea that Olivia might only need a distraction. So, I suggested the house party. We'd hoped having more people around her would help her find her light again."

"A month ago, after everything had been arranged and set into motion, I received another letter from Catherine. She said shortly after receiving letters of acceptance to their house party, something changed. Olivia started helping in her garden again. She brought fresh roses to her mother every morning and began riding and playing the piano forte. Catherine said it was like something clicked in her mind, bringing back her daughter." His mother stopped and looked around the room in self-contemplation before continuing.

"She still had times when she closed herself off from everyone, but not like before. I was told before we arrived Olivia was walking around the house singing."

William's father chuckled. "Your mother said Olivia hadn't sung a single note since her father's death, and Catherine had wondered if the change was brought on because you were going to be here."

He looked at his parents in question. "Lady Elmwood thought I was the reason her daughter had started singing again? But why? I don't understand."

"Isn't it obvious, my boy?" his father said. "She loves you."

William raised an eyebrow and stared at his parents in disbelief. "She didn't want anything to do with me when we left here last year. She did everything she could to avoid being near me. Why would you assume the change was because she loves me?"

His mother sighed. "I believe she avoided you because you made her feel happiness, and it wasn't how she wanted to feel. She was angry and hurting. Your attempts to heal her heart were too much for her at the time."

William thought back to their time here a year ago. He had done everything he could think of to try and help Olivia. The deep sadness he saw on her face every day had broken his heart. But no matter what he tried, she continually pushed him away.

"To answer your question," his mother said, a large smile on her face. "You couldn't find a more suitable wife for yourself. You are one another's light in a world filled with darkness. If Olivia is who you choose to spend your life with, we would be thrilled to have her as a daughter."

William smiled and kissed his mother's cheek, handing her a handkerchief when tears started to fill her eyes.

She beamed at him, squeezing his fingers tightly. "If she is who you want, William, do whatever you can to prove it to her."

William smiled. "I guess only time will tell."

Twelve

Olivia hadn't stopped smiling all day. She still couldn't believe what she had done. She caught William off guard when she initiated the kiss, but it only took him a second to realize what was happening. She touched her lips with her fingertips as she remembered the kiss, the smile on her face growing. She still felt the warmth where he had touched her skin on the back of her neck and when he pulled her to him.

"Would you like the green dress for dinner tonight, my lady?" Sally asked, stopping Olivia's wanderings.

Olivia cleared her throat. "Yes, I think the color will be perfect."

Sally walked out of the dressing room holding the silk gown and laid it out on the bed. Olivia always liked the dress. It made her skin look lighter than normal, and made her lips look darker. Sally took the brush from the dressing table and pulled and twisted her long strands in different directions. She told Olivia she had practiced a new style and thought it would be the perfect choice for the evening. Olivia never cared about having the perfect hairstyle, or the current style and dress of the *ton's* choosing. Yet tonight, she wanted everything to be perfect.

After an exhausting amount of time sitting in the same chair, Sally turned Olivia around to look in the mirror. Olivia gasped. It was like nothing she had ever seen before. The typical curls were surrounding her face and trailing down the back of her neck, but Sally had pulled off a hairstyle Olivia knew would soon be the desired coiffure of the *ton*. A single braid started at the top of her head and wound around the knot, making it look like the braid alone held everything together. Looking at the style, Olivia wondered if her maid had used any hairpins at all.

Once Olivia stepped into her gown and Sally had buttoned it up, she stood in front of the mirror in absolute shock. She didn't even look like herself. Her usually blue eyes held a green tint tonight, and her lips and cheeks were a rosy pink. In the candlelight, the twisted braid highlighted subtle sections of red hair which usually were hidden within the folds of her coiffure.

"Thank you, Sally," Olivia said in awe. "You obviously practiced the new look more than you let on. It's perfect."

Sally blushed. "Thank you, my lady. It's easy when your mistress is so lovely."

Olivia laughed, then hugged her maid. "I don't know what I'd do without you."

Olivia watched as a look of pure joy washed over Sally at her compliment, a tear slipping down her maid's cheek before she quickly wiped it away. "You best be going, my lady, dinner will start without you."

Olivia gave Sally one more grateful look before hurrying to the drawing-room. Tonight's dinner was to be a more formal affair, so Lewis had to announce her entrance. When all eyes turned toward her, she felt heat creep up her neck. She didn't enjoy being announced. Having all eyes in the room turn toward her made her extremely uncomfortable and she barely concealed her fidgeting fingers in the folds of her gown.

Her mother bustled over to her, grinning from ear to ear. "Good heavens, my dear, you look breathtaking. Is this a new gown?"

Olivia grabbed her mother's arm so they could move from the entrance. "No, Mama. It's the green one we bought in London during my Season."

"Well," her mother praised. "It's perfect on you."

Smiling brightly, she kissed her mother on the cheek before hurrying off to greet the other guests. Olivia stood in awe of her mother. She had been a rock to the entire family since father's death, even though she was grieving herself. Tonight, she donned a big smile, greeting everyone with joyous acceptance.

"How is a marquess to woo a lady when his own sister is the bell of the ball?" she heard Charles's teasing voice from behind her and spun around.

Olivia hugged him tightly, loving the relationship she shared with her older brother. It was rare for siblings to be so close to one another. "Don't be silly," she responded, smiling up at him with a mischievous grin. "I'm only trying to make sure I'm visible thru all your glory, my lord."

"Oh no, don't you dare go *my lording* me," he wagged a finger at her in disapproval, bursting into hearty laughter. "Seriously though, Livvie, you look happier tonight than I've seen you in a very long time. I'm grateful to whatever or *whoever* is responsible," he winked at her as he walked away.

Olivia scanned the room, looking for William. When she had joined the guests in the drawing-room last night, before she'd sought refuge from her stray pin, he hadn't been in the room. Tonight, he stood in the corner of the room talking to his friend Mr. Colfelt and Miss Bowman. Olivia laughed to herself at the thought of how many times Miss Bowman would mention Mittens, her orange tabby cat, during their discussions.

Olivia watched William for a minute. He wore a dark tailcoat with brass buttons on the cuff. His light-colored trousers had been finely pressed, his cravat tied in a perfect mathematical, and his boots shined in the light of the room. He stood tall and straight with his arms tucked behind his back, making Olivia blush as she remembered those hands pulling her into his embrace several hours earlier.

Directing her gaze away from him, she decided to find Miss Abbot. Olivia hadn't had a chance to get to know the young lady as she would have liked yet. She wanted to make sure Miss Abbot wasn't toying with her brother's heart in order to get his money and title. The young woman was sitting on a settee with Mrs. Abbot and Lady Pembrooke. They seemed to be in a deep discussion, probably over the upcoming ball, but Olivia decided to walk over anyway.

Upon her approach, the ladies ceased talking and looked up at her. She felt like an intruder until Lady Pembrooke smiled so warm and welcoming, Olivia couldn't help but return it.

"Good evening, my lady," Mrs. Abbot said, rising from her seat to greet her. "You look striking in that color."

Olivia returned the curtsy. "Thank you, Mrs. Abbot. I do hope you are finding your stay at Elmwood Manor pleasant."

"Indeed. It's a beautiful estate," she replied.

"Miss Abbot," Olivia said, turning to the younger woman. "It's nice to see you again. I'm thrilled you enjoyed the tour of the gardens this morning. Did you have a favorite rose?"

Miss Abbot dove into great detail about how much she loved the garden and how she couldn't believe there had been so many roses all around her. Olivia realized the beautiful, petite, Miss Abbot was not shy or afraid to talk in the least. Olivia listened, nodded, and replied when called for, but her mind was on the man standing a few short paces away. William still hadn't looked at her, and she began to wonder if he even wanted to. She turned back to the ladies' conversation which had turned into excitement about the upcoming ball.

Olivia was about to excuse herself when dinner was announced. She curtsied at the other woman. "If you'll please excuse me," she said, moving to stand behind her mother.

"Lord Hanley will be escorting you, Olivia," her mother grinned. "Smile."

Olivia rolled her eyes. "I don't think your reminder to smile is quite necessary," she teased, leaning closer to her mother so only she could hear. "Who wouldn't smile?"

Her mother's mouth twitched as she attempted to restrain her laughter. "Who indeed?" she said looking over Olivia's shoulder, her eyes twinkling. "Ah, Lord Hanley, a pleasure."

Olivia's eyes grew wide. She had no idea how long he had been behind her, but she hoped he didn't hear her last comment. She turned to him and tried to force her blush to stay hidden.

"Good evening, Lady Olivia," he said with poise and held out a single white rose to her. "I know lilacs are your favorite, but tonight, you are more lovely than a rose," he leaned closer to her.

Olivia felt her blush burn her cheeks. William chuckled. "I will never grow tired of seeing such a lovely response."

Olivia didn't know how much darker her blush could get, but she had a feeling she would find out tonight. She curtsied, then took the flower, lifting it to her nose and breathing in the sweet smell.

"Lilacs are indeed my favorite flower, but as you saw this morning, I also love roses." She said, slipping her arm into his as he led her into the dining room. He pulled her chair out for her, then took the seat next to her.

"Did you have a nice afternoon?" he asked her.

She nodded and moved to allow the servant to fill her goblet. "I did. Although the gloomy weather outside is not my favorite."

"Sometimes it takes a storm cloud for us to see the benefits of the sun," he uttered.

She was surprised by his philosophical answer. "Who said that?"

He puffed out his chest like a proud peacock. "It was the great philosopher, Lord William Hanley."

She laughed a bit too loudly, and the people sitting nearby stared at them both in question. She covered her mouth and tried unsuccessfully to smother her humor.

"I don't see how it's so funny." William teased, making her bite her cheek to hold back another laugh.

"Lady Olivia?" a female voice called from a few seats down. Olivia couldn't remember her name, but it didn't seem to show because the woman continued her question.

"Do you play whist?"

"Not well, I'm afraid."

"What a shame, Mr. Wolfort and I were just saying we would enjoy a game after dinner."

Olivia eyed the couple; she had a very vague memory of meeting Mrs. Wolfort when they first arrived. The woman was short and plump, with grey wiry hair. Mr. Wolfort was tall and had more bone than muscle. He sported thick sideburns and a bushy mustache. She didn't think the couple could be any more different from each other.

"I believe my mother is planning a night of games this evening. I am sure whist will be included," Olivia said.

The woman looked very pleased when she turned back to her husband, indicating to Olivia she had finished her questions.

"If you don't play whist, then what games do you enjoy?" William said, pulling her attention back to his dark brown eyes.

"You mean besides a friendly game of bantering with a certain gentleman?" she said flirtatiously. William's grin stretched across his face and it made her heart speed up. "I'm afraid games are not usually how I like to pass the time. I would much rather play the piano forte or sing," she responded truthfully, trying to get her heart rate to a much more normal pace.

"My mother said you have a beautiful singing voice. We will need an additional night of music soon so I can enjoy another of your many talents." His words seemed earnest, but Olivia rarely sang in front of anyone but her family.

"I do not believe anyone would enjoy my voice. I *can* sing, but it's not anything special."

"I highly doubt it," he muttered. "I have yet to see a talent you don't excel in."

She turned her attention to her plate in front of her, trying to hide the heat rising to her cheeks. She hated how she blushed so easily, but especially disliked how often she did with William.

"Will you go riding in the morning?" he asked before taking a bite of his rabbit stew.

Olivia wiped her mouth with her napkin and looked back at William. "I try to ride every morning, but it doesn't seem like the weather agrees with my plans."

"Did you ride this morning?"

She shook her head. "I had a difficult time sleeping last night, so I told my maid to wake me later than usual."

He looked at her in concern. "Was it because of whatever ailed you last evening?"

"Sort of," she answered. "But it was mostly unsettling thoughts."

The next course was brought in and Olivia's attention was pulled to other guests. Once the last course was finished, the women returned to the drawing-room as the men remained for port.

She walked to a chair against a far wall and took a deep breath to calm her labored breathing from being so close to William for so long. After this morning, she found it difficult to not reach for his hand or speak more openly than she was able to among the other guests. She looked at the rose he had given her before dinner. She had laid it on her lap during the meal, not wishing for a servant to take it away. She knew that if she weren't wearing gloves, the white petals would be soft against her fingertips when she gently touched them. She'd received roses from gentlemen before, but this single flower was by far the most romantic.

A footman entered carrying a silver tray. He moved to where she sat, and she took the small, folded letter from him. She turned the note over in her hands wondering who would be writing to her. She didn't recognize the two curled letters overlapping each other on the seal. It had been smudged, and she couldn't make out which letters they were.

She tucked the letter into her hidden pocket, planning to read it in private after the evening's entertainments were over. Olivia leaned back and listened to the murmuring of voices from the other women in the room, trying to ignore whatever gossip they were discussing. The night outside the window was dark, and the rain remained. Rumbles of thunder still sounded in the distance, and the occasional flash of lightning added a different ambiance to the candle-lit room. She closed her eyes, the ticking of the rain on the window smoothing her nerves. She could feel her beating heart in the side of her neck, and calmly counted its steady rhythm. It no longer beat erratically like it had during dinner, but was a nice slow tempo, comforting her mind of thoughts from the night before.

"My lady?" She opened her eyes to Mr. Colfelt and Miss Bowman watching her. She sat up straighter and hoped her maid's work on her hair wasn't a disaster.

"Good evening, Mr. Colfelt, Miss Bowman. I hope you are enjoying your evening," she said, stifling a yawn.

"Yes, very much," Miss Bowman agreed. "You have a lovely home, and the gardens are delightful."

Olivia gave the woman a look of gratitude. "Thank you. I know my brother will be pleased to know his guests are enjoying themselves."

"I saw a piano forte on my tour of the home," Miss Bowman said smiling. "Do you play?"

Olivia saw William walking toward them and turned her attention back to their conversation. "I do. I began playing as a young girl and haven't looked back since," she answered.

"Lady Olivia has a very outstanding musical talent," Mr. Colfelt praised. "She played a lovely piece a few nights ago."

"I believe my mother has a night of music planned tomorrow if I'm not mistaken," Olivia said kindly. "Miss Bowman, do you enjoy music?"

Miss Bowman's fan flipped around in her hand excitedly. "Oh yes. Although I'm not fortunate enough to have the talent, I do love listening to those who do."

Olivia's eyes flicked to William again. He'd been stalled by the duke and duchess but was moving toward her again.

She turned back to Miss Bowman. "What do you entertain yourself with at home?"

She instantly knew her mistake as Miss Bowman started talking about all of her animals. It seemed her orange tabby was only one of her favorites. Mr. Colfelt listened intently to her explanations of her chickens and Olivia wondered if he was truly interested in her or merely being very polite.

"Don't you think so, my lady?" Miss Bowman asked, staring at her.

Olivia had no idea what question she'd been asked and felt a moment of panic at her wool-gathering.

"I'm sure Lady Olivia enjoys the benefits of a laying hen," William said as he moved to her side. "Only this morning, I believe she even enjoyed an egg at breakfast."

Olivia nearly laughed out loud but managed to contain it. He must have known she wasn't paying attention and had come to her rescue.

"Oh yes," she said, playing along. "Hens are fascinating animals."

She watched William hide his amusement and her previously steady heart rate had flown into a new dance all over again.

"I'm terribly sorry, but Lady Olivia has promised me a game of chess," he said, holding his arm out to her. "Please excuse us."

Olivia had most certainly not promised him a game of chess, but at the moment, she was grateful she wouldn't have to come up with any more thoughts about chickens. William led her to a small table holding her father's ornately carved chess set. The darker and lighter woods of the pieces matched the board perfectly.

"I will have you know," William whispered as he pulled the chair out for her. "I'm a very good chess player."

She watched as he moved to the other side of the table. Immediately an idea formed, and she nearly giggled in delight. "Well then, I'm afraid this will be a very short game," she laughed lightly. "I don't know how to play at all."

"You don't know how to play chess, and you have an older brother?" he said in faux surprise. "I am appalled at Charles for not teaching you."

She stifled a grin. "Oh, he tried," she said in a serious tone. "But he had a very poor pupil."

He laughed. "Surely you are better than you would have me believe?" he said, giving her a sly half-smile.

"I assure you, I am not," she said, her breath caught as his eyes found hers and she had to blink to break his spell over her.

"Well, we need to fix such an oversight in your education," he said, leaning over the board. He grabbed one of her pieces and held it up for her to see.

William explained each piece, and its abilities and rules, watching her excitedly as he did. Olivia stared at him and had a brief pang of guilt roll through her. She knew how to play and had won quite a few games against Charles and her father. Only, she didn't want him to know yet. She'd planned on beating him with *beginner's luck*. She knew when he realized he'd been tricked, he would laugh at her, teasing her mercilessly. She would enjoy every single minute.

William played slowly at the beginning, allowing her time to figure out the rules of the game. She moved a couple of pawns into places where they were easily captured. Each time she did, William would explain why her move was a mistake. After half an hour, she decided to finish the game. A few quick moves later, she called 'check mate' to which he applauded her for her quick understanding of the game. After he lost the second game, he raised an eyebrow at her in suspicion and she only shrugged her shoulders, giving him an innocent look. It was after the fourth match he realized he'd been lied to. When realization struck him, Olivia burst into a fit of laughter.

"I believe, my lady," he said, shaking his head and she could see he was barely containing his mirth. "You have indeed played this game before."

His eyes were radiating happiness when she looked at him and she pressed her lips together in a thin line to try and hide her amusement.

"Did my sister tell you she couldn't play chess?" Charles said, his eyes full of mischief.

"She has done this before, has she?" William teased.

"She did it to me when I got back from school a few summers ago. She told me our father couldn't teach her how to play, and she wanted to learn. I lost several quid in the process," Charles said, raising an eyebrow at his sister.

"She hustled her own brother?" William tsked. "Here I thought she was an innocent debutante of the *ton*."

Olivia lifted her shoulders and sighed. "There is no such thing as an innocent debutante. Besides, you can't blame a girl for the talents she was blessed with."

They all laughed and spent the remainder of the evening sharing stories and mishaps of their childhood. Olivia glanced at William often, only to find him watching her. It made her blush every time. When the night was ending and guests began to retire to their bedchambers for the night, William escorted Olivia up the stairs to the hallway leading to her room.

"It was a pleasure, my lady," he said raising her gloved hand to his lips and kissing the back before turning it over to kiss her palm.

She smiled. "I'll see you in the morning, my lord." She quickly pressed a kiss to his cheek and turned to hurry down the hall.

William's hand slid down her arm as she moved, and he linked his fingers into hers before pulling her back to him and into his arms. She froze when he laid her hand on his chest. She found herself unable to breathe from the intensity of his gaze. He took the white rose from her hand he had given her earlier and tucked it behind her ear. "Goodnight, my beautiful rose," he said in a husky whisper before he released her.

William turned and disappeared in the direction of the guest rooms. She stood where he had left her, the feel of his kiss on her palm and his gentle grip about her waist, still fresh in her mind.

Her legs felt wobbly and she was having a difficult time getting them to move.

After several minutes, Olivia was finally able to make her way to her bedchamber. When she shut the door behind her, she smiled, placing a hand against her stomach to quell the feelings inside her. Olivia took the rose he had tucked behind her ear and moved it to her nose. She would never think of a rose the same way again after hearing him call her *his* rose. She had discovered tonight, and earlier this afternoon, that she loved being in his arms. She dropped her hands to her side and felt the forgotten letter in her pocket she had received after dinner.

She laid the flower on her bed, and walked to her small writing desk, sliding her finger beneath the seal.

Lady Olivia,
I look forward to continuing where we left off.
FG

She read the letter again, turning it over and looking for any indication of who FG could be. She couldn't remember anyone with those initials. She laid the letter on her writing desk and stared at it. A sick feeling began to form in the pit of her stomach. Something about the wording of the letter felt menacing, almost like a threat of some kind. She called for Sally and dressed for bed, her mind never far from the words on the page. She returned to the letter after her maid left for the night, and with a final glance, Olivia threw it aside, climbing into bed and hoping sleep would take over and release her from her worries.

Thirteen

William couldn't sleep. All he could think about was Olivia in his arms, and the smell of lilacs following him everywhere. He stood and paced his room, trying to clear his thoughts. Lilacs and roses had quickly become his favorite flowers, and he couldn't wait until he and Olivia were in her garden once again. It was absurd how quickly everything seemed to have turned for him as far as Olivia went. He could still picture her in his mind as a young girl with two braids and muddy skirts. Now, the vision of a beautiful woman with deep blue eyes, shining chestnut-colored hair, a brilliant smile, and too many talents to name dominated his every awareness.

William sighed. How was he supposed to ever sleep if all he could think about was the way she fit perfectly in his arms? He rang the bell for Sam and requested a cup of lavender tea. He hoped the warm drink would help him sleep. When Sam entered with the requested drink a few minutes later, he immediately began to relax as the liquid ran down his throat. He climbed into bed once finished and closed his eyes, letting the herb do its job.

Pounding rain woke William early the next morning. He didn't feel anywhere near rested and having another rainy day would only make things worse. He knew the dark skies would coax everyone into somber moods. His head ached and if he didn't take care of it, he knew he would end up miserable. William dressed without waiting for his valet and went to the breakfast room. The servants were setting the food on the table and bowed when he entered.

"Can you have a cup of ginger tea brought to me, please?" he asked a young maid before she left.

"Of course, my lord," she said in a quiet voice.

He grabbed a plate and filled it with some sausage and eggs along with some warm fresh bread. The food smelled good, making his stomach growl. He positioned himself in the window seat and watched the water from the rain pour down the windowpane like a small raging river. Sometimes England's weather fascinated him, but today's rain and darkness were the last thing he wanted. If it was raining, he wouldn't get the chance to ride Blue with Olivia. He nibbled on his food and thanked the young maid when she gave him a cup of hot ginger tea.

The dull headache was intensifying, so he asked for a second cup. Once the liquid settled in his stomach and the ginger worked to alleviate the pain in his head, he started to feel slightly normal again. Charles and his mother walked into the room, smiling and laughing about something.

"Good morning, William," Lady Elmwood said as he bowed over her hand. "It's a lovely morning, is it not?"

William glanced at the window, wondering how she thought this rainy day lovely.

She laughed. "Yes, I know about the rain. But there are so many other things which can make your day enjoyable."

He thought about her words, wondering what she had meant by them. She must have noticed his confusion because she giggled and shook her head.

"Don't worry," she said, her smile lighting her face. "Soon, you'll understand."

More confused than ever, he pushed his breakfast aside and offered to get her a plate of food. She thanked him, but declined his offer, claiming she wasn't quite up to eating at the moment. He turned to Charles. The man looked like a love-stricken buck. His eyes danced with merriment and a wide smile stretched across his too pink cheeks. William what could make a man look the way his friend did at that moment. He himself had experienced the exact sentiment yesterday.

"Did you enjoy Miss Abbot's company last evening?" he asked with a knowing smile.

If possible, Charles's smile grew, and he chuckled softly.

"Have you seen my daughter this morning?" Lady Elmwood asked.

William looked at the door at the mention of Olivia hoping she would walk in. He was disappointed when he didn't see anyone there. "Not yet. Do you expect she'll be down for breakfast soon?"

She smiled at him. "I'm sure she has already had breakfast. I would bet she is in the stables. Putting the last few months aside, I never could get her away from those animals."

William looked at her in surprise. "Does she often ride in the rain?"

"Oh, good gracious no," Lady Elmwood replied with a sigh of relief. "Olivia insists her horses *need* her daily attention. She has returned to tending to them no matter the weather. I don't understand, as I'm not a rider myself and don't care much for the animals, but she and her father were out there day-in and day-out. He would even sneak her out of her lessons when she was younger to ensure she had time in the stables or atop one of her horses." She gave a small smile, and William could see the pain of her husband's loss still seemed fresh in her mind.

"I didn't get to ride as often as she did," Charles complained with a smile. "Olivia eventually became so well trained on her horses, even father couldn't keep up." He and Lady Elmwood laughed. "I took her horse's bridle one morning when we were set to race, and dash it all if she still didn't manage to beat me. Blaze and I still didn't stand a chance."

"Yes, you told me she cheats," William smiled. "I believe you're right. I have yet to even come close. When I think I may pull ahead; her horse seems to mock me as she kicks dirt into my face and races off ahead of me. She confessed she has an unfair advantage when she rides Buttercup."

Charles shook his head and chuckled. "Yes, I lost a few quid there as well. I finally learned I can't trust her when she claims she doesn't know how to do something. She will usually win every time."

"She has definitely made her father proud with those horses," Lady Elmwood said in a calm quiet tone. "He would love all she has accomplished."

Charles put a hand and his mother's shoulder. "We always knew he was proud of us, mother. He told us every day."

A tear spilled from Lady Elmwood's eyes and rolled down her cheek. "Enough of this. Charles, we need to go to town soon and procure items for the ball."

Charles rolled his eyes at William and silently begged for his help to escape what he knew was going to be a torturous outing. He sighed in resignation when William shook his head while holding up a hand to indicate he wouldn't be getting involved. Defeated, Charles followed his mother to the table. William was grateful he and his own mother shared the same type of relationship Lady Elmwood did with her children. He had friends whose mothers had barely spoken to them because they weren't the heir. He couldn't imagine what it would be like to have a parent so detached. He excused himself and grabbed his coat and hat before running out into the pouring rain to find Olivia.

Before he made it too far, he stopped and looked toward the rose garden, an idea forming. Smiling, he turned and raced toward the garden. He entered the small building where he knew Mr. Smith would be. He was soaked through and shivered in the cold room.

"My lord!" the gardener said, bowing in surprise.

William grinned and slapped the man on the back. "Mr. Smith," he said conspiratorially. "I need your assistance in wooing a certain young lady."

The gardener grinned. "What did you have in mind?" he asked.

William explained his plan, which caused Mr. Smith's smile to grow.

"It would be my honor, my lord," he said bowing again. "If it's alright with your lordship, I would like to add a little something else as well."

Without hesitation William agreed before excusing himself, his heart lighter than it had been all morning. The rain hadn't lightened up at all, in fact, he believed it was coming down harder than before. He felt cold when he finally arrived at the stables, but he wasn't disappointed. A rather wet young lady stood before him, brushing Sweet Pea. Olivia looked up from her task and didn't seem at all surprised to see him. Her face turned a very becoming shade of pink before she turned her attention back to her mare.

"Didn't anyone tell you it was raining outside this morning?" he teased, removing his outer coat and wringing it out.

He saw the corner of her mouth twitch, but she didn't look at him again.

"I did notice, my lord," she said. "As you can probably see from my very disheveled appearance."

William heard her give a small chuckle, but she still wouldn't look at him. It was driving him mad. He entered the mares stall, and Sweet Pea whinnied in annoyance, but he didn't let it stop him from his objective. He moved quickly to her side and put his hand under her chin and lifted her eyes to meet his.

"Much better," he whispered, his thumb stroking her jaw line. "I can't bear not seeing your smile."

He watched her eyes turn from shy to completely playful. He looked at her cautiously, and before he could say a word, she gave him a very flirtatious smile and batted her eyelashes as she dropped her gaze to the floor. Of course, he had seen the same look a thousand times from every eligible debutante of the *ton* as they tried to get his attention. It had never affected him the way it did at this moment. His heart sped up and he fought the urge to pull Olivia into his embrace. Then she laughed and his jaw dropped.

"I'm so sorry," she said, gasping as she tried to stop laughing. "I know I should not attempt the ways of the *ton*, but you make it too tempting."

William looked at her in complete confusion, unsure of her meaning, but he was loving her laughter. Seeing the delight in Olivia's eyes and hearing her laughter became too much, and he turned her face to his and kissed her. Not slow and gentle the way he had yesterday, but with a passion he didn't know he could feel. He felt Olivia's arms wrap around his neck as she returned his gesture, sending shivers of pleasure down his body.

William pulled her closer and tucked his fingers into her wet hair, lilacs overwhelming his senses. Much too soon for his liking, Olivia pulled back, her breathing ragged, and her face flushed. She smiled, resting her forehead against his, then lowered her hands to his chest. William wrapped his fingers around hers, before pulling them to his lips.

"William," she whispered, "we're going to be seen."

She was right, William knew he had lost complete control, but he couldn't think about anything but her. He was in love with Olivia, and didn't mind the knowledge. He missed her when she wasn't with him and became enraptured by her lovely blue eyes. William reveled in the scent of lilacs and would never look at another rose without thinking of her. He loved her and was sure she cared for him as well. William wanted to spend the rest of his life with Olivia. He wanted to wake up with her beside him and watch their children run wild around the house. He wanted to run his fingers through her thick, soft tresses and be the one to put the pieces of her heart back together. William wanted her, all of her.

He cleared his throat, and placed his hand on her cheek, letting his thumb glide over her cheek bone. "What if I didn't mind being caught?" His voice was low as he spoke.

Olivia pulled further away from him and smiled. He reluctantly released her, immediately missing her touch. She reached down and grabbed the brush from the ground, which she had dropped when William had kissed her, and resumed her care of Sweet Pea.

"You're making me nervous," she said, giggling. "Either grab a brush and help me or see to Blue."

He smiled widely and reached around her to grab a brush, but he couldn't help but kiss her neck as he did.

"William!" she exclaimed happily.

He laughed, moving to the other side of the horse. He needed to put the mare between them, or he would not be able to stop himself from grabbing her and kissing her again. He watched her as she patted Sweet Pea on the nose and moved from the stall to greet Buttercup. The horse bobbed her head in pleasure as Olivia took a sugar cube from her pocket and held it out for the animal. Olivia scratched her horse between the ears and down her long nose as Blue enjoyed the treat. Leaning forward, Olivia rested against the mare and released a deep sorrowful sigh.

"I don't know if I would have made it, if not for them," Olivia said quietly. William wondered if she was talking to herself or him. She walked to Buttercup's side, her smile replaced by a look of pain and grief. "It took months after my father's death before I found my way back out to the stables. I found myself spending hours in their company, absorbing their energy, hoping it would chase away my demons. Sometimes I would sit here in the quiet. At times it would be to release frustration, or to confide in Buttercup and Sweet Pea." She pushed out a slow breath then turned to him and her smile returned. "You changed those feelings for me."

William stared at her, unable to move.

She walked up to him and grabbed his hand. "When I heard you and your parents had accepted the invitation to my mother's house party, something came alive inside of me." Her eyes filled with tears as she continued. "The darkness overpowering me for so long, was replaced by hope. A hope that your visit would bring joy and happiness back into my life. I didn't want to hurt anymore. When you arrived," she sniffed, "I wasn't disappointed."

He opened his mouth to respond, but she put two fingers to his lips silencing him. "I was so nervous you would have changed after our last meeting. I had treated you so poorly. I didn't recognize my actions until your family left, and I instantly regretted everything." She released her hold on him and moved back to her horse, a far-off look in her eyes. She paused briefly before continuing.

"I wrote so many letters to you trying to apologize, but threw them in the fire when I'd finished." She turned back toward him, and a sad smile formed on her lips. "Now, I have the opportunity to tell you in person. William, you will never know all you have done to help me. You unknowingly lifted the darkness plaguing me, and replaced it with a light I haven't felt for a long time." She stepped closer to him, and he inhaled the scent of lilacs and horses, and his heart swelled.

William wanted to reach out and pull her closer but resisted. She took another step, and he felt the edges of her skirt against his legs. Her eyes never left his own and eventually, she stood on her tip toes and smiled, placing a soft kiss on his cheek.

"Thank you, William," she said quietly before backing away.

He pulled her back to him and placed his mouth next to her ear. "Marry me?" he whispered.

She stiffened and shifted her eyes to his.

"Olivia?"

She stared at him, and took a step back, her eyes going from light to dark in anger. "What did you say?"

William wasn't sure what to say. Did she want him to ask her again, or was she repulsed by his offer of marriage?

"I don't ever want to leave you, Olivia. I—I want to marry you," he said, his voice low and quiet. He took a step toward her and reached for her hand that had dropped to her side.

She looked at him in question. "Why?"

William shot her a look of surprise, "Why do I want to marry you?" he asked, confused.

She nodded but didn't say anything else.

He pulled her toward him again. "Olivia," he whispered. "I love you. I have loved you since the moment I saw you at the afternoon tea our parents arranged in London four years ago."

She watched him wearily, but again, said nothing.

"Please Olivia, I can't live without you any longer. I need you," he kissed the tip of her nose. "You are my beautiful butterfly…You are my forever rose."

She stared at him. "I didn't tell you those things for you to pity me, my lord," she said, glaring at him.

"Pity?" his voice raised an octave. "Olivia, I'm not doing this because I feel sorry for you."

She eyed him suspiciously, but he could see the features of her face softening.

William rested his hand on her cheek and lifted her chin to make her look at him. "I love you, Olivia. I love everything about you."

She closed her eyes and leaned into his touch. When Olivia finally looked at him, she had tears in her eyes. "I want to believe you, but I'm afraid of being hurt, William. I don't think my heart would ever recover."

He let his finger slid along her jaw and down to link their fingers together. When she didn't pull away from him, he took it as a positive sign she was realizing his feelings for her were true.

"I would never hurt you, my darling. I want to be there for you. I want to be the one to comfort you and to make you laugh. I want to be the only man who kisses the small dimple on your right cheek," he touched the spot with his fingertips and smiled at her. "I want to be your husband, Olivia."

William saw the corners of her lips twitch. He let his thumb move slowly across her cheek, before tucking a curl behind her ears. Olivia watched him, and he saw the fear and worry melt away, replaced by a soft look of adoration. She nodded her agreement and William didn't have to be told twice, he lifted her into his arms and twirled her around the stables. "I love you, Olivia," he said before kissing her softly.

She started giggling and pulled away slightly. "I have waited four years to hear you say those words to me."

He shook his head, and smiled. "My beautiful rose, you are my perfect match in every way."

She tucked her lip between her teeth, then kissed him softly once more before stepping around Buttercup. "You'd better go. I'm not sure it is a good idea for us to be alone any longer," she said, glancing around the stable to show they were indeed without a chaperone.

He bowed, knowing she was right. "Of course, my love."

William moved slowly toward to the doorway. A small playful look spread across Olivia's face as she watched him. He grinned, and before he changed his mind, left the stable and ran back to the house, ignoring the cold rain. He was going to marry Olivia Barton, and he didn't believe he would ever stop smiling again.

Fourteen

There are times in every woman's life when she experiences a joy so great, she's positive there is nothing in the world to surpass it. William made Olivia feel such a way as he held her and told her he loved her. A burst of laughter erupted from her mouth. She couldn't remember a time in her life when something made her feel this way. Olivia left the stall and looked out of the stable, watching as William disappeared into the heavy rain. Her heart thumped loudly in her chest at the thought of becoming William's wife. Olivia grabbed the sides of her skirt and spun in circles around the stable, her laugh echoing against the walls.

"My lady," Henry said entering the stables, his coat dripping from the rain, sounding like he was holding back a laugh. "Are you quite alright?"

Olivia stopped. The room spun and she wobbled slightly before grabbing the gate to steady herself. "I'm more than okay, Henry. I'm perfect."

He smiled. "Have the horses been entertaining you this morning?"

She looked back toward her horses who watched her a few paces away. "No more than usual," she said giggling.

Henry raised an eyebrow then shook his head. "Do I even want to know?"

Olivia could feel her smile grow as she thought of why she was so happy. "Probably not."

He laughed. "Whatever you say, my lady. Can I saddle one of your horses for you?"

Looking back out into the cold wet rain she sighed. "Unfortunately, this weather will be keeping them indoors today."

"Aye, my lady. It's quite the storm." Henry said, moving to stand beside her.

Olivia sighed. "Would you mind making sure they have fresh straw in their stalls? I don't wish for any of the horses to catch a chill in this wind."

"Of course. I will be sure to give them all a few extra oats as well," he said, smiling at her.

She returned his smile and kissed his cheek, causing the man's eyes to grow wide in shock.

"Thank you, Henry," she said before grabbing her cloak from the hook near the door. "I will try and come check on them later if the rain stops."

Henry cleared his throat. "Would you like me to assist you back to the house, my lady?"

Olivia shook her head. "No, thank you. I wish to enjoy the rain on my own."

He stared at her in question but didn't say anything. Pulling the hood of her cloak over her head, Olivia tucked her fingers into her gloves, and raced out into the cold wet morning. She gasped when the water hit her face. The uselessness of her cloak was instantly realized. It absorbed the water and before she was halfway to the house, she was soaked to her skin.

As she neared the entryway, Lewis spotted her and raced out into the rain to help her up the wet, slick steps. He slammed the door once they were inside, and they both dripped water all over the front foyer.

"I'm sorry, Lewis, now you're all wet," Olivia laughed.

The butler grabbed a towel from nearby, apparently anticipating her arrival and wrapped her comfortably in its warmth. "My lady," he murmured. "Must you go out into the rain to see your horses?"

She laughed. "You already know I do."

He pushed her toward the stairs. "You best change before you catch a cold, my lady."

"Thank you, Lewis," she chuckled, and turned toward him again and took his hands in hers. "I also want to thank you for caring for me all these years. You've been like a second father to Charles and me."

"Go change," he demanded with a watery chuckle.

Grinning, Olivia hurried up the stairs, listening to the water slosh around in her boots and the snap of her wet skirts. She peaked around the corner of the hallway to make sure neither her mother, nor Charles, would see her. She knew they would scold her for going out in the rain. Olivia scurried to her door and pushed it open, but stuttered to a stop. Her hands covered the gasp of surprise that rushed from her mouth.

Roses of every color laid atop her bed, several dozen, at least, and a rainbow of matching petals were strewn across the floor. She walked slowly into the room, tears filling her eyes and spilling down her cheeks. A bouquet of lilacs had also been placed on her dressing table and a lavender bouquet was on her writing desk. She heard herself giggle as she moved around her room, smelling the two purple bouquets before moving to her bed. Olivia picked up a single red rose which had a note tied to its stem with a white ribbon. Removing it, she smelled the rose before gently laying it back down to her bed. She moved to her writing desk where a candle had been lit and slipped her hand under the flap and pulled it open.

O my Luve's like a red, red rose, That's newly sprung in June: O my Luve's like the melodie, That's sweetly play'd in tune! As fair thou art, my bonnie lass, So deep in love am I: And I will love thee still, my dear, Till a' the seas gang dry:

I couldn't let you miss your garden on this rainy day.
Yours Always,
William

Olivia covered her mouth and stared at the note. Robert Burns had always been one of her favorite poets. She and her mother would sit in the library and read his poetry on rainy days, like today, romanticizing over the words. Olivia didn't know how William knew she liked his poetry, but he couldn't have picked a poem more suited to them both. Wiping the tears in her eyes, she sat down on the chair nearby. Olivia's heart was full and complete. William made sure she could have her flowers, even with the cold and rain. Her fingers slid lightly down the words on the letter, then she looked back at the flowers lining every available space in her room. It was truly magical. Never in her life had she seen something so beautiful, and William had done it for *her*.

A loud gasp pulled Olivia's eyes to the door of her bedchamber which had been left open. Her mother stood with both hands covering her mouth, much the same as Olivia had done and tears also filled her eyes.

"Oh, Olivia," she squeaked. "It's beautiful!"

Olivia could only smile.

"Did William do this?" she asked, walking in to admire all the flowers.

She nodded. "He said he didn't want the rain to keep me from my garden."

Her mother put her hands together in a ball against her chest, and her lip quivered as she tried to hold back more tears. "How very thoughtful."

Olivia smiled. "That isn't all, Mama."

Her mother had been dabbing at her eyes with her handkerchief, and her eyes shot in her daughter's direction.

"He asked me to marry him," she told her mother, the grin only getting wider as she spoke.

Her mother screamed in delight and rushed over to Olivia and wrapped her in a tight embrace. "Oh, my sweet darling," she cried, her tears falling more now than before. "I can't tell you how happy I am for you."

Olivia giggled. "I can't tell you how happy *I* am."

Her mother pulled back from her and looked at her daughter. Olivia could see the pure joy behind her mother's deep blue eyes. "Your father would approve most heartily," she said, patting Olivia's cheek. "We always wished for you to marry William. But we decided to allow you to choose for yourself."

Olivia pulled her mother in for another hug. "Thank you, Mama," she said, her voice cracking with emotion.

Her mother grabbed her hand, pulling her daughter toward the door. "We must go tell Victoria."

"Mama?" Olivia said, stopping her mother. "I think I shall like to change first," she pointed to her wet gown.

"Oh! Of course," her mother said, looking down at her own gown, now wet from their hug. "I think I shall also need a new gown."

Olivia smiled. "I shall meet you in the front parlor when I've finished."

Her mother squeezed her hands tightly and kissed Olivia's cheek, before turning and leaving the room, pulling the door shut behind her.

Olivia walked to her writing desk and picked up William's letter. She read the poem again, focusing on his signature. The two words, yours always, warmed her heart. She would marry, William. Then he would truly be hers always and forever. She loved the idea of being by his side every day.

The next several hours were spent in the front parlor with her mother and Lady Pembrooke as they discussed the ball with the other ladies staying from the house party. Everyone was excited for the dance, but she could see the excitement more on Miss Abbot and Miss Bowman's faces. She had grown to enjoy Miss Abbot's company and had begun to hope she and Charles would marry. Much to Olivia's surprise, even though it had only been a few short days, she started considering Miss Bowman to be a dear friend as well; cat stories and all.

As the ladies conversation turned to other things, with some women leaving to work on their embroidery projects in other rooms, Olivia turned to her mother and future mother-in-law. They'd expressed a desire to discuss wedding details and decided Olivia and William would announce their engagement at the ball tomorrow night. Olivia thought they should include William in the decision, as it was to be his wedding as well. Both ladies laughed and without a pause, continued the plans. Olivia was the only daughter and William the only child. She knew their mothers would go crazy.

Lewis gave a light tap on the door, and entered the room. "My lady," he said addressing my mother. "A package has come for Lady Olivia."

Her mother looked from Lewis to Olivia. "Please bring it inside, Lewis," she said.

Lewis brought in a large box, and Olivia knew in an instant it was her new gown she'd ordered for the ball. She jumped up and took the box from Lewis with thanks and hurried to her mother and Lady Pembrooke.

"It's your new dress!" her mother said, clapping her hands in front of her. "I was beginning to worry it wouldn't arrive in time."

"Well, let's see it," Lady Pembrooke said, leaning closer.

Olivia slid the lid off and peeled back the paper protecting the material. She reached in and pulled out a beautiful white gown made of the softest silk Olivia had ever felt. Lace was sewn around the neckline and sleeves, and white floral embroidery cascaded down the front of the sheer fabric, covering the entire dress. A matching pair of embroidered slippers complimented the gown.

"Oh!" both mothers cooed when Olivia held it up for them to see.

"Olivia, it's exquisite," Lady Pembrooke said, letting the soft fabric slide through her fingers. "The embroidery is the perfect addition."

Olivia beamed; it was exactly as she had pictured it would be. She looked at every detail, loving each new thing which caught her eye. The box also contained new stockings, a pair of long white gloves, and a smaller box neatly wrapped in a soft pink ribbon. Curious, she pulled it from the dress box and pulled off the ribbon holding the lid in place.

"Mama!" she gasped, holding up a beautiful red coral necklace.

A smile lit the marchioness's face. "Do you like it?"

Olivia nodded. "Yes, but where did it come from?"

Her mother sighed, and took the necklace from her daughter. "Your father picked it out the day before we left London to come home. It was delivered to our townhouse after we had already departed. I decided to have it sent here with the gown, rather than waiting to give it to you the next time we went to Town."

Olivia's eyes began to feel the familiar sting of tears. "This is from father?" she asked reverently.

Her mother wiped tears from her eyes as she looked at the gift. "He knew the color would look stunning on you. I even tried to talk him out of it, but he told me he wanted to spoil his only daughter." Tears rolled down her face and quiet sobs burst from her lips.

Olivia laid her dress gently back in the box and wrapped her arms around her mother. They sat for several minutes, both crying quietly. Lady Pembrooke excused herself, giving Olivia a moment to grieve alone with her mother.

"Thank you, Mama," Olivia sniffed. Her tears still falling. "I love it."

Her mother placed a hand on each side of Olivia's face and looked into her eyes. "He loved you so much," she said dreamily. "I'm happy you will have William to love you as much as your father loved me."

Olivia smiled and kissed her mother on the cheek. "I better take the dress to Sally so she can get it pressed for tomorrow evening."

Her mother smiled. "You are going to be even more beautiful than you always are."

Olivia gave her mother one more small smile before asking a footman to take her items to her room. She followed him out of the parlor.

"My lady?" Lewis called before she could ascend the stairs.

She turned around and waited as the butler approached with a letter on a silver salver.

"This was just delivered for you," he said, holding it out to her.

Olivia took the small missive and thanked him. Turning the letter over, she saw the same smudged seal as the one she'd received a few days earlier. She tapped the letter on her other hand, wondering who the sender could be. She still hadn't figured out who FG was, and until this moment had honestly forgotten about the first letter.

She hurried up the stairs and arrived at her door as the footman was leaving. Her dress box was lying on her bed, surrounded by the colorful roses, which had now been placed in vases all around her room. Olivia closed the door and moved to her writing desk. She slid her penknife under the seal and pulled back the folded paper. She stared at the writing and saw it was signed again by FG.

I'll be seeing you very soon.

FG

Olivia searched her mind frantically for anyone she knew who would send such a strange letter. The brief message felt ominous, and she wondered if it was time for her to give the two letters to her brother. She read it again, then folded it, and put it with the other letter in the corner of her desk. She needed to think about this before she worried her family.

Olivia pulled her new dress out of the box again and laid it gently on the bed, clenching the soft, thin, fabric lightly between her fingers. She took the necklace from her father and sat it atop the dress. The red coral would be the perfect addition to her white gown.

She tugged the bell pull and instructed Sally on what to do with her gown, then put the necklace back into its box and tucked it into her dressing table drawer. A bright light stretched across her floor, and she hurried to the window. The clouds were moving off, and a small bit of sun shined and glimmered against the droplets of water on her window and the grass.

Olivia could feel the pent-up energy from staying indoors coursing through her. She needed an escape. It would be too muddy to ride the way she wanted, but she could take the horses for a walk in the sunshine before England's weather decided to change again. Her eyes drifted back to the letters she'd received, and she decided it would be best to have Sally take them to Charles while she went to the stables. She changed into her riding habit, in case she got the opportunity to truly ride, then Sally left with the dress and letters.

Olivia hastened down the stairs and out the door to her garden, then proceeded down the pathway. She tried to avoid any puddles of water and mud, but a few weren't easy to side-step. She entered the stables and went directly to her red mare. Sweet Pea stared at her, then whinnied when Olivia pulled out a sugar cube for her. She did the same to Buttercup, who nudged Olivia's hand when she finished it, asking for more. Olivia chuckled and ran her hand down Buttercup's long nose, pausing so she could rub the soft velvety skin. Olivia thought if a modiste could find fabric as soft as Buttercup's nose, the shop would become the most popular in England.

She turned to look around the stable, wondering where Henry had gone. Not seeing him anywhere, she saddled Buttercup on her own. Even though it was muddy, Olivia wanted to take her for a brief walk around the stable and paddock.

A few minutes later, her horse was ready to ride. Rubbing her hand down the horse's long sleek neck, she sighed at the sense of peace such a large animal brought her. She adored her horses.

"Horses really are beautiful creatures."

Olivia froze; the hair on the back of her neck standing on end at the sound of a man behind her. It was a voice she never thought she would have to hear again, a voice which filled her with fear on more than one occasion. She spun around; the man leaned against the side of the stable with a satisfied smirk on his face.

"Lord Greenly?" she said in a hoarse whisper, her heart pounding in her chest.

"Ah, so you do remember me," he said coldly with a wicked grin.

"What are you doing here?" she said, realizing she had no way to escape.

"Surely you received my letters," he said, his smile growing.

"*You* sent me those letters?" she hissed. Nothing was close enough for her to use as a weapon. He had timed his arrival perfectly.

"Who else could it be? You and I had such a connection last year in London. I was quite disappointed when you left so suddenly."

"We had nothing," she spat angrily.

He tsked and pushed himself from the wall, walking slowly toward her. "But of course we did. We were in love before your father took you away to the country. But we don't need to worry about him anymore, do we?"

She gasped. "How dare you speak of my father!" She snapped.

His smile fell from his face and a darkness swept over him. "Considering I was the one who took care of said problem, I believe I have a right to speak of the poor dead man."

Her face paled as her worst fears came true. She truly was the reason her father had been killed. She took a deep breath. "What?" her voice broke as she mumbled the word.

He looked at his fingertips, then smiled so wickedly, it made her shiver. "Oh, didn't I mention it? It was too easy, I mean, did he think a different carriage would fool me? My only regret is I wasn't able to kill your mother as well."

She felt the room start to sway and she shook her head, she couldn't faint, not now.

"But…why would you kill my father?" her voice cracking as she tried to hide her fear.

"He was in our way, my dear," he said shrugging his shoulders. "Now we can be together like we planned."

She glared at him. "I'm not going anywhere with you."

He moved forward quickly and wrapped his fingers around her neck. "Oh, but you are. As you can see, there is no one here to prevent it. I've been waiting for this moment since your blasted brother and his friends stopped me the night of the masquerade ball," his hot breath made Olivia's nose scrunch in disgust as Lord Greenly continued to speak. "I tried several other times over the last year to get to you, but you rarely came outside and were never alone. I was also annoyingly followed for months by a Bow Street Runner," he growled angrily.

"However, a few weeks ago I heard about a ball being held at Elmwood Manor. It would be the perfect distraction. No one would be paying attention to one more guest. I came here every day, but you always had too many people around," his voice was deep and low as he spit out each word. "Then, to my surprise, your incompetent stable master gave the other stable boys the afternoon off because of the rain, and you so conveniently came alone, as I hoped you would. Who would have thought the rain would lead you directly into my arms?"

She tried to pry his fingers from her neck and gasped when he squeezed harder, making it difficult to breathe.

He relaxed his grip, knowing she had nowhere to go and no one to help her. She quickly wiggled from his hold and tried to run past him, but he grabbed her hair and yanked her back, forcing his mouth onto hers. When he pulled away, she turned her head and spat on the ground at his feet, disgusted by his touch. He sneered as the back of his hand slammed across her face, sending her sprawling to the ground. Olivia's head made contact with the ground with a loud crack, making her inhale sharply as pain seared across her cheek. She could feel the warm blood from the blow trickling down her face and into her mouth. Her vision blurred and she felt nauseous. She gently placed a hand on her cheek and watched as the dark red liquid dripped to the ground. Pushing herself backwards, she attempted to put some distance between them, but he yanked her leg and pulled her up from the ground, then hit her again, this time her face crashed into the floor and dirt filled her mouth and eyes.

She shook her head, trying to clear the pain and darkness trying to overwhelm her and making her too weak to fight for her freedom. Her vision filled with black spots and she struggled to focus but knew she needed to get away. She heard a rip as he tore strips of fabric from her skirt and tied a gag to her mouth, leaving her unable to scream for help. He picked her up, and she kicked her legs and hit him anywhere she could reach, but it didn't deter him. He set her on Buttercup's back then strapped her hands together with a rope from the wall of the stable.

He pulled a gun from his boot and pointed it at her. "If I were you, my lady," he murmured, his eyes red with anger. "I wouldn't move."

Olivia stared at him, rage building in her chest. She looked frantically around but could see no way to escape. She shifted in the saddle as he led her horse outside and away from the house. She could see his horse tied to a small tree nearby, and Lord Greenly moved quickly toward it. He mounted then kicked the horses into a run. The animals struggled in the muddy conditions, but Lord Greenly didn't seem to care. She turned to look behind her and watched as her only hope for rescue disappeared. Fear crippled her mind as she struggled against the ropes.

No one knew where she was or how to find her. The crazed man holding her captive killed her father and now had come back for her. Tears began rolling down her cheeks before being swept away in the wind as the two horses raced down the path toward her own death. She knew if she didn't escape, he would kill her. Maybe not right away, but even being forced to marry him would end her life. She was trapped, stuck with a murderous lunatic who wanted to do unspeakable things to her.

Alicia Rivoli

Fifteen

William felt like he could fly. He was going to marry the woman he had unknowingly loved for so long. He watched from the end of the hall when she'd returned from the stables and saw her reaction to his surprise. Mr. Smith had done very well. The petals he had added to the floor were the perfect touch, and her response had been more than he could have imagined. His smile hadn't left his face since.

He joined the men later the same morning for a hunt on the estate. It was still raining, so they opted to walk instead of riding the horses, but the dreary weather didn't stifle his mood. He listened to the hound's barking and braying as they chased their prey and scattered the startled birds into the sky. Several men had hit their intended target, and he knew they would be having grouse for dinner tonight. When they had returned, Charles had asked William to join him and the other men in the billiard room later.

He knew Olivia would be with her mother, which meant he wouldn't get to really talk with her, so he found his way toward the billiard room. He hadn't seen much of his father in the last couple of days and was looking forward to spending a little time with him. When he entered the room, he was immediately greeted with the heavy smell of pipe tobacco. He wasn't a smoker himself, he quite despised it, but he knew some of the other men enjoyed it. He sighed and walked to his father who was standing in the corner near Charles and Robert. Two men were fully engaged in a game of billiards and others were sitting around a small table playing cards, drinking, and smoking. He shook his head; he would never understand the desire people had to gamble their lives away.

His father smiled up at him. "Good afternoon, son."

"Afternoon," he replied. "Isn't it beautiful outside?"

Charles looked at him with a sideways glance. "Are you daft? It's raining," he said in a tone suggesting he thought William had gone mad.

William chuckled. "Even the rain can't dampen my mood today."

His father grinned. "Why is that?"

William checked to make sure they were far enough from the other guests that they would have a modicum of privacy. Even though he was sure Charles would give him and Olivia his blessing, there was an inkling of doubt still lurking in his mind. "Actually, Elmwood, I need to ask you a question," he answered, his voice low.

Charles looked at him with a side-ways glance. "What question?"

"I want to marry your sister. She has agreed, but I wanted to ask you for your blessing."

Charles's lips turned upward. "What if I said no?"

William shrugged, his stomach dropping at the mere suggestion of being told no. "I guess I would leave it up to your sister."

Charles stood and stretched forth his hand. "Welcome to the family."

William shook it vigorously, and Robert slapped him on the back.

His father embraced him. "Congratulations, William!"

"I wasn't sure you'd get the nerve to ask her," Charles said after a moment. "Weren't you afraid she might reject you?"

He shrugged; it had worried him. "A little," he replied. "You can never be too sure about a woman's feelings. They are a strange sex."

His father laughed loudly. "Oh, you don't even know the half of it."

The three men turned to look at the earl, eyes narrowing.

"Marriage is not as easy as it looks, there are a lot of things you need to learn about each other which can sometimes cause problems. If you stick it out and work your problems together, then life will be much easier and you'll find yourself more in love than you ever thought possible," the earl said, sighing loudly. "Women are indeed fickle creatures, and their moods are sometimes as turbulent as a stormy sea, but every day you get to live together, is a new adventure. Love makes all the difficulties seem like nothing more than a brief irritation."

William shook his head. "Maybe you should have given me such advice before I made an offer of marriage," he teased lightly.

"I don't think anything could have stopped you from wanting to marry Lady Olivia," Robert said. "You have been in love with her for several years."

He looked sideways at his friend. "What are you talking about?"

Robert smiled mischievously. "You talked about her constantly, my friend. The first time I met her, I half expected to find a goddess."

William glanced at his friend. "I was not so obvious."

His father chuckled. "Even your mother and I knew."

Charles raised his hand in the air and laughed. "So did I."

William gawked at them. "Here I thought I was being so subtle."

"Yeah, as subtle as Mr. Bowman's gambling," Charles said, throwing a look over his shoulder. The man looked like he had run his fingers through his hair more than once during the game of cards he was playing.

"He is rather obvious when he has a good hand," Lord Pembrooke said, smiling. "I don't know how he hasn't run his estate into the ground by now."

Robert looked at them. "Miss Bowman said her father loves cards but knows when to quit. I don't think he has a desire to lose everything."

"Miss Bowman, huh?" William teased, happy to shift the attention onto someone else.

Robert's face split into a wide grin, then he shrugged. "I don't know. She is beautiful to be sure, but she's so quiet."

William nearly choked. "Quiet? Robert, I haven't heard the girl stop speaking since her family arrived."

The door to the billiard room opened, and Olivia's lady's maid entered. She moved quickly to Charles and handed him two letters.

"Lady Olivia asked me to give these to you, my lord. She didn't know what to think of them and thought you should see them," Sally said in a quiet voice so the others wouldn't over hear. When Charles took the two notes, the maid gave a brief curtsy and hurried back the way she'd come.

Charles turned the letters over and looked at the broken seal, before holding them out so William, Robert and Lord Pembrooke could see the design. "Do any of you know anything about this seal?"

William's father reached for the letters and stared at the red wax. "I'm afraid it's too smudged to tell what it says."

Charles nodded then opened the first letter. William watched as his friend's face turned white and his mouth dropped.

"Charles," Lord Pembrooke asked. "Is everything alright?"

Charles opened the second letter and collapsed in a nearby chair.

"Charles," William exclaimed. "What is it?"

He held the letters out to him. "Olivia…"

William grabbed the letters and read the words on each page before cursing under his breath.

"Who are they from?" Robert asked, looking from Charles to William.

"Lord Franklin Greenly," the two men hissed in unison.

William's father took the letters, read them, then handed them to Robert.

"Where is she now?" Charles asked William.

He shrugged. "I think she is with our mothers in the parlor."

The four men raced out the door, leaving the other gentleman staring after them. They hurried down the hall and descended the stairs two at a time. Charles reached the door to the room and swung it open.

"No one's here," he said, looking around frantically and tugging on the bell pull.

Lewis came around the corner, and seeing the looks on their faces, picked up his pace. "Yes, my lord?"

"Lewis," Charles barked. "Where is Lady Olivia?"

"I believe she went to the stables. Shall I send for her?" Lewis asked nervously.

Charles gaped at William. "We have to get to her. Now!"

William nodded then ran with Charles toward the stables.

Please let her be there, he thought to himself.

He ran through the open wooden doors and looked around. Buttercup was gone.

"Henry?" Charles yelled when he entered behind William.

There was no answer. They looked at each other in alarm and moved to the back office.

"Henry?" William called as he pushed the door open.

The room was dark and cold. Charles grabbed a lantern and lit the wick. The light poured out and bathed the room in an eerie yellow glow. A man lay in a heap on the ground, a pool of blood surrounding his body.

"HENRY!" Charles yelled.

William's entire body trembled with both rage and fear as he saw a large gash across the back of Henry's head. Things were scattered all over the small room, suggesting there had been a struggle.

A moan escaped Henry's lips and Charles slowly turned him over, dark streaks of blood stained his face and the front of his shirt.

"Henry," he whispered. "What happened?"

The man's eyes fluttered open and he took a deep breath. "Man came…took Lady…" his words drifted off as his eyes closed again.

"Henry?" Charles called. "Henry, where is Olivia?"

The man didn't answer, but William could see his chest rising and falling with shallow breaths.

"Charles! William!" Robert called from outside the room. "You better take a look at this."

William hurried to where Robert and his father were bent over, staring at the ground.

"What is it?" Charles cried out, joining them.

The ground had long drag marks and drops of blood were scattered in the dirt. William's heart flew into his throat.

"Olivia…" he moaned, dropping to his knees and raking his hands thru his hair and down his face.

William's father moved to the door and gave a shrill whistle. A short time later, several footmen entered the stable.

"Send one man for a doctor and another for the constable. Henry's been injured and Lady Olivia is missing," Lord Pembrooke said calmly. "We also need stable hands to saddle as many horses as they are able for a search party."

"Yes, my lord," a footman answered.

"I need my dogs readied as well," Charles told them, grabbing his horse from the stall and moving to the tack area.

Robert moved to Charles's side. "Where do you think he could have taken her? The blood isn't quite dry, they can't have gone far."

Charles didn't look at him, instead, he focused his attention on the stable boys running toward them. "I don't know, but my dogs will."

William looked up from the ground. "We're going to need weapons."

Charles and Lord Pembrooke both nodded. Several stable hands ran into the building and took over saddling the horses.

"Bring them to the house when you're finished," Charles called. "And you," he pointed to the smallest of the boys. "Tend to Henry until the doctor arrives."

The boy nodded and went to the back room. The three men ran from the stables and headed for the manor. They burst through the door and both Charles and William ran up the stairs. Charles headed to the room where the weapons were kept, and William went to his own chambers. He was grateful he had thought to bring his sword with him to Elmwood so he could practice his fencing with Charles. Normally a foil would be used, but William preferred the feel and thrill of an actual sword. He strapped it to his belt then stuck the small knife he always carried when he traveled, into his boot. When he arrived in the foyer, the entire area was full of men; both servants, and guests awaited orders.

"What's happened?" Lady Elmwood said, panicking as she moved quickly down the stairwell.

William looked at her, not sure how much to tell her, and was rescued as Charles joined them. He had her sit down so she wouldn't faint, and quickly explained everything. William watched as the marchioness's face went white. Lady Pembrooke immediately wrapped her arms around her friend.

"No!" she whimpered. "Charles, you have to find her."

"I know mother," he said, laying a hand gently on her shoulder.

"Your horses are ready, my lord," Lewis called from the front door.

The search party hurried to the gravel path and their allotted mounts. The braying of hounds echoed around the courtyard. William looked back and saw a pack of dogs being held by a single servant. The man gripped tightly to small ropes which had been secured around the animals' necks.

"I will have the dogs attempt to follow Olivia's scent. I'm hoping they won't have any trouble with the wet conditions," Charles explained to the group of men. "We need to assume Lord Greenly is well-armed, and will more than likely kill her, rather than let her go."

William groaned. His entire frame shook from fear and anger. Charles whistled, and their party hurried across the estate, sliding wildly in the muddy conditions.

Alicia Rivoli

Sixteen

Olivia's wrists were bleeding and sore as she twisted and pulled at the ropes binding her. She'd begun to form an escape plan, but if she failed, she knew she wouldn't get another opportunity. They'd been riding for a while; the muddy path had forced them to go at a slower pace than her captor wanted. The horses were breathing hard from the exertion of riding through the thick mud. They needed a break, but Lord Greenly didn't seem to care whether or not the animals struggled. He'd been avoiding roads and maneuvered around homes and farmland. As Olivia looked around, she recognized several landmarks and knew which way she would need to go to get back to Elmwood.

She lifted her leg toward her hands and pulled her skirt up slightly. She ripped off a small piece of the fabric and let it fall behind them like she'd done since leaving the stable yard. She hoped Charles would use his dogs to track her down, although these would allow him to find her without them if he didn't. She looked toward the sky at the dark clouds forming in the distance, indicating another storm was approaching. She prayed it wouldn't hinder the rescue party from locating her.

Her mouth was dry from the gag, and she could feel the side of her lips cracking under the pressure of the fabric. She could also feel significant swelling and pain around her eye and on the right side of her face. She heard a growl from Lord Greenly as he kicked his horse in the side, trying to force it to move faster. Olivia turned her head in the direction he'd been looking, hoping there would be someone there, but she saw nothing.

Buttercup's reins were tied to the other horse, giving Lord Greenly a hands-free way to lead her away as quickly as possible. There were small rolling hills facing the west, and when she looked to the north, she could see the tips of the trees from her forest. It was a long way from where she was now, and her horse was already tired. She hoped if she could somehow get free, she could make it to the trees. She knew the forest better than anyone, and Lord Greenly would have a difficult time finding her there.

Lord Greenly cursed under his breath when he heard a howl in the distance, and Olivia sighed in relief. Charles was coming for her, *and* he had the dogs. They would be able to catch her scent. Lord Greenly pulled a pistol from his trousers and stared in the direction the howl had come from. Olivia had been waiting for the right moment, and as her captor was distracted by the howling, she knew now was as good a time as any.

When she was sure he wasn't watching her, she pulled hard on the ropes encircling her wrists. Eventually, thanks to how long she had been working to loosen them, and Lord Greenly's inexperience at tying knots, she was able to pull her hands free. She winced in pain from the cuts the ropes caused, and rubbed them for a moment, smearing blood onto her hands. Olivia looked at Lord Greenly, and when he had looked again toward the horizon, she leaned as far forward as she could over her horse's neck and unbuckled the throat latch. She stretched her hands to Buttercup's headstall, which was tucked behind the horse's ears. Olivia needed to get close enough to push the leather over Buttercup's ears. It would then fall to the ground, freeing her horse and giving them a chance to escape.

She felt the leather beneath her fingers and pushed. Buttercup threw her head in confusion causing the bridle to slip back into place. Olivia dropped her head and took a deep breath. When Lord Greenly continued to stare off into the distance, she tried again. She used two fingers and pushed the strap hard, sliding it easily this time over the horse's ears. The headstall dropped to the ground with a quiet thud thanks to the muddy ground, releasing Buttercup from Lord Greenly's saddle.

Olivia slowly coaxed her horse to stop with a few simple cues and watched as the viscount moved ahead of her, unaware Olivia was no longer behind him. When she believed he was at a far enough distance to give her a good head start, she urged Buttercup to turn around, and she gave her mare a tap with the heel of her boot. The horse responded immediately. Olivia had never been more grateful her father had encouraged her to teach Buttercup leg reining. The horse took off, her speed increasing as they headed back in the direction of the house. She had only gone a short distance before a loud curse reached her ears. She looked behind her and watched as Lord Greenly chased after her.

Olivia convinced Buttercup to move faster, and she felt the horse's feet slide in the mud. Buttercup soon found her footing, and even though the horse couldn't reach her top speed, she flew across the damp earth. Olivia chanced a look back, hoping she was far enough away from her captor that she could lose him. She gasped as she saw his gun aimed toward her.

A loud explosion filled her ears, followed by an agonizing pain in her right shoulder. She let out a muffled scream as dark red blood seeped through the fabric of her jacket. Another crack echoed around her and she braced herself for the impact of the next bullet, but no pain came. When she looked back, she saw the viscount falling further behind. She pulled the gag from her mouth and dropped it to the ground, inhaling sharply when the movement caused a sharp pain to run up her shoulder.

As she crested a hill, she saw the large oak trees standing majestically a mile or so ahead of her, leading into a densely packed forest. She rubbed her horse's neck, whispering words of encouragement to keep Buttercup moving. The horse snorted, her chest rising and falling in quick successions. Olivia knew her horse wouldn't be able to maintain this speed much longer, but Lord Greenly was still attempting to catch up to her.

Olivia continued to use the pressure of her legs to rein Buttercup, getting her to change directions and turn toward the trees where she knew she could enter the woods and hide. She reached up and touched her shoulder. It was warm and wet, the pain becoming more intense. When she pulled her hand back, her vision blurred at the amount of blood marring her palms. She shook her head, trying to clear the daze. The tree line was only a few hundred feet away now. She looked behind her, Lord Greenly had gained some ground and was closer than she hoped he would be.

Olivia gave a loud whistle when they reached the trees, and Buttercup skidded to an abrupt stop, her hooves digging deep into the mud. Olivia slid to the ground and slapped her horse on the hindquarters, knowing her mare couldn't run anymore with a rider. Olivia was hoping Buttercup would run home. She could hear the pounding of hooves as Lord Greenly got closer. She darted into the dark, dense forest without another thought.

The sun had begun its descent, causing eerie shadows and unknown noises to surround her. The trees were so close together, it was difficult for her to find a path she could use. Olivia could hear Lord Greenly tromping thru the brush behind her, so she pushed deeper into the trees. With each movement, the searing pain in her wounded arm was becoming increasingly hard to ignore. Her dress and hair continually snagged on branches and thorns, a few times she heard a loud rip as her skirt tore further. After several twists and turns, she found the path leading to her waterfall and ran forward. The loud crashing of branches behind her made her stomach roll; she didn't have a lot of time.

A tall oak tree stood before her as she burst into the open area surrounding the river. Olivia sprinted toward the waterfall, the loud roaring drowning out the thuds of Lord Greenly's pursuit. She didn't dare look back. Knowing she only needed to get a little farther before she would be well hidden, she pushed her body forward. Clenching her teeth against the pain she was feeling, she put her boot on the small outcropping of rocks along the cliff's face, and slid against the wet slick surface until she was able to pull herself through the powerful torrent of water. The force almost knocked her into the swirling, raging river below. Her aching shoulder shook in protest as she tried to hold onto the wet cliffside, but she knew she had no time to stop.

With one final step, Olivia lunged forward, losing her balance on the slick stone. Her knees crashed into the rocky floor of a hidden cavern, sending shooting pains up her legs and back. Her dress was soaked through, making it heavy and cumbersome as she tried to scramble deeper into the small space. She hadn't gone far before a wall of stone stopped her movement. She pressed her back up against the cold hard surface, and began sucking in air as she struggled to get oxygen into her burning lungs.

She didn't know if Lord Greenly has seen her go behind the waterfall, but this was the only place she could think to hide. She had found the small cave after a drought had plagued the area several years earlier. The river had nearly gone dry, exposing the small cavern. She came here whenever the water allowed, seeking refuge from her thoughts or anything else plaguing her. She'd never been behind here while the waterfall gushed so violently over the cave and she was relieved she was even able to make it inside.

Olivia tucked her legs against her body and shivered in the darkness. The air was turning colder the longer she waited, making her teeth chatter uncontrollably. She knew she needed to get warm but had no way of doing so. The crash of the waterfall became the only sound she could hear. Her cold wet gown made her shudder violently as it pressed against her body.

"Please help me," she prayed quietly.

A bright flash followed by a loud rumble made her jump. The storm had returned. *Perfect*, she thought to herself, rolling her eyes at the ceiling, knowing more water would only make it more difficult for her to escape her hiding place.

Time ticked by, and Olivia felt her body growing tired. After several different positions, she felt herself droop, exhaustion taking over her weak body. She slid to the wet floor of the cave, her eyes drifting closed.

Seventeen

They had tracked Olivia's path, but the mud made it more difficult. William rode Blue hard, forcing him through the thick mud. The dogs ran in front of their search party, leading the way. The animals had picked up Olivia's scent at the house and had been following it for a while. At one point, Charles whistled and jumped from his horse. He bent down to the ground, pulling up a small piece of torn fabric.

"That's my girl," William said, as they continued to find more pieces of torn fabric.

Seconds later, they heard a gunshot ring in the distance. The entire party pulled to a stop and listened. He saw several men pull their weapons out, prepared for whatever situation came next. The group pushed forward, the dogs flying across the ground when a second shot pierced the air. William's heart stopped, but he kept pushing his mount harder across the ground.

"My lord!" a servant called. "Look!"

All eyes turned toward where the man was pointing. In the distance, William could see a horse racing across the field, no rider on its back. Charles and William glanced at each other, and

Charles barked orders for one of the men to catch the horse and bring it to them. The man didn't take long before he returned, Olivia's horse following behind.

"It's Buttercup, my lord," the servant said, leading the mare to Charles. "She 'as some blood on 'er, but I don't think she's hurt."

"The blood isn't from the horse?" Charles asked, his face pale.

"No, my lord."

William swallowed hard. "Take the horse back to the stables and take care of her."

The servant nodded and turned back toward the house, leading an exhausted Buttercup away.

William looked up at the darkening sky. "Let's go, Charles. I don't want the rain to wash away any chance we have of finding her."

Charles ground his teeth together. "When we find him, I'm going to enjoy watching him die a slow death."

The dogs led them over the crest of a hill, and toward a forest. They rode hard, searching the area around them, hoping for any sign of where Olivia might be. When the trees became clearer, Charles pulled his horse to a stop and whistled to his dogs. They came bounding back to their master, howling and barking with excitement. He pulled some meat from a pack on his saddle and tossed a piece to each animal, praising them for their work thus far. The dogs lapped at his hands when they finished, hoping for more.

"Soon, boys," Charles told his dogs. "You may have anything you want if you find my sister."

William knew Charles was reaching his breaking point. He could see the darkness clouding his eyes, but also heard the hitch in his friend's words when he spoke. Watching him pat each dog on the head before mounting his horse again, Charles shouted another order to the animals. They immediately put their noses to the ground and were gone.

Charles pulled to a stop and pointed to a small area at the edge of the forest when they approached it. William peered to where Charles had indicated, and not far from where they stood, he could see a tall, black horse at the edge of the trees. He was strapped to the branch of a tree, but there was no one around.

A flash of lightning lit the sky, startling the men and the animals. William leapt from his saddle and tossed the reins to a waiting servant before racing into the woods. He hoped he could find the trail the owner of the horse left behind. He quickly came upon broken branches and disturbed ground leading further into the crop of trees. He didn't know if it was Olivia and Lord Greenly but knew he needed to try to follow the path.

"Charles, see if your dogs can find her scent here," he said, moving to allow them to pass.

He held out a piece of Olivia's dress, and the dogs immediately rushed into the trees. They paused often and changed direction multiple times before William realized where they were headed.

"She went to the waterfall," he yelled.

Charles nodded and picked up speed. The dogs suddenly stopped and growled into a darker part of the forest. William looked into the thick brush but couldn't see anything in the fading light. Charles bent low to the lead dog, said something to the animal and it sprinted off into the trees. Another shot pierced the night air, Charles watched for his dog, waiting. Seconds later, they heard a loud crash and a yelp, followed by the grunt of a man.

William and Charles looked briefly at one another before running after the dog. Charles held tight to the remaining hounds as they moved around fallen trees and thick roots. The yell of a man in pain bounced off the trees around them. Charles released the other dogs who immediately bounded after their mate. Soon William heard the loud snarls and snaps as the dogs trapped their prey.

Coming around a corner, William nearly shouted for joy when he saw Lord Greenly standing with his back pressed against a tree, his gun several feet away. He was trying to fend off the dogs with a stick, but the beasts were smart and came at him from multiple directions at the same time. One of the dogs leapt toward Lord Greenly, knocking him to the ground, yanking the stick from the viscount's hands and shaking it ferociously. William smiled in satisfaction. The man had large gashes across his arms and legs where he'd been bitten, and his clothing was torn in multiple places. William pulled his sword from his belt and approached the beaten-down man, pressing the tip of the blade into his throat. Charles called off his dogs and had a servant restrain them. He pulled a gun from his jacket pocket and joined William, holding the weapon against the side of Lord Greenly's face.

"Where is my sister?" he snarled.

Goosebumps raced up William's arms as Lord Greenly smiled wickedly and looked at them with hatred in his eyes. The other men approached, but remained at a safe distance behind them, their own weapons ready if needed.

"I won't ask you again," Charles growled and pulled back the hammer of his weapon. "What have you done with my sister?"

"Come now, Elmwood, I did you a favor," he sneered. "With the death of your father, you are now the marquess, and an extremely wealthy man. Taking your sister off your hands frees you to do whatever you want."

Charles slammed the butt of the gun into Lord Greenly's face with a loud crack. Blood drained from his nose and a red welt streaked across his face. Greenly wiped at his nose with the back of his sleeve and chuckled as he shook his head back and forth. Charles grabbed the lapels of the man's coat and yanked him back up, pushing his pistol into the side of Lord Greenly's skull.

William moved forward and narrowed his eyes. "What do you mean you did Charles a favor?"

A wicked laugh escaped Lord Greenly's mouth, and he shrugged. "No one gets in the way of what I want, including a nosey marquess and his stodgy wife."

William's eyes grew wide in horror. "It was you!"

The man grinned wickedly. "You thought your runner could keep tabs on me. You scoured the country for months, not even realizing what was right under your nose. It's only a shame I had to kill him when your sister wasn't in the carriage. I couldn't have them telling anyone it was me, now could I?"

Charles moved the pistol under Lord Greenly's chin, and William realized the viscount had all but admitted to murdering Olivia's father.

"Who else was with you?" he snarled, the barrel of the gun digging deeply into Lord Greenly's skin.

"His brothers," Lord Pembrooke said from behind them. "They have always fit the description your mother gave us and their involvement always seemed plausible, but the Runners claimed that they were out of the country. I pushed aside my concerns of Lord Greenly's family, and looked for other's who could have been implicit in Elmwood's murder."

William's mouth dropped open. "This coward has brothers?"

His father nodded. "A malicious group. If you remember, William, I had Greenly's family investigated, but his brothers were out of the country. I should have had the Runner's double check."

"Father," William began, but the sound of his friend stopped his words.

"I should shoot you right here. It would be easy. All I have to do is pull the trigger," Charles snarled.

William rushed forward and grabbed Charles's arm, pulling him back and stepping in front of him.

Charles glared at him. "He deserves to die!" he yelled. "He killed my father, shot my mother, and now has done something to my sister."

William nodded. "I know, but if we kill him, we won't have the pleasure of watching the bounder hang."

Charles looked from William to Lord Greenly and glared. "You better hope I find her alive."

"Or what?" the viscount grumbled. "Are you going to kill me if you don't?"

William turned around and with a flick of his sword, sliced a deep gash down the man's face, from his forehead to the bottom of his chin.

"If he doesn't, I will," William growled angrily.

Lord Greenly put a hand up to staunch the bleeding and glared at William. "Neither of you have it in you. If you wanted to kill me, you would have already done it."

William put his sword back in his belt, and after taking a deep breath, slammed his fist into Lord Greenly's nose. With a loud satisfying crack, he knocked the viscount out, and the cad crumpled to the ground.

"Tie him up and take him back to the horses. The constable will arrive soon and can take him to prison," Charles told a couple of the stronger servants.

"I'll go with them," Lord Pembrooke said. "I want to make sure the constable knows of all his crimes. Now that Greenly has confessed to murdering a marquess, a judge will have no choice but to convict him."

Charles shook his hand and thanked him.

The servants picked up the motionless body of Lord Greenly, Lord Pembrooke following close behind them.

"Charles, we need to find Olivia. See if the dogs can find her scent again," William suggested. "The storm is moving in and it's getting cold."

Charles ran his hand through his hair, and sighed. "What if he killed her and threw her in the river, William?"

William shook his head. "We can't think in such a manner. Send the dogs."

Charles nodded and called for his hounds. He held out the same fabric from earlier, said a word William didn't recognize, and the dogs yapped excitedly as they ran through the trees toward the waterfall. By the time they reached the clearing, the rain was coming hard and the wind howled in the trees. William hoped the rain wouldn't wash away the scent the dogs had been tracking. They searched along the riverbanks and in the surrounding forest but found nothing.

William didn't know what to do. It had been hours since Olivia had disappeared. The sun had descended, and with the storm, he was losing hope they would find her alive. The servants returned with lanterns, telling Charles the constable had taken Lord Greenly. He nodded his approval, but William could see the agony on his friend's face. An hour later, more servants, people from the surrounding villages, and tenants on the estate had come to help search for Olivia. William could see bobs of light and hear calls and whistles in every direction, but the sound of the storm drowned out most of it.

"Olivia!" he called, not for the first time. "Olivia, where are you?"

As each minute ticked by, the temperatures continued to drop and he knew if she were injured or wet, she wouldn't be able to survive much longer. He put his lantern down and wiped the rain from his face and peered into the darkness.

"Come on, Olivia, call out. Where are you?" he whispered to the trees.

Eighteen

As she came to, Olivia realized her head was pounding, and her entire body ached as memories of the day rushed back to her. Blinking several times, allowing her eyes to adjust to her surroundings, she was met with nothing but darkness and cold. She felt as though ice were running through her veins making her shiver violently, her teeth hit together so hard, it hurt. Movement was almost impossible. Her muscles had weakened significantly, and every attempt at movement was met with a shock of pain.

A faint noise came through the roar of the waterfall. She strained her ears, hoping it wasn't Lord Greenly. The distinct yap of a dog, muffled and quiet penetrated the small area. The sound sent a surge of hope through her. She tried again to move, but her body refused to cooperate.

"Charles!" she tried to yell, but the only sound to escape was a hoarse squeak. She cleared her throat and tried again but had the same outcome. Frustration swelled inside her, but she knew she had to keep trying. She tried to coax her voice a little louder but knew it would never be heard over the sounds of the water spilling over the cliffside and down to the river below. Tears rolled down her cheeks as the fear of not being found flooded her thoughts.

"Olivia!"

The male voice was close. She tried again to call for help, hoping her quiet pleas would be heard. After several attempts, she could feel her body weakening further and darkness clouded her vision. She didn't know how much longer she would be able to remain awake. She tried desperately to get to the voice calling out to her, but every part of her refused. She breathed through her teeth as another shot of pain pulsed through her frame, making her already blurred vision, dim even more. She groaned.

"Olivia!"

Her eyes began to drift closed, and she tried to force them to remain open but felt herself slipping into unconsciousness.

"I'm here," she said almost silently before her mind went black.

One of the dogs was frantically barking and digging at the dirt and rocks near the cliff when William and Charles reached the servant who'd called to them. William looked over the edge and down into the water but couldn't see anything through the mist and darkness. The dog continued its crazed barking, but instead of digging in the ground, he had moved to the rock face and yapped loudly at the waterfall. Charles moved to stand next to his dog, peering through the darkness. William waited, hoping the dog wasn't barking at the moving water.

"I think I hear something," Charles called to the group. "Everyone be quiet."

William hurried over and Charles silenced his dog. They waited, straining to hear any other sounds besides the rushing water.

"There!" he called again. "Did you hear it?"

William shrugged his shoulders and stepped as close as he could to the rocky face. Cold water vapors seeped through his already soaked shirt, making him shudder even worse than he already was. After a few seconds, he heard a faint female voice. He called to her but couldn't see her. He searched and spotted a small narrow outcropping of stone which jutted out unevenly leading behind the waterfall.

"Charles, I think there's something behind here," he said, stepping carefully onto the wet, slippery ledge. He shuffled his feet, careful to make sure his feet were stabilized before moving further into the waterfall. It cascaded down his back and along his bare skin, chilling him to the bone. He continued and after a few more inches, found himself standing behind the waterfall inside a pitch-black cavern of sorts.

"Olivia!" William called into the darkness, a blast of cold air making him tremble uncontrollably.

"I'm here."

William nearly choked as the very faint sounds of Olivia's voice shook him to the core. He could tell from the tremor in her voice she was weak, and from the cold he was experiencing after only a few moments in this blasted cave, knew she was in serious danger. He dropped to his knees and felt around in the darkness, trying to find her. The loose rocks shifted and moved under his hands and jagged stones protruded from the floor slicing into his flesh. When his hand connected to the wall, he moved back in the other direction and sighed in immediate relief when he felt the soft wet fabric of a woman's dress.

"Olivia?" he said, moving his hand up to find her face. "Olivia, answer me."

His hand brushed a piece of torn fabric and found the bare skin of her arm. He inhaled sharply; she was ice cold. He moved quicker, finding her face, then her neck. He leaned down over her mouth and could feel the warmth of her breath, but it wasn't strong. He slipped one arm under her neck and the other beneath her legs and lifted her from the ground, keeping himself hunched over slightly so he didn't hit his head on the ceiling of the cave.

"Hang on, sweetheart. You're safe now," he whispered into her ear and held her as tightly as he could, trying to share his body heat. He looked toward where he had thought he had come from, grateful when he could see the bob of a lantern outside somewhere, giving him an idea of where he needed to walk. His feet slipped as he shuffled forward, forcing him to slow his pace. He could finally see the outline of Charles who stood on the other side of the ledge holding a lantern. He breathed a sigh of relief.

"Charles," he yelled to be heard over the roar of water. "I've got her, but she is unconscious. I need you to help me get her out of here."

"What do you need?" Charles called.

"I can't carry her over those tiny rocks, we are going to need a safer path."

"Hang on," Charles called. "I'll be right back."

William pressed his cheek to Olivia's. "Hold on, Olivia. We're going to get you out of here."

"Move back!" Charles called to him. "We've found a dead tree which should work."

William moved his feet carefully so he wouldn't fall over the edge of the cliff. A loud crash shook the floor, followed by a few shouts.

"William," he heard Charles call to him. "Can you see the log?"

He squinted, barely making out the round object blocking the ledge. "I see it."

"I'm coming to you," Charles yelled.

William stared at the tree and saw a tall figure move into his line of sight.

"We are going to form a chain," Charles said. "Pass her to me, and I'll pass her to the others until she is safely out."

William shuffled toward the figure and held Olivia out to him. He felt a pair of strong arms take hold of her and she was lifted from his arms. He could hear the faint sounds of men calling to each other, and then a cheer erupted.

"She's out," Charles called to him. "Let's get her home."

William didn't hesitate. He found the edge of the tree and lifted himself up, slowly following Charles from the cave. As soon as his feet landed on the soggy ground, Charles had reached Olivia and had taken her from a tall man William couldn't remember the name of.

William hurried to their side. "Bring me a blanket!" he yelled to a few others standing nearby. A small boy hurried up and handed him a thick wool blanket.

He and Charles were able to move Olivia enough to wrap her tightly in the warmth the covering provided. As soon as she was secure in her brother's arms, they all ran into the forest.

A servant approached with their horses as they broke from the confines of the trees. William moved to Blue's side and climbed into the saddle. "Hand her to me," he said, reaching down to take her. Charles easily placed her in William's hold and as soon as he had her safely tucked into his arms, he kicked his horse into a full gallop toward the house. He could hear the rumble of hooves pounding the ground as Charles and the others in the search party followed behind them.

The ride to the house seemed to take far longer than it should have, thanks to the soggy conditions. When William approached the front door, Charles had already jumped from his horse and raced to take his sister, hurrying inside the house and disappearing up the stairs. William followed, his wet boots slipping on the stone floor. He heard sounds of people in Olivia's bedchamber moving things around and logs being thrown into the fire. They needed to make the room as warm as possible. Charles laid her down in her bed when Lady Elmwood turned and pushed both of them out of the room.

"We need to get her out of those wet clothes. I'll send for you when you can come see her," she said, slamming the door, leaving Charles and William panting for breath outside in the hall.

Charles leaned against the wall, then slid to the floor. He rested his elbows on his knees and dropped his face into his hands with a loud groan.

"Her body was so cold," he murmured. "Her lips had turned blue."

William had also noticed the bluish hue on Olivia's mouth.

Charles raised his head and looked up at him. "Thank you, William."

William collapsed on the floor beside him. He leaned his head back and stared at the ceiling. "What if we were too late?" he said quietly.

Charles turned, the look on his face showing his concern. "She'll be okay, she has to be. I can't lose her," he said in a rough whisper.

The doctor ran down the hall toward them and without a word, opened the door and slammed it shut again.

Lord Pembrooke and Robert joined them a few minutes later, both dripping wet. A servant brought chairs from a different room and placed them against the wall for the men to sit on and then handed each of them a warm blanket. They waited in silence, none willing to talk. The same servant brought up cups of hot tea, small cakes, and some biscuits. William knew he wouldn't be able to eat anything, but as he was still in his wet clothing, he willingly took the warm drink.

An hour later the door opened and Lady Pembrooke walked out and closed it with a quiet click. William and Charles both flew to their feet.

"Is she okay?" Charles asked, hope surging in every word.

William's mother gave a very heavy sigh. "Olivia was shot at some point in this ordeal. She lost a lot of blood from the wound and also has several other large cuts. Dr. Campbell stitched as many as he could. Olivia also has a very deep gash below her eye," she explained and held a hand up as William opened his mouth to speak. "She is suffering the effects of being out in the cold for too long, but the doctor believes as long as there aren't any further complications or she becomes ill, she will recover with a lot of rest."

William blew out a breath, the tension in his body easing. "Can we see her?"

She looked at them. "Only for a few minutes. The doctor has given her a dose of laudanum so she can sleep peacefully."

William followed Charles through the door and walked to Olivia's bedside. The glow of the candles around the room illuminated a deep purple and black bruise around Olivia's eye and down her nose. There was a large gash across her cheek and one on her lip as well. She was pale and still had a slight blue coloring on her lips. She was propped up in her four-poster bed surrounded by pillows and blankets. Her arms, both covered in scratches and bruises, had been laid across her chest.

William clenched his teeth, anger building inside him. He knew if Lord Greenly were still here, he would have killed the man. He gently took one of Olivia's hands in his own and placed a kiss on her knuckles.

"She needs to rest now, boys," Lady Pembrooke said quietly. "You can visit her after you have all changed into warm clothing and got some sleep."

"Thank you," the faint voice of Lady Elmwood said from a chair near the bed.

Charles kissed his mother on the cheek, and William smiled kindly at her. William gave Olivia one final kiss on her hand, before following Charles from the room. His heart was heavy with worry, but knowing she was alive gave him hope.

Nineteen

The warmth of the blankets, and the fire were a welcome sight when Olivia finally opened her eyes. She was groggy, and her head felt heavy. Olivia had never felt so tired and miserable in the whole of her life. Her entire body felt bruised and battered, and she had a splitting headache. The light in the room sent a sharp pain to her eyes and even though her vision was blurred, she could make out a bottle of laudanum on the table beside her bed. She wondered how much of her misery had come from the contents of the bottle and how much from her injuries.

With considerable concentration, she was able to clear a little of the dizziness after a few brief attempts. She had a vague memory of her mother holding her hand at some point. The hand holding hers now wasn't soft like her mother's though, and not nearly as dainty.

She blinked several more times before William came into focus. He wasn't looking at her, so she was able to watch him silently without his notice. He rubbed the back of her hand lightly with his thumb and flipped the page of the book he was reading with the other. His face was serene and his eyes a lighter brown than usual. He wasn't wearing a jacket, only his starched white shirt and no cravat, which left his neck and part of his chest exposed. She felt herself blush and was grateful he hadn't known she was watching him. She could see he was tired and knew he probably hadn't been sleeping well. He had dark lines under his eyes, and his hair was mussed like he had run his fingers through it several times.

She tried to shift without his notice but ended up sucking air through her teeth when pain surged through her shoulder, and she began coughing forcefully. William was up in an instant and once her coughing fit had settled, she smiled slightly at the look of panic on his face.

"Please tell me I don't look as bad as I feel," she said. Her throat was dry and scratchy, so her words came out more like a strained whisper.

He smiled and lowered himself to kiss her forehead. "You are more beautiful than ever."

She cocked an eyebrow and rolled her eyes, regretting it immediately. "I know you're lying, but I appreciate it." She coughed again, wincing from the pain of the movements.

He handed her a glass of water and helped her take small sips. It was difficult for her to swallow and even harder to move her head. He tucked a stray hair behind her ear and stared at her. She didn't know what he saw, but she knew she couldn't look very appealing. She could feel her swollen cheeks and a stabbing pain under her left eye which made it more difficult to open than the other.

"What happened?" she asked, after finally getting comfortable again. "How long have I been asleep?"

He took her hand back in his and gently raised it to his lips, pressing a light kiss to each one of her fingers. Then he began explaining, making sure she understood Lord Greenly was in prison and would hang for his crimes.

She frowned. "William," she coughed. "He killed my father."

He nodded. "He told us as much, bragged actually. We were afraid he had done the same to you. It took a long time to find your hiding place. We have Charles's dogs to thank for finding you or we may never have," he took a step closer to her and put a hand against her forehead, nodding when he felt she wasn't feverish.

He sat down beside her on the bed. "Don't ever do that to me again," he whispered, gently rubbing several locks of her hair between his fingers.

She cocked an eyebrow before remembering her swollen face and flinched. She closed her eyes and laid back on the pillow. "Didn't you know? I got kidnapped on purpose just to make you worry."

"That's not even funny," he said. "I thought I had lost you."

She looked at him and felt a warmth burn through her. She shook her head and squeezed his hand. "I'm still here."

He smiled brightly before placing a brief kiss on her lips. "I have never been more grateful for anything in my life."

"Okay you two," Charles said as he walked into her room. "I don't want to call you out William, but I will."

William chuckled, but immediately turned his attention back to her. She looked at him briefly before turning to her brother.

"I hear your dogs saved the day," she wheezed. "Maybe you do have a little talent after all."

"Yep," he chuckled. "She'll be fine." He kissed the top of her head. "We thought we lost you, Livvie. I can't tell you how happy I am you're here."

"Well, this is quite the party," Dr. Campbell said as he walked in. "And how is our patient this afternoon?"

"Afternoon?" she croaked.

Charles smiled. "Leave it to you to miss your own ball. You've been asleep for two days."

"I missed the ball?" she asked, disappointed at the thought. "I was looking forward to wearing my new gown."

William laughed heartily and stroked her cheek. "Oh, you will get your chance. Your mother postponed it. There wasn't a soul alive who could change her mind and cancel it. She had already put in too much work, and knew you would never want to miss such an event," he winked at her.

She gave a small giggle. "Well, that's good. Although I'm not sure I'll be up to dancing for a while."

"She will reschedule as soon as you are feeling up to it," Charles said. "I can't believe you would think otherwise."

"I'm afraid, gentleman," the doctor said, bringing their conversation to an end. "You'll have to excuse us. I need to check on her injuries."

Lady Elmwood screamed when she walked in and saw Olivia awake. She hurried to her daughter's side. "Oh, my dear girl! How are you feeling? Are you alright? Can I get you anything?"

"I'm fine, Mama, only a little sore," she murmured when her mother tried to contradict her. "I promise." She heard Charles and William laugh as they excused themselves, shutting the door behind them.

"Well, if you're sure," her mother said, kissing her forehead, then moving to allow the doctor to inspect her injuries.

Dr. Campbell gently touched her cheek under her eye, causing her to flinch. "Do you remember how you got this?" he asked, pointing to what Olivia assumed was where her face felt tight and sore.

She thought back to the stable and remembered all to clearly being knocked forcefully to the ground and the taste of blood in her mouth when Lord Greenly had struck her. She nodded and her mother gasped when she told the story of Lord Greenly's attack. Olivia felt like rolling her eyes at her mother's theatrics, but she was so happy to be home, Olivia found she didn't mind having her mother fret over her.

"And this?" he lifted her shoulder and gently unwrapped the white linen encircling her arm. She cringed but tried not to show how much the movement hurt.

"I got shot when I was escaping on my horse," she explained.

He nodded. "You have many more injuries, some deep cuts and gashes, others only small scrapes. Your knees are badly bruised, and the effects of the cold will take time for you to recover from. You'll probably cough for some time as your body heals. I'm hoping it's only lingering effects from the cold, but if it gets worse, we may need to get you some herbs and other concoctions to try and clear any infection which may exist," he explained calmly, not leaving out any details. "Are there any other injuries I don't know about?"

He looked at her in question, but Olivia couldn't think of what he could mean. She opened her mouth but didn't know what she would say, so she closed it again.

"Lady Elmwood," the doctor said quietly. "I know this will be against what is normal, but I would like to talk to your daughter in private for a moment—if you'll allow me."

She looked from Olivia to the doctor, then focused on Olivia, her eyes betraying her fear of leaving her alone with a man, even a doctor.

"It's fine, Mama," she said soothingly. You can wait right outside the door and when we are finished, you can come right back."

Lady Elmwood hesitated, then nodded and left the room.

Dr. Campbell waited a moment before turning back to Olivia and looked at her. He sighed and rubbed his hand over his eyes.

"When you were brought in, you were blanketed in blood, covered with more than a few small cuts, and your riding habit was shredded," he said in a calm tone. "Did Lord Greenly hurt you in any other way?"

She stared at him in confusion. "He only did what I've already mentioned. Nothing else happened." she insisted.

He nodded. "That's very good to hear. Some aren't so fortunate in such a situation. I expect you'll be very sore for several days and it will take even longer for your energy to return, but I can't see why you won't make a full recovery."

"Thank you, Dr. Campbell," she said. "I'm grateful to you for all you've done."

He grinned. "It's a pleasure to have you home and so well, my lady." He bowed, then turned and left the room.

Her mother rushed back inside. "Are you sure you don't need anything?"

She looked lovingly at her mother. "I love you, Mama. Thank you for taking such good care of me."

Olivia could see her mother's chin quivering and her eyes filled with unshed tears. She smiled reassuringly to her, and her mother dabbed at her eyes and smiled.

"The doctor said if you're up to it, you should eat," her mother said, watching Olivia carefully.

Olivia nodded.

Her mother clapped her hands in obvious approval. "I'll have Cook make you your favorites for dinner," she exclaimed, her earlier emotion no longer visible. "The entire staff has been worried about your recovery, but Sally assured them you would be well in no time."

"I really am quite hungry," she said, her stomach growling at the thought of food. "Would you mind having some tea and a few small cakes sent to my room? I think I would like to get something small in my stomach before I attempt to eat dinner."

Her mother grinned at having something to do and hurried from the room in a swirl of skirts. Olivia chuckled and laid her head back against the pillow. She closed her eyes and tried to remove the memories of her capture from her mind.

"She's been a complete mess you know," William said.

Olivia looked over and saw him standing with his back against the wall, his arms folded across his chest. Her cheeks warmed and she felt breathless at the look he was giving her.

"I have no doubt," she said once she was able to catch her breath. "I will have to make it up to her."

He pushed off the wall and came back to the bed. "Do you mean to make it up to me as well?" he teased.

Olivia had no idea how she would ever function if she continued to completely melt when William touched her or looked at her as if she were the only other person in the world. Her heart thrummed inside her chest, and she dropped her gaze to hide her blush.

"What would it require?" she asked after composing herself a little.

He grinned so impishly, she laughed out loud causing her to cringe and cough at the same time.

"Maybe I don't wish to know," she said giggling. "I don't know if I would be able to meet your expectations."

He tucked his hand under her chin and gently raised her eyes to meet his then lowered his mouth to her ear. "If you keep looking at me in such a way, your brother may end up really calling me out," he whispered. His breath sending chills of pleasure through her body.

She had no idea what he was talking about, but she chuckled all the same. "Maybe that's my intention." Her words came out so quiet, she barely heard them.

She heard him groan, then he pressed his lips to hers, careful to not hurt her. She put her uninjured hand on the side of his face when he pulled back. She gave a small laugh and smiled at him.

He chuckled and shook his head. "I didn't realize I was being funny."

"You weren't. I was only wondering which dueling pistols my brother will choose when he gets to call you out," she said mischievously. She pulled him back into her embrace and released a sigh when she felt the tension in her body disappear at the touch of his lips on hers.

Four weeks later, Olivia stood in front of her dressing room mirror and groaned. Her bruises had long since faded, but for a few small light-yellow spots in different areas of her body. The cut on her cheek, caused by the hand of Lord Greenly, was nearly healed but still showed a rather significant scar. Even after everything, her mother insisted they move forward with the ball.

To be honest, she wasn't sure she wanted to attend any longer. She had toyed with the idea of feigning an illness, but she knew it would only upset her mother. She would also more than likely be carried or dragged from her room by either William or Charles. She sighed as she watched Sally twist her hair into an elaborate knot and finish it off with a plethora of tiny white flowers. The smell of lilacs surrounded her, making her smile. She knew it had become something William loved. He had brought her fresh lilacs or roses every day while she was recovering.

Once she awoke from her ordeal, she had plenty of visitors. Every houseguest had visited on more than one occasion. Some came to talk, or give their well wishes, but others would sit and read to her. The duchess would bring in her book of poetry she'd composed. It was something Olivia had looked forward to. She hadn't known Her Grace had such a talent, but every single poem gave Olivia chills or made her laugh. Some even made her cry.

Reliving the night was something she didn't enjoy. She had had to explain the detail of her capture to several different people, including a couple of Bow Street Runners and a magistrate. What really bothered her was when she was alone.

Nightmares plagued her every time she tried to sleep, causing her to wake in complete panic or screaming for help.

There were also moments where she would shake uncontrollably, no matter how warm the room was, how close she sat by the fire, or how many blankets were wrapped around her. Dr. Campbell thought it was some lingering effects of the amount of time she'd spent in the cold. She was thrilled when it finally stopped happening and she began feeling more like herself. However, her nightmares remained. The only person who knew about them was Sally. Olivia made her maid promise to keep her dreams a secret. Her mother rarely left her alone, and if she knew Olivia was having terrifying dreams, she would probably insist on sleeping in her bed with her. Olivia hoped time would stop them from being so overwhelming, but so far, they were always the same.

Her nightmares were always full of darkness and cold, but nothing else. No sounds, no light, no walls or floor, only her mind completely trapped in a shroud of black icy memories. She assumed it was from being so cold in the dark cave behind the waterfall, but lately, she had wondered if it was the same darkness she had felt after her father had died, but in a different way. It wasn't making her sad or cry, only scared.

William was the perfect gentleman. He rarely left her side, read to her, and when she was feeling especially downtrodden, he would play his guitar for her. She had convinced herself if he hadn't already asked her to marry him, she would have asked him if only she could hear him play as often as she liked. It was always soothing and sweet, and he often played the song he wrote for her, which made her cry. He insisted he wouldn't keep playing for her if she couldn't control her tears because it made him feel helpless. She had laughed and kissed him, several times.

William took her for walks in her rose garden when she was finally feeling well enough to get out of bed. He would kiss her by their statue and tuck a rose behind her ear, always a different color from the day before. Now here she stood, dressed in her finest, ready to dance the night away. Usually, the thought of being in William's arms would have thrilled her, but she was desperately trying to figure out a way to escape facing the other guests.

"Sally," she asked. "Can you grab the coral necklace my father gave me, please?"

Sally retrieved it and helped her clasp it around her neck. Olivia felt a pang of emotion tug at her heart as she thought about her father choosing this especially for her.

"Well," she said with a sigh, "how do I look?"

"He won't be able to take his eyes off you, my lady," Sally said, smiling.

Olivia chuckled. "I guess I'm ready then."

She took a deep breath and opened her door, stifling a scream when William wrapped his arms around her waist from behind and pulled her to him.

"William!" she exclaimed, as she attempted to hold in her laughter. "What are you doing here?"

He took a rose the same color as her necklace and tucked it in her hair, then he leaned back to look at her.

"I continually forget how beautiful you are when we are apart and am in awe each time I see you," he placed a lingering kiss on her hand.

Olivia giggled. "Don't be ridiculous."

He looked at her intently and rubbed his fingers along her cheek. "You were right," he said after a brief silence. "It would have been a shame to miss seeing you in this gown. Dressed all in white, you remind me of an angel."

She blushed and lowered her head to try and get herself under control. William lifted her chin and Olivia shifted her eyes back to his. She stared up at him and felt herself relax. William tilted her head and kissed her so affectionately, she felt her emotions tug at her heart.

He shook his head as he pulled away. "I don't think I will ever tire of having you in my arms."

She kissed him once more and then wrapped her arm through his. He led her down the stairs toward the ballroom, keeping her close to his side.

"One more week, my beautiful rose, and we will never have to be apart again."

William had come to refer to her as *his rose* anytime they were together. She found she quite enjoyed the term of endearment. He had also reminded her daily of their upcoming wedding. They had posted the bands and planned on getting married as soon as the last ones were read. The wedding plans were all that had been discussed between Olivia's and William's mother, and Olivia was more than happy to have them plan everything. She had thought she had wanted to be a little more involved, it was her wedding after all, but she decided she would much rather spend time with William, rather than in a stuffy sitting room.

They entered the ballroom and walked around casually, greeting the guests. William had, even though it was highly improper, filled her entire dance card and wouldn't allow her out of his sight. She had teased him, but in truth, she was completely fine only dancing with her future husband. Whenever they found a moment alone, he would brush a kiss on her cheek, or her hand, and whisper how much he loved her in her ear. He held her close as they waltzed around the room and sat with her when she was too tired to continue dancing. As they moved into dinner, she was grateful for the reprieve. Shortly after the last course had been served, Olivia's mother stood and began to address all those in attendance.

"We are so pleased to have everyone join us tonight and are grateful to each of you for understanding when the ball had to be postponed," she said, a smile lighting her face. "As I am sure you are all aware, Lady Olivia and Lord Hanley have announced their engagement and will have their wedding in a week's time. I am also pleased to announce my son Charles has asked Miss Lyla Abbot for her hand in marriage, and she has agreed."

Olivia stared at her brother who had risen from his chair and held his betrothed with an arm wrapped around her waist. He had the same look in his eyes William had when Olivia looked at him—complete adoration and love. Olivia's heart warmed to see him so happy. She had been nervous about Lyla when she had first arrived at Elmwood Manor, but over the last couple of weeks, Olivia had witnessed how much she loved her brother and found she wholeheartedly approved of Charles's choice of wife.

The crowd cheered and offered their congratulations to the couple. Olivia had known Charles was fond of Lyla, but she didn't realize he had already proposed.

"Did you know about this?" she asked William as he returned her to a quiet corner of the ballroom.

He smiled and slid his fingers across her cheek and down her neck, making her body shiver in delight. "I have known for weeks, my love."

"Why didn't you tell me?" she said, clearing her throat as a surge of energy ran thru her body when he touched her bare skin.

He shrugged and smiled at her. "Because I was too busy falling madly in love with his sister."

Twenty

When Olivia awoke the morning of the wedding, her stomach rolled and twisted in nervous anticipation. Her wedding gown had been hung nearby to limit any creases which may occur if pressed against her other gowns. The cream-colored satin gown had ruffled sleeves, a low neckline trimmed in lace, a thick full skirt with embroidered patterns around the hem, and a sash to go around the bodice. On the dressing table lay a crown of purple lilacs Lyla had given to her for her hair. Olivia stood and felt the soft slick fabric and smiled. She was getting married today.

Sally entered her room with a light tap to the door. "Good morning, my lady," she said, grinning happily. "Would you like something to eat before you get ready?"

Olivia shook her head. "I'm too nervous to eat," she said with a light chuckle.

Sally nodded and moved to stand beside Olivia. She held out a long white box. "I'm to give you this, my lady."

Olivia looked at the box and then at Sally. "Who is it from?" she asked warily. After Lord Greenly's letters and her abduction, she had been very cautious about every delivery or letter.

"I'm not to say," she said, lowering her head so Olivia couldn't see her eyes.

Olivia took the box and stared at it. Maybe she should take it to Charles or William before opening it. Olivia shook her head; she was being silly. Sally wouldn't be so secretive and shy if she didn't know the person it was from.

She shook the box slightly and heard a little clink against the side. Her curiosity burned inside her, and her hands shook nervously as she reached to remove the lid. She hovered over the box before she pulled on the ribbon tying it together, revealing what awaited her. Inhaling sharply, her hand flew to her mouth. Olivia pulled out a gold pendant in the shape of a rose, hanging on a long golden chain necklace. In the center of the petals was a stunning purple stone.

"It's beautiful!" she screeched, tears pooling in her eyes.

She laid the golden rose inside her palm and ran her fingertips across the jewel. She had never seen anything like it in any of the shops she had visited.

"There is also this, my lady," Sally said, holding out a folded letter.

Olivia took it quickly and set the necklace back into the box. She walked to the light that was spilling into the room from the window and opened the letter, smiling brightly when she saw the signature on the bottom of the page.

There isn't a rose in the world that compares to the one who holds my heart. Two more hours.

Love Always,
William

Olivia held the note to her chest and exhaled dreamily at his words. She looked out into the bright morning sunshine. The unpredictable English weather had decided to allow the sun to glow today, giving every flower in her garden a shimmering effect from the droplets of dew on their petals. It made for a perfect day. Touching the wavy glass, Olivia was pleased when she felt warmth radiating into her room. She was glad the summer warmth had finally decided to stick around. Laying her letter from William on her writing table with a deep breath to calm her fluttering stomach, Olivia allowed Sally to prepare her to become Lady Olivia Hanley.

The churchyard was quiet when she and Charles arrived in the carriage. He had been unusually silent on the short ride. Olivia laid a hand on his arm and glanced up at him. He looked at her and Olivia could see several different emotions flash in his eyes; love, sadness, trepidation, pride, and something else she couldn't name.

"Charles," she said quietly as he led her across the stone path to the church's large wooden doors. "Is everything alright?"

He stopped and laid his hand on top of hers. "I was only thinking how much father would have loved to be standing here with you on his arm, instead of mine."

Careful not to move her flower crown or one of the many pins holding her curly coiffure in its knot, she laid her head against his shoulder. "I miss him too. But I know you have made him proud," she said quietly.

She felt him kiss her forehead. "I wouldn't have been able to let anyone who wasn't up to father's standards take you from us, but Lord Hanley has proven himself a loving and caring man. I believe you will be very happy in your marriage."

"Thank you, Charles," was all she could say. She knew if she attempted to say anything else, she would cry, and red puffy eyes would not go very well with her gown.

Olivia straightened and took a deep slow breath. Her stomach rolled as she thought about walking down the aisle toward William. Sally had done her magic, and she felt as prepared as she was going to be. She raised a hand to the necklace William had given her and smiled as she felt the jeweled pendant.

"You look beautiful, Livvie," Charles said as he watched her fidget with the pendant. "Just breathe."

She chuckled. "We will see how you are feeling when the tables are turned."

He laughed, then pulled her thru the doorway of the church. She heard the sighs and praises from their closest friends as she entered, but she only looked to where William stood. He was dressed in a black tailcoat, white shirt and silk cravat, black waistcoat, and matching trousers. He looked at her in awe and gave her a playful grin when she met his eyes.

"Perfect," he whispered in her ear when she stepped up beside him.

The vicar was polite and quite winded, but when he finally pronounced them man and wife, the tension she had felt all morning dissipated. She found herself being held tightly in her new husband's embrace. She returned his kiss to the cheering of the crowd. Although it wasn't a long kiss, it was one of the most important they would ever share.

As soon as the ceremony was over, he assisted her into the carriage and took the seat beside her. Olivia felt her heart race when he wrapped one arm around her. When they pulled from the courtyard, he turned to face her and gently lifted the pendant from her neck.

"It suits you," he said, smiling. "Do you like it?"

She stared into his eyes and laid her hand against his cheek. He let the necklace fall back into its place. Her lips rose slightly before she leaned in close to him and pressed her lips to his. He wrapped his arms around her and pulled her so close to him, she could feel his heart racing. When he pulled back slightly, both of their breathing had increased and she was positive her crown of flowers had fallen from her head to the floor, but he only shook his head.

"You are stunning, my love," he said in a hoarse whisper.

Olivia kissed him lightly again. "I love you, William," she said in a hushed tone.

"I love you, *Lady Hanley*," he said tracing her jawline with his fingertips.

She shivered in pleasure. The softness of his eyes trapped her in his gaze. He was perfect, and he was hers. He pulled her back into his arms, kissing her the way a husband in love kisses his wife.

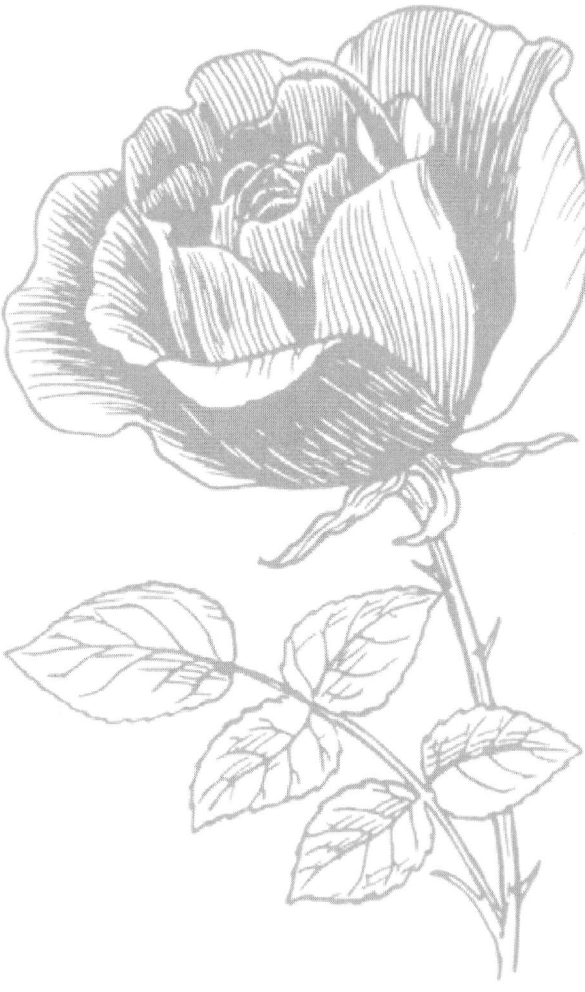

Epilogue

Five Years Later

Olivia leaned against the wooden railing of the fence and watched the horse move gracefully around the paddock. She had been out here most of the morning seeing to some of the newer horses who had recently come from a breeder in Derbyshire but stopped to watch as Mr. Trenton worked. The pure white coat of the new mare shined with sweat. The horse snorted and threw her head impatiently as the stable master urged her to trot around in a wide circle.

"She will be a fine horse when she's trained a bit," he yelled across the paddock.

Olivia smiled. "If anyone can tame her, it's you."

"Should I be jealous?" William said from behind her, a small child sitting on his hip.

She smiled. "Should I? It seems I'm the one with the competition." she said, as she moved to take their daughter from him.

William leaned down and kissed her. "Do you think she will be the right horse for her?" he asked, nodding toward the white mare.

Olivia nodded, then turned her daughter toward the paddock. "Do you see the horse?" she asked.

Clarissa stared wide-eyed at the animal and nodded.

"Her name is Willow," she said, sitting Clarissa on the fence so she could see better. "When she's a little older and Mr. Trenton has trained her, you will get to ride her."

Clarissa beamed. "She's mine?"

William laughed. "Yes, darling girl. But not until you are both a little older. Willow is still young and needs to learn some things before you can ride her."

The child nodded, her deep brown curls bouncing down her back. "Miss Beth told me I needed to learn to be big, but Francis said he was already big, and Miss Beth tickled him."

"Papa? When do I get to ride?" Francis said, holding onto the nurse maid's hand as they walked toward them.

Olivia smiled and wrapped her arm tightly around her daughter before setting her on the ground so she could stand next to her brother. The twins looked quite similar with the same curly hair and light brown eyes, but they couldn't have been more different in personality. Clarissa was calm and always giving everyone a hug and kiss. She constantly told her parents she loved them and had a laugh which sounded like the tinkling of bells. Francis was more like his father, stubborn, persistent to a fault, too adorable to ever get into trouble, and like William, rarely ever let Olivia out of his sight. The one thing Francis had in common with his mother was his desire to get into mischief.

He seemed to always be in one scrape or another, and all Olivia could do was laugh.

William pulled his son into his arms and pointed to a spotted grey horse tied to a post outside the paddock. "Your mother has also selected a very nice horse for you," he said, smiling. "His name is Juniper."

Francis squealed with delight. "Really, Mama," he cried. "Is Juniper for me?"

Olivia smiled and touched the tip of her son's nose with her fingertip playfully. "Only if you behave for Miss Beth." They had hired the nursemaid shortly after the twins were born, and she was a delight to the entire household. The children adored her and Olivia had managed to find a friend in Miss Beth.

"Oh, I will, Mama. I'm always a good boy." Francis said, his excitement bubbling over as he wiggled around in his father's arms.

William adjusted his hold. "Would you like to go see him?" He asked.

Francis nodded emphatically and clapped his hands. "Yes, please!"

William laughed and in a quick motion sat the boy on his shoulders. Francis grabbed hold of William's ears to steady himself and Olivia laughed.

"Seems he is already a great rider," she teased. "He has learned the trick to lead his trusty horse."

William cocked an eyebrow at her, his lips rising slightly at the corners. "Be careful, love," he said. "I would hate to have to tell the cook you are the one responsible for stealing the biscuits from her kitchen."

Olivia nearly choked as she laughed, swatting him playfully on the arm. "I can't believe after all these years, you are still teasing me about stealing those biscuits. I'm going to give Charles a piece of my mind for telling you the story when they arrive later today. His only saving grace will be his new baby girl, Brianna. I'm dying to see her."

William grinned mischievously and leaned down to kiss his wife's cheek. With the hand not holding his son, he touched the gold pendant around Olivia's neck. "I still say there isn't a rose in the world which compares to you." He whispered, then flashed her a brilliant smile.

She giggled as the man who stole her heart took off at a pretend gallop, their son giggling on his shoulders.

"Mama?" Clarissa said, putting her little fingers into Olivia's hand.

She bent down and arranged her skirts around herself so her daughter could come closer. "Yes, darling?" Olivia pushed a curly lock of hair away from the girl's forehead waiting for Clarissa to ask her question.

"Will baby Brianna get a horsey too?" she asked, putting a hand on each of Olivia's cheeks.

"That will be up to your Uncle Charles and Aunt Lyla," she answered. "Do you want Brianna to have a horse?"

Clarissa nodded her head dramatically. "Oh yes, but not my Willow."

Olivia's heart warmed at her daughter's reference to her horse as *my Willow*. It seemed at the young age of four, she was going to be as much in love with horses as her mother.

"Not your Willow," she said, pulling Clarissa into an embrace. "Now, should we go catch your Papa and see if he will give you a ride like Francis?"

Clarissa's face exploded into a grin and she grabbed Olivia's hand and pulled her toward her father who was still running around in circles with Francis on his shoulders. She rubbed her hand across her belly and smiled.

"William?" she called to him. He came running over to her, his breathing ragged and his cheeks flushed.

She laughed and nodded toward their daughter who was grinning up at her father in expectation.

He shook his head and set Francis on the ground then put his daughter on his shoulders and turned to continue their game.

"Oh, and darling," she said, grinning when he turned back toward her. "I hope you save some of your energy for the baby."

He looked at her for a second in confusion then his eyes grew wide. "Baby?"

She smiled and bit her bottom lip. He quickly set Clarissa down and grabbed Olivia around the waist and spun her around in a circle before setting her down and kissing her gently.

"I love you, my beautiful rose," he said in a rough whisper.

Olivia smiled and kissed the tip of his nose. "I love you as well, but I think your daughter is going to start throwing a tantrum if you don't pick her back up and play with her."

William laughed and kissed her quickly before returning to Clarissa, whose giggles echoed off every surface surrounding them as her father tossed her playfully up into the air.

"We are very fortunate, my beautiful child, to have such a man in our lives," she said rubbing her expanding belly. She chuckled as William nearly tumbled to the ground when their son latched onto his father's legs, begging for another turn.

"Very fortunate indeed."

Acknowledgments

Writing historical fiction can be extremely difficult for all authors. We wish to maintain as much accuracy as possible, but there are times when our stories take on a life of their own. Please keep in mind that this story is fictional, as are all the characters and places. I have also pushed the boundaries of what was socially acceptable during the early Regency Era as William and Olivia's relationship grew, which I felt necessary for their personalities and to keep the storyline flowing freely.

This story took many hours of research, and I enjoyed each and every one of them. When I decided I wanted William to be able to play the guitar, I wanted to find just the right sound for his performance and came upon a video by Cristina T., and Luis M. C.

As I listened to the two performers, the pianist playing Bach's Prelude 1 in C Major, and the guitarist strumming the tune to Ave Maria, I couldn't help but fall in love with it. To hear this beautiful rendition, please visit https://bit.ly/3FXz6lr. It was then that I knew I had found William's song.

Even though in the story William claims to have written it, Ave Maria was actually composed by Franz Schubert in 1825 as part of his Op. 52, a setting of one of seven songs from Walter Scott's 1810 narrative poem, Lady of the Lakes. You can read more by visiting https://en.wikipedia.org/wiki/Ave_Maria_(Schubert).

I also would like to give a shoutout and heartfelt thank you to everyone who helped me along my journey. My Beta Readers, Colette H., Kimberly L., Erica L., Haley B., and Cammy B., I couldn't have done this without your insights and critiques. Your help is invaluable! I also had a tremendous amount of assistance from Laura B. who willingly put up with my endless questions. My editor, Amanda, did a wonderful job of helping me polish the story and make sure it was ready for readers. My cover designer, Melody Simmons, did a wonderful job of capturing the essence of the story with her work. I also would like to extend my love and gratitude to my family. Writing takes a lot of my time, and because of this, I spend hours in front of a computer ignoring life around me. Thank you for your patience and assistance.

All Authors love to hear from our readers and we always love feedback. Please leave an honest review of A Rose Worth Saving on Amazon, and/or Goodreads.

About the Author

Alicia Rivoli was born and raised in a small town in Idaho. She grew up riding horses and helping on the family farm and ranch, but now resides in the beautiful Ozark Mountains. She discovered her love of books as a teenager, but didn't start reading for fun until she was married. She received the inspiration for her stories in a dream and through an active imagination. She is a stay-at-home mom with two handsome boys and an amazing husband who helped her dream of being an author come true.

See other works by Alicia Rivoli by visiting her website or Social Media platforms.

www.aliciarivoli.com
www.facebook.com/AliciaRivoli
Instagram: aliciarivoli
Twitter: @AliciaRivoli

Made in the USA
Columbia, SC
13 September 2022